Tyler saw what he thought was a mirage

Walking toward him was a grown-up version of Diana Smith, the girl who'd broken his teenage heart. He blinked, expecting the woman to disappear, but she kept coming.

Her figure was curvier, the glossy brown hair she'd once worn parted in the middle feathered around her face and her features overall were more mature, but there was no mistake about it. It was Diana, who'd left Bentonsville–and him–ten years ago.

Her step didn't falter, her slight smile didn't waver, as though seeing him again hadn't affected her. "Hello, Tyler," she said, her voice still low, still smoky.

"Hello, Diana." He knew he was staring, but couldn't help it. Although her oval-shaped face appeared virtually the same, her eyes seemed different, as if they'd seen more than she'd bargained for.

"This is quite a surprise," he said."I hadn't realized you were in town visiting."

"I'm not visiting, Tyler. I've come home...."

Dear Reader,

Have you ever done the wrong thing for the right reasons? Does trying to do what's right lessen the gravity of our mistakes? These are two of the questions that inspired *A Time To Come Home,* the sequel to *A Time To Forgive.*

Diana Smith is far from the perfect heroine, which is obvious from the opening pages when she abandons her much-loved daughter at her brother's home. It's the latest in a long line of Diana's missteps, for which she's trying to redeem herself.

Which brings up some more interesting questions. Can we expect others to forgive us when we can't forgive ourselves? And can love survive the sins of our past? Please read on as Diana and Tyler re-create their special bond.

All my best,
Darlene

P.S. You can visit me on the Web at www.darlenegardner.com.

A Time To Come Home

Darlene Gardner

TORONTO • NEW YORK • LONDON
AMSTERDAM • PARIS • SYDNEY • HAMBURG
STOCKHOLM • ATHENS • TOKYO • MILAN • MADRID
PRAGUE • WARSAW • BUDAPEST • AUCKLAND

ISBN-13: 978-0-373-71396-7
ISBN-10: 0-373-71396-7

A TIME TO COME HOME

This edition published by arrangement with Harlequin Books S.A.

www.eHarlequin.com

Printed in U.S.A.

ABOUT THE AUTHOR

Darlene Gardner has worked as a features reporter and then a sportswriter for daily newspapers in South Carolina and Florida before deciding she'd rather make up quotes than solicit them. She's been published by several Harlequin and Silhouette Books lines since she sold her first novel in 1992. Darlene, a Penn State graduate, lives in Virginia with her journalist husband and two children.

Books by Darlene Gardner

HARLEQUIN SUPERROMANCE

1316–MILLION TO ONE
1360–A TIME TO FORGIVE

For my son Brian and my daughter Paige,
because writing this book drove home for me
how precious our children are. And for my
husband, Kurt, for giving them to me.

PROLOGUE

WITH ONLY THE DIM GLOW of the bathroom night-light to guide her, Diana Smith moved silently through the upstairs hall of her older brother's pricey town house. The low heels of her boots sank into the plush carpeting, muffling her footsteps.

Shifting the weight of her backpack more comfortably on her shoulder, she stopped in front of the bedroom where her nine-year-old daughter Jaye slept and carefully eased open the door. The hinges groaned in protest, the sound gunshot-loud in the quiet house. Diana froze, her breath catching in her throat.

She glanced down the darkened hall to her brother's bedroom door, waiting for Connor to emerge and find her awake and fully dressed. But the door remained closed.

She exhaled, her breath coming out ragged. Careful not to nudge the door, she peered around the crack into the room.

Jaye was still asleep but stirred restlessly, turning over onto her side. Diana stood perfectly still until the girl settled into position and her chest expanded and contracted in a rhythmic motion. Weak moonlight filtered through a crack in the blinds, bathing Jaye in soft light.

Her face was relaxed, her cheeks rosy and her full lips slightly pursed as she slept. Her long, blond hair spilled over the pillow like a halo.

A wave of love hit Diana hard. Three days ago, she'd decided on the course of action she must take. Gazing upon her daughter now, however, she wasn't sure she had the strength to carry through.

She was reminded too vividly of another place, another time and a man whose features she glimpsed in the sleeping child. She'd done right by Tyler Benton, too, but the doing had shattered her heart.

From necessity and long practice, she shoved Tyler from her mind and concentrated on the moment. Before she could muster the will to retreat, she broke into a cold sweat, her muscles and her very bones aching. She fought off a bout of nausea as her stomach pitched and rolled.

If she needed a sign that leaving Jaye was the right thing to do, her physical condition couldn't have provided a better one.

Since losing control on a slick stretch of road and slamming her car into a towering oak tree, she'd felt ill, but not due to injuries sustained in the crash. She'd walked away from the one-car accident remarkably unscathed, considering she might have died if she'd struck the tree a few inches left of impact.

The police had attributed her accident to bad luck, but Diana feared the pain pills she'd popped after leaving her job at a Nashville clothing warehouse had been the true cause.

She'd been using the drug since straining her back six months before, devising new and clever ways to secure the tablets long after her prescription ran out.

Horrified that Jaye could have been in the car with her, she'd faced the fact that she was addicted. Then she'd flushed the rest of the Vicodin down the toilet, only to find a new stockpile a few days later in one of her hiding places.

Since then, she'd lost her job after failing a random drug test at work and confronted some more harsh truths. She needed help to kick her habit and she wasn't fit to be around her daughter.

After much thought, she'd packed up Jaye and the child's meager belongings and boarded a bus for the two-day trip from Tennessee to Connor's town house. They'd arrived in Silver Spring, Maryland, not even six hours ago, surprising a brother she hadn't seen in years.

Jaye made a sweet, snuffling sound in her sleep and hugged the soft, stuffed teddy bear that Diana had bought her when she was a toddler. Diana longed to rush over to the bed and kiss her one last time, but couldn't risk waking her.

"I'm sorry, baby," she whispered.

Tears fell down her cheeks like rain as she memorized the planes and angles of the sleeping child's face before moving away from the door. She left it ajar, unwilling to risk making another sound.

She crept down the hall and descended the stairs as silently as a ghost. When she reached Connor's state-of-the-art kitchen, she turned on the dim light over the stove, dug Jaye's school transcripts and birth certificate out of her backpack and set them on the counter.

After locating a pad and pen, she thought for long moments before she wrote:

Connor, I need to work some things out and get my head on straight. Here's everything you need to enroll Jaye in school. Please take good care of her until I come back. I don't know when that will be, but I'll be in touch.

She put down the note, read it over, then bent down and scribbled two more words: *I'm sorry.*

A fat teardrop rolled from her face onto the notepaper, blurring the ink of the apology.

Wiping away the rest of the tears, she headed for the front door. Her chest ached. Whether it was from being without Vicodin or from the hardest decision she'd ever had to make, she couldn't be sure.

Within moments, she was trudging down the sidewalk by the glow of the street lamps toward the very bus station where she and Jaye had arrived.

She knew that abandoning her child was unforgivable, just as what she'd done to Tyler Benton ten years ago had been unforgivable.

But it couldn't be helped.

She'd been barely seventeen when Jaye was born, no more than a child herself, grossed out by breastfeeding, impatient with crying and resentful of her new responsibilities.

A tidal wave of love for her daughter, which gathered

strength with each passing day, had helped Diana grow up fast. She tried her best, but harbored no illusion that love alone would make her a good mother.

Diana waited for the sparse early-morning traffic to pass before crossing a main street, placing one foot in front of the other when all she wanted was to turn back. But she couldn't. Not only did she lack the courage to confess to her brother that she had a drug problem, she couldn't risk having him say Jaye couldn't stay with him.

Despite his bachelor status, Connor represented her best hope. Her parents, to whom she hadn't spoken to in years, were out. She had no doubt that her brother would take good care of Jaye. Until Diana kicked her habit and put her life back on track, Jaye was better off with him. And without Diana.

She blinked rapidly until her tears dried, then turned her mind to her uncertain future. Once she spent a portion of her dwindling cash on a return bus ticket to Nashville, she'd need to find a cheaper apartment, search for a job that paid a decent wage and somehow figure out how to get into drug treatment.

Even now she craved a pill. She reached into the front pocket of her blue jeans, her fingertips encountering the reassuring presence of the three little white Vicodin tablets left from her stash.

Despite her desire to do right by her much-loved daughter, she couldn't say for sure whether the pills would still be in her pocket when she reached Nashville.

CHAPTER ONE

Six months later

DIANA SMITH WIPED away the bead of moisture trickling down her forehead with the pad of her index finger. It felt warm against her skin, a marked difference from the drenching sweats that used to chill her body when she denied herself the Vicodin that held her in its grip.

It had been months since she'd stopped desiring the prescription pain pills, longer since she'd done an abbreviated stint in detox and then gone through the hell of withdrawal. And longer still since she'd crept from her brother's town house in the dark of night while Connor and Jaye slept.

The air had been crisp then, cold enough that she could see her breath when she exhaled. Now it was stagnant and sultry, the kind of heat typical of Maryland in the waning days of August. But the heat wasn't what had Diana sweating.

She sat in the driver's seat of her secondhand Chevy with the driver's-side window rolled down, a good half block from her brother's brick town house. No lights shone inside as far as she could determine, suggesting nobody was home. She had no way of knowing if anyone would arrive soon, although it was past six o'clock on a Friday.

She waited, her entire body on alert whenever a car appeared. But it was never the silver Porsche her brother drove. She counted up the months since she'd last been here in Silver Spring, surprised that six of them had passed. It felt twice that long, because every day without her daughter seemed to drag to twice its normal length.

She hadn't spoken to Jaye once in all that time. She'd picked up the phone countless times, but fear had paralyzed her. How could she expect a child to understand she'd done what she thought best when her own adult brother didn't?

She'd left phone messages on Connor's answering machine to let him know she was okay but had only spoken to him the one time, after he'd tracked her down through a private investigator.

Connor had kept his temper in check, even offering to put Jaye on the line. Diana had ached to hear her child's voice and longed to promise her they'd be together soon. But she'd resisted the allure, unable to face the questions about why she'd gone or when she'd be back.

As she waited, she heard birds singing, the distant sound of a stereo playing and a quiet that made little sense. A neighborhood like this should be alive with activity late on a Friday afternoon, after businesses shut down for the day. Only holiday weekends followed a different pattern.

"Oh, no," she said aloud, as the importance of

today's date sunk in. The last Friday in August. The start of the long Labor Day weekend.

Connor could have gotten off work early and headed somewhere with Jaye to enjoy the last gasp of summer. She might not glimpse her daughter today after all.

Her hopes rose when she heard the whoosh of approaching tires on pavement, but a blue compact car and not her brother's Porsche came into view. Before discouragement could set in, the car pulled into Connor's driveway.

Diana slouched down in her seat, her right hand tightening on her thigh. Both doors opened simultaneously. A woman with short, dark hair emerged from behind the wheel, something about her vaguely familiar. But Diana barely spared her a glance, her attention captured by the passenger. By Jaye.

The little girl reached inside the car and pulled out a number of plastic shopping bags. Her hands full, she bumped the door closed with her hip, then came fully into view. Her long gilded hair was the same, but her skin was tanned by the sun and she appeared a few inches taller. A growth spurt, common enough in a nine-year-old. But Diana had missed it.

The sun was low in the sky. It backlit Jaye so that she looked ephemeral, as out of reach to Diana as if she were an other-worldly creature.

Diana remembered the unexpected wave of love that swept over her the first time she held Jaye in the hospital. The love no longer surprised her. She braced herself for it, but it still hit her like a punch.

The dark-haired woman joined Jaye at the foot of the

sidewalk and took a few of the bags from her. The woman said something, and Jaye giggled, the high-pitched girlish sound traveling on the breeze. Diana's lips curved. She leaned closer to the open window, closer to Jaye, forgetting her notion to be inconspicuous.

The woman ruffled the top of Jaye's blond head, and then Jaye skipped up the sidewalk to the front door of the town house.

The woman followed, a small object that could only be a house key in her free hand. Despair rolled over Diana, settling in the pit of her stomach. The woman unlocked the door. A cry of protest rose in Diana's throat. Feeling as though she was choking, she watched helplessly as the woman opened the door.

Jaye scampered inside, out of sight. The woman closed the door behind them. This time it was a tear and not sweat that slid down Diana's cheek.

A sharp tapping interrupted her thought. The knocking came again. Faster. Louder. Diana turned toward the sound—and saw her brother's handsome, scowling face through the passenger window.

Her stomach pitched as she mentally called herself all kinds of a fool. Checking her rearview mirror, she spotted the silver Porsche parked behind her car. She'd been so absorbed in Jaye that she hadn't heard Connor pull up.

He rapped sharply on the closed window again. "Diana, unlock the door," he ordered.

The temptation to flee was so sharp that Diana's foot moved to the gas pedal, but she suppressed it. Her brother deserved better. She reluctantly pressed the unlock button, and Connor opened the door and slid onto the worn fabric of the passenger seat, not bothering to close the door behind him.

He was dressed as though he'd come from the brokerage firm, in a navy silk tie, a long-sleeved blue dress shirt and dark, tailored slacks. But his resemblance to a cool, collected stockbroker ended there.

"I don't know whether to hug you or yell at you," he said in a low-throated, angry growl. "My P.I. told me you quit your job and moved out of your apartment. Where in the hell have you been?"

She tilted her head. "You're still using that private eye?"

"Off and on. I need someone to tell me what you're up to. You certainly won't. Do you know how worried I've been about you?"

She gazed into her lap and fought tears. She'd been on her own for so long it hadn't occurred to her that he'd worry. "I'm sorry," she said without raising her head. "I should have let you know I was moving."

"Hell, yeah, you should have. You should return my phone messages, too," he said gruffly, his voice thickened by emotion. "You didn't even call after I told you about Drew Galloway being denied parole."

The date Galloway could have gained his freedom seared into her memory, Diana had discovered the outcome of the parole hearing before she received Connor's message. But her throat had swelled at the mention of her brother's killer, so she didn't tell Connor that.

Connor heaved a sigh and ran a hand over his forehead. "It must be a hundred degrees in this car. Come into the house so we can talk where it's cooler."

"No." She punctuated her comment with a firm shake of her head. "I can't come in."

"Want to tell me why not?"

In a softer voice, Diana said, "Jaye's in there."

"Isn't Jaye the reason you're here?"

She nodded. "Yes. But only to see her, not to talk to her."

"What?" The word erupted from him, like lava from a volcano. "My God, Diana. I was planning to fly to Nashville next week to talk some sense into you. You haven't had any contact with her since you discarded her."

Guilt, her constant companion, slithered through Diana before she reminded herself of her reasons. "I didn't discard her. I left her with you."

He shifted in his seat, turning more fully toward her. "A bachelor with no experience taking care of a child."

"The best man I know. And I was right to do it. I saw her just now. She looks happy, Connor. You've done a wonderful job." She dug into her purse and removed an envelope containing cash she'd managed to set aside from her two jobs. "I was going to mail this to you. It's not much, certainly not enough, but I'll never be able to repay you for all you've done."

His lips thinned, a manifestation of the stubborn streak he'd developed way back in childhood. "I'm not taking your money, Diana. If you really want to repay me, come inside and talk to your daughter. Spend the weekend with us. We're driving to the Maryland shore tomorrow."

"You don't know how much I'd like to but I can't."

She swallowed, then stared at him, silently pleading for understanding. "But I will talk to her. Just as soon as I get my life organized."

"Isn't that what you've been doing for the past six months?"

"It's what I've been trying to do." After a brief stay at a detox center, she'd run short of cash to pay for treatment and stayed off the pills through sheer strength of will. The withdrawal symptoms had lingered for months, but she'd managed to secure a secretarial position and then work a second job as a waitress. "But I can't see Jaye. Not yet."

"Why?" His eyes seemed to bore into her, where her secrets lay buried. "What is it that you're not telling me? Are you sick? On drugs? Is that what this is all about?"

Shame billowed inside Diana, the same humiliation that had engulfed her when she'd attended the Narcotics Anonymous meetings. She hadn't been able to own up to her addiction in a room full of strangers. Admitting to her problem was downright impossible in front of her strong, self-assured brother.

"I'm not on drugs," she said. *Not now. And hopefully not ever again.* "But this isn't about me. It's about Jaye. It's a lot to ask, but I need you to keep her a while longer."

She read resistance on his face, and the enormity of what she'd done struck her. "Oh, my Lord. It didn't even occur to me that you might not want her."

"Not want her?" He made a harsh sound. "I love her like she's my own daughter. Abby loves her, too."

Relief caused Diana's limbs to feel boneless. "Abby? Is she the woman I saw with Jaye?"

He nodded. "Yeah. She's Jaye's violin teacher. We're also getting married in October. I would have told you about her if I could ever get you on the phone."

"Congratulations," Diana said in a small voice, ashamed she hadn't known about this major development in her brother's life. She sensed he was about to say something else about his fiancée, then heard herself speaking her next thought aloud. "I didn't know Jaye played the violin."

"That's my point, Diana. You've missed too much of Jaye's life already. Abby and I are happy to take care of her, but she's *your* daughter. You need to be in her life."

"I can't," Diana said miserably. "Not yet."

"You still haven't given me a good reason why not." He practically spit out the words.

Because I'm afraid.

The words imprinted themselves on Diana's mind, but she felt too raw to admit her fear to Connor. He'd always been the strong one in their family, the one who followed the straight and narrow path and never disappointed anyone. He'd never find himself in her situation.

"I want her back so much it hurts. You've got to believe that. And I have a plan to get her back. But I can't face her until I know everything will work out. I'll call her. I will. Just as soon as I settle in."

"Settle in where? What's this plan you're talking about?"

"I enrolled in a career training program in Gaithersburg. I'm going to study business administration.

I also lined up a waitressing job. And I have a lead on an apartment, too."

She deliberately left out the most difficult part of the plan, the piece that involved Tyler Benton.

"In Gaithersburg?" His eyebrows drew together. "I can't figure you out, Diana. That's not even twenty miles from here and only thirty from Bentonsville."

"Thirty miles can be a long way."

"So you're not planning to visit Mom?"

Unwilling to confide she had a more important visit to make, she dodged the question. "I'm not moving to Gaithersburg because it's close to Bentonsville. I'm moving there because it's close to Jaye."

He was quiet for long moments, then said, "You'll call and leave a number where I can reach you?"

"I will." She sensed that he didn't believe her. "I promise."

"What am I supposed to tell your daughter in the meantime?"

Making a snap decision, Diana again reached into her purse, this time pulling out a sealed envelope she'd planned to mail when she got to Gaithersburg.

She extended the envelope to him, her fingers shaking slightly. "Could you give this to Jaye? But don't tell her you saw me. It already has a stamp, so she'll assume I mailed it."

He took her offering, his expression grave. "Are you sure about this, Diana?"

The lump that hadn't been far from her throat since she pulled into the neighborhood formed with a vengeance. "I'm not sure of anything."

Least of all the portion of her plan that would enable her to set the rest in motion. Nobody knew better than Diana what a struggle raising a child alone could be, but there was no longer any reason for her to be solely responsible for Jaye.

She hadn't returned to Bentonsville since she was a pregnant sixteen-year-old, but she needed to go back home now. Not to see her mother, but to tell Tyler Benton she'd lied ten years ago when she claimed she'd slept with half the guys at Bentonsville High.

In reality, she'd only had one lover—Tyler.

THE AIR-CONDITIONED COOL of the town house contrasted sharply with the oppressive heat inside Diana's Chevy. So, too, did the cheerful chatter drifting into the foyer from the family room.

Connor hung his suit jacket on one of the brass hooks beside the front door and followed the noise, easily identifying Jaye's girlish voice. "I like the folder with the Redskins on the cover the best, but the one with the pink unicorn isn't bad."

Then he heard Abby's somewhat deeper voice, light and teasing: "I'm surprised a girl as musical as you pays any attention to football."

"I like how the players crash into each other," Jaye stated with enthusiasm. "It's way cool."

Connor rounded a corner and the two females came into view. His niece balanced on her knees beside a coffee table stacked with folders, packages of pens, pencils and binders. Abby, sitting on the love seat dressed in a yellow sundress, looked as pretty as a summer flower.

"Hey, Uncle Connor." Jaye smiled at him with her eyes as well as her lips. "We went shopping for school supplies."

"I can see that," he said, moving deeper into the room.

"And I just discovered Jaye has a passion for football." Abby rose to her feet and walked into his embrace, looping her arms around his neck.

He kissed her, his passion heading in a direction that had nothing to do with football, as it always did whenever he touched her. But he kept the kiss brief because Jaye was in the room.

"Jaye watched a Redskins preseason game with me the other night," he remarked. "Now she's hooked."

"Oh, no," Abby said dramatically. "That means I'm outnumbered. What am I to do?"

"Learn to like football," Connor said. "Jaye has."

"I'd do just about anything for you, Connor Smith." Abby batted her long, dark eyelashes at him, then scrunched up her face. "But not that."

He smiled at her antics, wishing he didn't have to break the lighthearted mood. The envelope in his hand felt as though it was scorching his skin. He held it out to his niece. "I have something for you, Jaye."

"Really?" Her eyes brightened with the excitement of somebody who never got mail. "Who from?"

"Your mother."

The color visibly ebbed from her face, the pleasure in her expression gone. Connor glanced at Abby, whose anxiety came across as tangibly as the sick feeling in his gut.

He extended the envelope to Jaye, praying she didn't

possess enough knowledge of post office procedure to notice the stamp hadn't been cancelled.

It appeared for tense moments as though Jaye would refuse his offering, but then she tore the envelope out of his hand, ripping the plain white paper open as though it contained a Christmas present.

She unfolded a single sheet of paper and read, the hope he'd briefly glimpsed on her young face vanishing. Her mouth formed the mutinous line he hadn't seen in a very long time. In one swift motion, she ripped the letter in two, letting the pieces drift to the floor.

"I hate her," she exclaimed before brushing by him and running up the stairs.

His heart dropping like a stone in his chest, Connor picked up the two parts of the letter and pieced them together. Abby came up beside him, touching his arm. "What does it say?"

"Only that she loves her and will make things up to her one day."

Abby glanced at the now-empty path Jaye had taken when she'd sprinted from the room, then regarded Connor with worry etched into her features. Their minds often operated on similar wavelengths, but never more than now.

"I don't think your sister realizes how difficult making things up to Jaye is going to be."

WAY BACK in what seemed like another lifetime, Diana's mother used to say there was no time like the present...to do her homework, to clean her room, to practice the piano.

The saying had been Diana's first coherent thought

upon awakening in her hotel bed. Possibly because Diana was geographically closer to her mother than she'd been since running away to her aunt's house as a pregnant teenager.

Or maybe because there was no time like the present—to tell Tyler Benton about Jaye.

The realization that she had to come clean with Tyler had dawned on her slowly, the same way she'd accepted her need to rectify the mess she'd made of her life.

It had gradually become clear that the future she planned to build for her daughter should include more than a better-educated mother with a higher-paying job. Diana had never been close to her own father, but that didn't justify her in keeping Tyler and Jaye apart. She supposed that, deep in her heart, she'd always recognized that father and daughter deserved to know each other.

Especially because the very valid reason she'd had for keeping Jaye a secret from Tyler no longer applied.

"No time like the present," she said aloud in a scratchy morning voice that no one besides her could hear.

She had nothing else on her agenda. She couldn't start her waitressing job at the Gaithersburg location of the national chain she'd worked for in Nashville until Tuesday, the same day classes began. The apartment building where she planned to live wouldn't have a unit available until Friday.

Today was Saturday, the official start of the Labor Day weekend.

Nothing was stopping her from getting in the car

and making the short drive through the Maryland countryside to the town where she'd grown up and Tyler still lived.

Nothing except cowardice.

A memory of the unhappiness she'd glimpse on Jaye's face in the last few months they'd spent together flashed in Diana's mind. To be worthy of reuniting with her daughter, she needed to start somewhere.

She sat up and swung her legs off the bed.

As she drove over rolling hills and past lush, green fields inexorably closer to Bentonsville a short time later, she reassured herself that this was the right thing to do. Just as she'd been right years ago when she'd lied to Tyler about her sexual history and left town without telling him she was pregnant.

He'd been such a good friend, sticking steadfastly by her after her brother J.D. died—even after she'd sunk into a dark place where none of the other students at Bentonsville High had dared follow.

He'd kept her company on the black nights when the thought of going home to the house with the empty bedroom her brother would never occupy again had been too painful.

He'd rubbed her back the night she'd gotten so wasted she'd spent half of it emptying the contents of her stomach.

And he'd held her when she cried.

How could she have let him take responsibility for her pregnancy when it would have tarnished his excellent prospects for a bright future? Especially after he'd gushed about being accepted at Harvard?

He hadn't been just any seventeen-year-old, but along with her brother J.D., he was one of the golden boys of Bentonsville High. Everybody knew Tyler Benton, honor student and all-around great guy, was destined for great things. The town had been named for his great-grandfather, his father was the Laurel County state's attorney and the senior class had voted Tyler Most Likely to Succeed.

Everybody also knew Diana had gone off the deep end after her brother died: skipping school, shoplifting, drinking. Before Tyler, she'd also made out with a few boys who'd greatly embellished how far they'd gotten with her.

She still remembered the hurt in his eyes when she'd confirmed the false rumors about her loose reputation, the utter look of betrayal on his face the night before she'd left Bentonsville for good.

She blocked out the image, replacing it with the beauty of the countryside. The deep, rich green of the grass hinted at a summer generous with its rain. Wildflowers in purple and yellow added splashes of color. Horses grazed near white-framed homesteads and cool, blue ponds.

The transformation from rural to urban happened gradually, with a gas station and a convenience store announcing the small town ahead. She drove the lightly traveled street past the timeless brick beauty of the town hall, what looked like a newly built fire station and a quaint shopping area where not much had changed.

Cutaway, where her mother had taken her and her brothers for haircuts, still occupied a corner building.

She also recognized Bentonsville Butchers, the local dry cleaner and the convenience store where she'd been caught shoplifting cigarettes and beer.

At a red light, she glanced down at the piece of paper lying on the passenger seat. The address she'd gotten from the white pages of an Internet search engine jumped out at her in black, bold letters: 276 Farragut Street.

She'd mapped the location, again on the computer, to help her remember how to get there. Tyler's neighborhood was grander than the one where she'd grown up, but the suggested route took her through her old haunts.

The cut-through street was long and winding, the houses spaced a fair distance apart. If she turned right at the next corner, she'd reach the house where the mother she hadn't seen in more than ten years still lived.

She braked at the stop sign, but then continued straight ahead on a road that transported her back in time. For there was the playground where she and her brother J.D. used to compete to see who could swing the highest. Heavy wooden equipment with plastic toddler swings had replaced the metal swing set, but the weeping willow nearby was the same.

Diana remembered sitting motionless on one of the swings after J.D. had been stabbed to death by another teen during his senior year of high school. She'd stared at the tree, wondering how she could feel so miserable without actually weeping. The playground had later become the place she met Tyler when she snuck out of her house.

Not that her parents, consumed by their own grief, would have noticed had she strolled out the front door. Later, her mother had all but pushed her out, screaming that she'd shamed the family instead of recognizing that what her pregnant daughter needed most was support.

She stepped on the gas pedal, driving faster than she should past the playground with its collection of memories, some sad, some merely bittersweet. Within moments, the tenor of the neighborhood changed. The yards became more spacious, the houses bigger, the very feel of her surroundings more exclusive.

She would have known Tyler had fulfilled his early promise even if she hadn't researched him on the Internet. A third-generation graduate of Harvard Law, he worked as an assistant state's attorney in the same Laurel County office as his father before him. Tyler had already distinguished himself by winning a number of high-profile cases.

She rolled her car to a stop in front of an impressive two-story Colonial she thought was his, except another man hosed down his golden BMW in the driveway.

Spotting her parked in front of his house, the man turned off his hose and approached her car. Trim, gray-haired and wearing tailored shorts and a polo shirt, he looked like someone who would have his car washed for him. She hit the automatic control that rolled down the window and breathed in the scent of freshly cut grass.

"Can I help you?" The man bent at the waist to peer into the car. "You look lost."

He didn't know the half of it, she thought. "I'm looking for 276 Farragut."

"You're in front of it."

"Then Tyler Benton lives here?"

"You're looking for Ty?" Interest bloomed on his face, but he merely pointed down the street. "You must have transposed the numbers. He lives at 267. Four doors down on the left. The only Cape Cod in the neighborhood. You can't miss it."

"Thanks." She rolled up the window, not taking a chance that curiosity would get the better of him, and drove on.

She soon spotted a pale yellow house with blue-shuttered windows, a wide, inviting porch, a spacious lawn and lots of charm. Exactly the kind of place she'd choose if she could afford to buy a single-family house.

Two people stood on the porch, one with wheat-colored hair she instantly recognized as Tyler. She braked, her palms growing slick on the steering wheel. Taller and broader than he'd been at seventeen, he towered over the woman whose hand lightly touched his chest. Her face tilted up to his, her long, black hair cascading down her back.

They both wore sunglasses and casual clothes, as though heading for a picnic or perhaps a day on the water. Tyler's parents, she remembered, had kept a motor boat docked at a marina on the Potomac River.

With the backs of her eyes stinging, Diana pressed her foot down on the accelerator. Now, obviously, was not the time to approach Tyler. Especially considering the woman might be his wife. She could have discovered his marital status easily enough on line, but she hadn't thought to check.

Diana blinked rapidly a few times until her eyes felt normal again. She couldn't let whether or not Tyler was married matter. Not when she'd given up her foolish dreams of a future with him when she was sixteen.

In retrospect, it had been naive to expect Tyler to seek her out after she'd taken refuge at her aunt's house. Still, she'd envisioned him getting wind of her pregnancy and showing up at the front door. She'd imagined him claiming to know in his heart that he was her baby's father.

But Tyler never came. He never even called.

She supposed his silence had been understandable. What high school boy sought to be saddled with a baby—or the stupid girl who'd dreamed of becoming his wife?

But she hadn't considered Tyler to be a typical teenage boy. She'd thought he was…special.

She pushed aside the long-ago hurt and tried to view the new development dispassionately. She needed to think about whether the possibility of Tyler being married impacted her decision to tell him about Jaye. She supposed not. He was either the kind of man who'd seek to develop a relationship with his daughter—or he wasn't.

She knew from experience that not all men made good fathers, whatever the circumstances. She'd spent most of her formative years in a traditional household with two parents, and she'd never been close to her own father.

Denny Smith had been a good provider, but he'd focused most of his attention on ensuring that J.D.—the second of his three children—developed his amazing physical gifts.

Her mother had explained that Denny had passed on his dreams of playing pro football to his son. Unlike his father, J.D. had a spectacular arm, superior coordination and good speed. Armed with a full scholarship to Penn State, J.D. had also had an excellent chance of making his pro-football dream come true.

Diana didn't remember resenting J.D. for being the favorite or her father for favoring J.D. That's just the way it was. In his own way, she knew, her father loved her. When Diana had lived with her aunt during the first years of Jaye's life, her father had regularly mailed checks to help with baby expenses.

He still wanted to send her money. She'd called him on a lark yesterday, expecting to be grilled about her ten years of silence. Instead he'd talked her ear off about his pregnant second wife and the athletic accomplishments of his young son. Then he'd asked what amount he should fill in on a check she'd had too much pride to accept.

She expected Tyler to be more involved in Jaye's life than her father had been in hers, but she'd misjudged Tyler before.

She drove on auto pilot, reaching the edge of town before it registered that her fuel gauge light shined at her like a beacon. She sighed, the high cost of gas doing nothing to improve her spirits.

She pulled into the gas station, selected the cheapest

grade of fuel, then put the gas pump on automatic. As she watched the dollar amount on the display head quickly upward, a man called her name.

"Diana Smith. Is that really you?"

She glanced up to see a man striding away from a car she assumed was his. About her age with extremely short dark hair and eyes that hinted at his mother's Asian heritage, she would have known him anywhere.

"Oh, my gosh. Chris Coleman," she cried.

He met her halfway, picking her up and swinging her around as though she weighed almost nothing. She giggled, feeling like a kid again. After the three-sixty, he set her down but still held her by the shoulders.

"What happened to your hair?" she asked, wondering if she'd ever had such a clear view of his distinctive cheekbones, long straight nose and straight brows. His hair had hung down to his shoulders in high school, with much of it falling into his face.

"I decided to get a clearer view of life," he said.

She laughed.

"You look good." His friendly gaze roamed over her, perhaps comparing her to the emotional wreck she'd been when she left town. He hadn't been in much better shape, his sorrow heightened because he and J.D. had drifted apart in the months before her brother's death. "With your mom still living in Bentonsville, I hoped I'd run into you one of these days. And today's the day."

She didn't correct his mistaken impression, loath to explain, even to Chris, why she was really in Bentonsville.

"So you never left town?" she asked him.

"I left to go to college in Pennsylvania, a small school called East Stroudsburg."

"On a football scholarship. I remember you and J.D. talking about it," she commented as it came back to her. Chris and J.D. had been the only two players on the Bentonsville High team good enough to play at the next level.

"My scholarship paled next to J.D.'s." Chris fell silent, possibly thinking the same thing as Diana. That J.D. had never played football at Penn State. Or ever again.

"So you returned to Bentonsville after college?"

"Yeah, which is ironic since my parents retired to Florida. I majored in social work. When it came time to look for a job, I found out I was a Maryland boy at heart. How about you? Where have you been all these years, Diana Smith?"

"In Tennessee, mostly," she answered evasively.

She heard the click of the gas pump turning off and automatically glanced toward her car.

"No way," he said, sensing the direction her thoughts had taken. "I was heading out of town to spend the weekend with friends, but they're not expecting me at any specific time. So you're not getting away until I find out what you were doing in Tennessee. There's a Starbucks around the corner."

"A Starbucks? In Bentonsville?"

"Things have changed," he said. "So how about a cup of joe?"

Why not? she thought. Not only had she always enjoyed Chris's company, but he'd know exactly how much things had changed since she'd left Bentonsville. Not only with the town, but with Tyler Benton.

CHAPTER TWO

DIANA SIPPED from her caramel-flavored frappuccino, nearly shutting her eyes in delight. She'd managed to rid herself of most of her vices over the years, but not her love of coffee.

With its rich wood-themed interior and strong scent of brewing coffee, the shop resembled any of a hundred other branches of Starbucks. But as Diana settled into a slat-backed chair across from Chris at a table for two, the setting seemed unreal because it was within the borders of her hometown. A place to which she thought she'd never have the guts to return.

She glanced around at the half-dozen or so other patrons, relieved not to recognize any of them. Maybe she was still lacking in the guts department.

Chris leaned back in the chair that looked too small for his frame, grinned and asked, "So what have you been doing with yourself, Tag-Along?"

It had been so long since anyone had used the nickname, she'd forgotten about it. Chris and J.D. had come up with it when they were high school freshmen and Diana was a mere eighth grader. Nothing had seemed cooler than hanging out with the two boys and their friends.

She smiled wryly. “Not following the fun, that’s for sure.”

“Oh, no. Why’s that?”

Regretting her too-frank answer, she affected a shrug. “Life’s not as simple as it was when we were kids. I have responsibilities now. I didn’t go to college. I’ve worked secretarial jobs mainly, with some waitressing thrown in. But making enough money is always a struggle.”

“You’re a single mom, right?”

Diana nodded. She’d left Bentonsville before her pregnancy showed, so she couldn’t be sure how many people knew about Jaye. But Chris wasn’t just anyone. Growing up, he’d spent so much time at her house he’d seemed like a third brother.

“Yeah. Her name’s Jaye.” From the look that passed over Chris’s face, she gathered pointing out she’d named her child after her late brother was unnecessary. “She’s smart and sweet and the best thing that ever happened to me.”

“I’d love to meet her.” He sounded sincere, a quality she’d always associated with him. “Is she with your mother?”

She hesitated only briefly before saying, “She’s staying with Connor in Silver Spring until I get settled.”

Her brain spun, devising new replies should he ask follow-up questions but he fastened on something else.

“Until you get settled? What do you mean by that?”

“I’m in the process of moving to Gaithersburg. I’m starting classes this week at a career training center not far from there." Before he could ask when Jaye would join her, she continued, "But enough about me. What are you up to?"

Chris had always been shrewd. His dark piercing gaze told her he still was, but he let her get away with changing the subject.

"I'm the director of a community center that started up a few years back. I love it. We've got programs for seniors, aerobics classes, day care, community theater and meeting room space. We're always hopping."

"That's great, Chris. It seems like you've found a job that suits you."

He tapped a finger on his chin. "Is that another way of saying I'll never be rich and famous?"

"As though you want to be," she teased. "If making money was important to you, you never would have gone into social work."

He lifted both of his hands, palms up. "You've got me there."

She perched her elbows on the table, balanced her chin in her hands and made her eyes dance. "Okay. On to the good stuff. Are you married? Engaged? Seeing anyone?"

His hesitation was so brief she thought she might have imagined it. "Nope, nope and nope. How about you?"

"Ditto," she said, removing her elbows from the table. She'd dated some over the years but had never felt as intensely about anyone as she had about Tyler. She'd forced herself to put him out of her mind a long time ago, spurred by the crushing knowledge that despite the lies she'd told he would have come after her had he really loved her. "I always thought I'd get married some day, but I'm starting to think I was wrong."

"I hear you," Chris said.

Her brain whirled as she tried to figure out how to bring the topic around to Tyler. The more she knew about him, the better prepared she would be to tell him about Jaye. "I imagine a lot of people we went to school with are already married."

He nodded. "That's true."

What to say? Diana wondered. *How to say it?* "Funny, I just happened to see one of our ex-classmates when I was driving through town. Tyler Benton."

This time she was sure she didn't imagine Chris's body stiffening. She tried to sound nonchalant. "Is Tyler married?"

The seconds ticked by before Chris answered, marked by the heavy beating of her heart. Things would go more smoothly if Tyler wasn't married, she told herself. Not all wives would be accepting of a child from another relationship.

"No," Chris finally said, causing the knot in her stomach to unfurl. "Although I don't expect he'll wait much longer."

The knot balled up again. "Do you mean he's engaged?"

Chris fidgeted in his seat. "Not as far as I know. I meant the right kind of wife can help further the career of a guy like Benton, and the woman he's dating fits the bill. Any particular reason you're so curious?"

"Not really, except we used to be friends," she said

quickly while she wondered what kind of impact the sudden appearance of a child would have on Tyler's life.

"That's right," Chris said. "I vaguely remember that now that you mention it."

"We weren't all that close," she said, deliberately downplaying the connection. Until she told Tyler about Jaye, she couldn't afford to get tongues wagging, not that Chris had ever struck her as a gossip. "I probably wouldn't have much to say to him even if I had stopped and talked to him. Because, like I said, we weren't close."

Shut up, Diana, she instructed herself.

It appeared as though her long-winded explanation had piqued Chris's curiosity instead of sating it. But when he spoke, it wasn't of Tyler. "Getting back to the career training center you mentioned, what are you planning to study?"

She relaxed slightly. That question was simple enough to answer. "Business administration."

"Do you have a job lined up?"

Another easy question. "Yeah. I was waitressing at a Scarlet Pimpernel in Nashville. Do you know the chain? There's a restaurant in Gaithersburg."

He tapped the top of the table with the fingertips of one hand, and she could almost see gears turning in his brain. "What I'm going to say might sound crazy, but would you consider working for me instead?"

She felt her jaw drop. "Here in Bentonsville?"

He smiled. "That is where the community center is located."

Bentonsville was also the place of so much hurt for her, the place where Tyler and her mother still lived.

Merely driving here had been emotional. "Working in Bentonsville never occurred to me."

"That's because you didn't know I'd offer you a job. My office manager left last week. Doing both jobs is getting to be a strain. I wouldn't expect you to step into her position right away, but I could sure use the help, and from someone I know I can trust."

"You're serious." She read the verification on his face. "But don't you have an application process where you need to interview other candidates?"

"We're a nonprofit organization that operates under a grant that comes up for review every few years. I don't answer to anyone other than myself on personnel issues."

"But you don't know anything about me anymore."

"That's not true," he said. "I know you're a single mom with secretarial experience who used to live in Bentonsville. I also know you're the sister of the guy who used to be my best friend."

Chris and J.D. had once been as tight as two people could be, hanging out in the weight room, on the football field, in the halls at school. But they hadn't been close at the end. If guilt festered inside Chris, it was a different variety than the kind Diana lived with every day of her life.

"This is just about J.D., isn't it?" she asked quietly. "That's why you're offering me a job."

He glanced briefly away before his eyes settled on her once again. "I've always felt bad about how we drifted apart. So, yeah, J.D. has something to do with it. The fact that I used to think of you as a kid sister does, too. But the bottom line is I need to hire somebody soon, and you need a job."

"I have a job lined up."

"Not in the field you're planning to study, you don't. I'll show you the ropes, teach you some things about running an office. Think of it as on-the-job training." He named a figure on par with what she expected to earn as a waitress. Then he threw in better benefits.

She had to admit the job sounded like a godsend, but the allure of the position warred with panic at the thought of being back in Bentonsville. "I couldn't work nine to five, because my classes are in the mornings."

"Then work one to nine. Nine o'clock is when the community center closes. We're open seven days a week, but you can have two days off. Say, Sunday and Thursday."

"That would mean driving back to Gaithersburg every night on the dark, country roads."

"Don't live in Gaithersburg. Live in Bentonsville. You could even stay with your mother." He must have picked up on her tension, because he added. "Or rent an apartment. Housing costs in Bentonsville are relatively cheap. I might even know of a place."

She fidgeted with her coffee cup. The people who remembered her would recall that she'd been pregnant and unmarried when she left home, subjecting Jaye to unwanted curiosity once the child moved in with her. But while Diana's mind rejected Chris's suggestion that she live in Bentonsville, she didn't entirely dismiss the idea of working in town. It might be awkward for her, but she'd faced a lot worse than awkward the last few months and survived.

"I'm tempted," she said, thinking aloud.

"Wait 'til you see the center. There's not much going on today because of the holiday weekend. But come with me, have a look around first."

"You sure you have the time to give me a tour?"

"For you, Tag-Along, I'll make the time." Chris stood up, extending his hand to her. "So what do you say?"

The safe thing would be to refuse on the spot, but instead she placed her hand in his. What could it hurt to look?

DIANA INSERTED a chicken marsala frozen dinner in the compact microwave, set the controls on high for five minutes, then flopped down on her hotel bed.

A rerun of the pilot episode of *Everybody Loves Raymond* played on the television set across from the bed. As she watched the hectic beginning scenes, she vaguely remembered the plot. Ray's wife's birthday was approaching, and she wanted peace and quiet away from ringing phones, demanding kids and friends and family dropping by unannounced.

Three shrill beeps signaled her food was ready. Diana grabbed the remote and flicked off the TV before getting up from the bed.

Spending a quiet birthday wasn't all it was cracked up to be. She should know. She'd had one last month. It had been only slightly more bearable than the lonesome Labor Day weekend that was finally coming to an end. But she had only herself to blame for that. If she were really through being a coward, she'd have accepted Connor's invitation to spend the holiday with him. And Jaye.

Setting the packaged dinner down on the desk, she removed a cola from the small refrigerator and sat down. Through the walls, she could hear a young girl's high-pitched giggle and the deeper voices of a man and a woman.

She glanced at the streamlined phone by the bedside, longing to pick it up and make a connection with her own daughter. But the reason she'd given Connor for not being in touch with Jaye still stood.

She was like a leaf swirling in the wind, without a place to touch down. How could she even think about having Jaye with her until she'd landed?

She cut off a piece of chicken with her plastic knife, put it in her mouth and chewed. The taste didn't compare to the chicken marsala served by the Scarlet Pimpernel, which is what she could be eating tomorrow night after she'd attended her first day of classes and started her new job.

But the position the restaurant manager in Nashville had lined up for her no longer seemed as attractive. Supposedly the Scarlet Pimpernel had prospective waitresses lining up at the door, but Diana kept thinking about the Bentonsville Community Center.

She'd make about as much money as she would at the restaurant, which would still enable her to afford a nice-sized unit in the apartment complex she'd chosen. But not only would she have more scheduling flexibility, she'd have better health coverage for Jaye.

She heard a door opening, then closing, and the voices of the family that had been in the next room growing softer as they moved down the hall toward the elevator. Then the quiet was so pronounced, she could hear herself chew.

When she and Chris stopped by the community center on Saturday, the place had been, to use one of Chris's words, hopping in spite of the holiday weekend. Small children and their parents had gyrated to the music in one of the all-purpose rooms hosting a Mom & Me exercise class. Senior citizens had congregated in the great room for their weekly Saturday afternoon bingo game. And a raucous basketball game had been going on at an outside court.

Pushing her half-eaten container of food away from her, Diana got to her feet and picked up her purse from the floor beside the bed. She rummaged through it, finally pulling out a business card.

Not giving herself time to change her mind, she punched in the number on the hotel phone and counted the rings. One. Two. Three.

"Hello," Chris Coleman said, his voice coming through bright and jovial. Commotion reined in the background, as though the community center had hit a particularly busy spell.

"Hi, Chris. It's Diana Smith. Is the job you offered me still available?"

TYLER BENTON RUSHED through the Bentonsville Community Center in the direction Valerie, the receptionist, had directed, aware of minutes ticking by that could be spent preparing for trial.

It couldn't be helped. He needed to take care of this today.

The high-pitched chatter of the children in center-based day care mingled with the rusty voices of seniors playing bridge as he stood at the head of a large room, scanning the crowd.

"Yoo hoo, Tyler." The greeting came from one of the women at the nearest card table: his sixth-grade teacher, the white hair piled on her head adding inches to her height.

"Hello, Mrs. Piper." He tamped down his impatience and smiled at her. The other women at the table looked up from their cards. Tyler knew two of them, who he greeted by name. Mrs. Piper introduced him to the third, Mrs. Ruth Grimes, a plump woman with old-fashioned horn-rimmed glasses.

"Tyler here is an assistant state's attorney," Mrs. Piper told her, "although we all know he's destined for even better things."

Mrs. Grimes peered at him with interest over the top of her glasses. "Oh, really? Then perhaps you'd like to meet my granddaughter. She's a peach."

"I'm afraid that adorable Lauren Fairchild got to him first." Mrs. Piper lowered her voice as though confiding a secret. To Tyler, she said, "I saw you two together at church on Sunday. You make a lovely couple."

Tyler's father, who'd invited the omnipresent Lauren to sit with them, had voiced the same sentiment. Tyler let Mrs. Piper's comment slide, the same way he'd ignored his father's verbal shove in Lauren's direction. If he claimed not to be serious about Lauren, he'd find himself on a blind date with Mrs. Grimes's granddaughter.

"Have any of you seen your director?" he asked. "I've got some business with him."

"I wondered what you were doing here in the middle of the day." Mrs. Piper craned her neck just as Chris Coleman stood up from a chair he'd pulled up to one of the other tables. "There's Chris now. He's such a sweetheart."

The three other woman nodded, their assessment of Chris unanimous.

"Don't let me interrupt your bridge game any more than I already have," Tyler said, his mind on taking care of business and getting back to work. "It was a pleasure to see you ladies."

He moved toward Chris, who excused himself from the foursome to whom he'd been talking. The charming smile the director had bestowed on the ladies of Bentonsville disappeared.

"Benton," he said in lieu of a greeting.

"Chris." Tyler inclined his chin. "I've got to talk to you."

"Now? It couldn't have waited until tonight?"

Tyler spent some of his very limited free time on the center's outdoor basketball court, playing ball with the teen boys who congregated there. "I can't make it tonight. Or any time soon, I'm afraid. I'm about to go to trial."

"Then what's so important you're here now?"

Tyler looked around, encountering a half-dozen sets of interested eyes. He indicated a nearby hallway with a jerk of his head. Receiving his silent message, Chris walked with him until they were out of hearing range of the card players.

"Okay, what's up?" Chris asked.

The director's manner was friendly. His eyes were not. Although they'd never run in the same social circles, Tyler had graduated from high school the same year as Chris. The animosity he sensed rolling off the director hadn't appeared until recently. Lately, it seemed as though Chris plain didn't like him. Well, Tyler didn't like what Chris had done.

Tyler carefully kept his next statement non-accusatory. "Jim Jeffries told me you backed out of buying his pool tables."

Jim owned a bar and two regulation-size pool tables he was about to replace. He would have sold them to the center at well under retail. Tyler should know. He'd negotiated the price.

"That's right. I took a closer look at the budget and decided the center couldn't afford it." Chris crossed his arms over his chest, as though reluctant to explain himself. That didn't make sense. Chris often stated that the community deserved a say in matters concerning the center.

"Jim says he has another offer. The center can't afford not to buy those pool tables," Tyler argued. "As soon as the nightly basketball game's over, the kids scatter."

"Pool tables aren't enough to make them stick around."

"They're a start," Tyler snapped. He ran a hand through his hair, frustrated at himself for raising his voice. Every good lawyer knew cool logic got better results than heated words. "We're on the same side here,

Chris. We both want to keep kids off the street. But how can we do that if we can't keep them at the center?"

"I don't disagree." Chris's body language said differently. "But I have to consider what's good not only for the teen program, but for the center as a whole. Our grant's up for renewal in a few months. How can I justify spending such a large chunk of money on our least represented group?"

"By explaining that you're trying to increase attendance."

"Except I believe you can't solve a problem by throwing money at it. Look at some of the things we've tried since the center opened. Paid speakers who talked to mostly empty rooms. Dances where nobody came. A study lounge hardly anybody uses."

Tyler addressed only his last concern. "That's because there are no computers in the study area."

"Computers cost money, which we don't have much of. I've got a tight budget. And, like I said, a lot of other programs to consider."

"Then I'll donate the pool tables," Tyler said, surprised the solution hadn't occurred to him before now. He'd sunk most of his disposable income into the house he'd bought last year, but he could afford used pool tables. "And maybe you could do some fund-raising for the computers."

"Any fund-raising I do is global, benefiting the center as a whole. I can't—"

"What if I get somebody to donate the computers?" Tyler asked, although he could ill afford the time. His work schedule was jammed.

Chris transferred his weight from one foot to the other. "That'd be great. But I'm still skeptical that pool tables and a couple computers will increase attendance."

"It can't hurt."

"I hope you're right," Chris said, then nodded to him. "Now if you'll excuse me, I have some things I need to do."

Without another word, Chris headed down the hall. Tyler turned to leave and saw what he thought was a mirage. Walking toward him was a grown-up version of Diana Smith, the girl who'd broken his heart. He blinked, expecting her to disappear, but she kept coming.

Her figure was curvier, the glossy brown hair she'd once worn parted in the middle feathered around her face and her features more mature but there was no mistake about it. It was Diana, who'd left Bentonsville—and him—ten years ago.

Memories slammed into him. Of Diana's tears dampening his T-shirt while she cried over her dead brother. Of her hazel eyes reflecting the attraction he hadn't been able to deny. Of her face infused with pleasure and passion as he made love to her.

Of her lips telling him she'd cheated on him with countless other guys.

The last memory was the strongest, perhaps because it had been the impetus he'd used to get over her.

And he had gotten over her. Years ago. But that didn't mean he hadn't thought about her and wondered what had become of her. Especially recently when her mother had been on a quest to keep her brother's killer from getting parole, gathering signatures on a petition in front of the grocery store and placing ads in the local newspaper.

With her clear skin, apple cheeks and gently arched brows, Diana had a natural quality that had always captivated him. She'd gotten even more appealing with age, something his infatuated teenage self wouldn't have thought possible.

Her step didn't falter, her slight smile didn't waver, as though seeing him again hadn't unduly affected her. It could have been because she'd done the spurning, although he could no longer blame her for that. With the wisdom that comes with age, he understood that she'd turned to him out of grief. But it still stung that he hadn't mattered much to her while she'd been vital to him.

"Hello, Tyler," she said, her voice still low, still smoky.

Annoyed at his reaction to her, he tried to pull himself together but still couldn't manage to smile. "Hello, Diana."

He knew he was staring, but couldn't help it. Although her oval-shaped face appeared virtually the same, her eyes seemed different, as though they'd seen more than she'd bargained for. His gaze slid downward to the tiny mole to the left of her mouth that he used to like to kiss. Before she'd told him he hadn't been the only guy she'd granted access to it.

The thought snapped him out of his embarrassing stupor. He wasn't a teenager anymore but an accomplished adult who prided himself on his poise. He could deal with the unexpected appearance of a girl from his past.

"This is quite a surprise," he said, pleased his voice sounded the way it always did. "I hadn't realized you were in town visiting."

A few beats of silence passed before she shook her head. "I'm not visiting. I'm working here at the center."

"You're working at the center?" he repeated numbly, barely keeping the incredulity out of his voice. "Since when?"

"Since today, actually." She slipped one of her hands in the front pocket of her slacks, where she seemed to be fiddling with something. He tried to wrap his mind around the startling revelation that she wasn't only back in Bentonsville temporarily. She was back to stay. "I'm going to school in Gaithersburg. My plan was to work there, too. But I ran into Chris over the weekend, he offered me a job and here I am."

Yeah, here she was. Back in Bentonsville for a reason that had nothing to do with him.

Blindsided that he'd subconsciously wished she'd returned to town because of him, he felt the need to put space between them. He wasn't that naive kid who'd once stupidly confused a grieving girl's dependence for something it wasn't.

But for the life of him, he couldn't make himself move.

"How about you?" She broke the deafening silence between them. "What are you doing here?"

"I needed to talk to Chris." His spinning brain furnished a reason why he was still frozen in place. Should he prepare himself to run into her around every Bentonsville corner? "Are you living here in town?"

"No, I'm not. I'm in a hotel right now but I'll probably get an apartment in Gaithersburg."

"I hope it all works out for you," he said shortly. *Move, Tyler,* he told himself. *Leave before you say something you'll regret.* "If you'll excuse me, I need to be getting back to work."

"Oh, of course," she said, taking a step sideways so he had more room to pass. The way she turned her head subtracted years from her face, peeling the decade away and taking him back to the time he was trying to forget. A time when he'd dreamed of a perfect girl, a girl he cared about and who cared about him.

He walked determinedly past her, banking his urge to speed up. His vaunted poise hadn't held up as well as he'd hoped, but a hasty retreat might give her the idea that her long-ago betrayal still hurt.

Which, unfortunately, it did.

CHAPTER THREE

DIANA SAT on the tall stool behind the welcome counter during a temporary lull, nursing her third cup of coffee of the day and turning over and over a smooth, flat stone with a psychedelic design.

Jaye had painted it last year during art class, then gravely presented it after Diana crashed into the tree. Amidst all the upheaval in their lives, Diana had forgotten the stone's existence—until she'd found it inside a box last night, its bold slashes of red, blue and yellow demanding to be noticed.

Her daughter had insisted it was a good-luck charm. After Diana's earlier encounter with Tyler, during which she'd held onto the stone like a lifeline, she seriously doubted it held hidden power.

She'd wondered if Tyler had thought to ask about her child, paving the eventual way for her to tell him he had a daughter. But he'd been silent, showing no more interest in the subject than he had a decade ago.

Disappointment rose up in Diana. He'd seemed like a stranger and not the boy she'd loved.

She hadn't remembered him being over six feet, but then he'd been young when they were together and possibly still growing. His chest and shoulders had filled out, changes apparent despite his well-cut gray suit. His face was different, too. The shape more rectangular, his clefted chin squarer, his blue eyes warier.

Once she'd been able to tell him anything, but she'd had a hard time getting out any words at all, let alone about Jaye.

She pushed off the floor with her right foot, sending the stool revolving in a complete three-sixty. She couldn't let their difficult first meeting deter her. Her reasons for telling Tyler about Jaye hadn't changed. Clearing her conscience so she could start her life anew constituted only a minor part of it. Doing right by her daughter—and, by extension, Tyler—made up the rest.

When the stool faced frontward again, a vaguely familiar woman with dyed red hair and a matronly figure was approaching.

"Aren't you Elaine Smith's daughter, Diana?" the woman, who was probably in her sixties, asked in a voice Diana recognized at once.

Diana's hand closed around the stone. She'd told Chris filling in at the welcome desk while the regular receptionist went on lunch break wasn't a problem, but she'd lied.

She'd gotten through her initial meeting with Tyler, but she wasn't ready to face her past and the rest of the people who populated it.

Please, God, she prayed, don't let the woman have worked at the high school. Teachers talked, and Bentonsville High's insulated community ensured that everybody knew Diana had been trouble. After Diana abruptly left town amidst rumors that she was an easy lay, speculation that she was pregnant must have been rampant.

"You're right," she admitted slowly. "I am Diana Smith."

The woman smiled broadly, causing the tension in Diana's shoulders to ebb but not entirely abate.

"I thought that was you. Elaine and I used to volunteer together in the school library when you were in elementary school. Have you worked here long?"

"Chris just hired me."

"He's such a dear, isn't he?" The woman didn't wait for her answer. "I'm Jake Wilson's mother. You remember Jake, don't you?"

Diana faintly recalled a boisterous kid with strawberry-blond hair, but Mrs. Wilson chattered on before Diana could respond. "Jake's an engineer in Baltimore. He's married with two adorable kids. How about you?"

Diana squeezed the stone tighter. "I have a daughter."

Mrs. Wilson's expression softened. "I know, dear. It's too bad about your fiancé dying in that car accident right after your brother died, God rest both of their souls. What a tough time that must have been, with you being so young."

Her fiancé?

"Your mother was beside herself, poor dear, especially because she was the one who insisted it'd do you good to get away from Bentonsville. You went to live with an aunt, didn't you?"

Speechless, Diana nodded. That was the only true part of the entire story.

"I'd love to meet your little girl one day," Mrs. Wilson said. "Please tell your mother I said hello and that she should give me a call. Or, better yet, I'll call her."

Diana had yet to inform her mother she'd returned to Bentonsville, a fact she wouldn't have revealed even if her mind hadn't been on the fiction the older woman had spun. Was Mrs. Wilson's version of events what everybody in Bentonsville thought had happened? Is that what Tyler believed?

Mrs. Wilson chatted blithely on for a few more moments before announcing she was off to a pottery-making class, stopping along the way to talk with Chris. Diana nearly rushed the pair so she could drag Chris away and interrogate him but waited to flag him down until he finished talking.

"Tell me something, Chris," she said before he reached the counter, not able to hold off another second. "What do you know about what happened to me after I left Bentonsville?"

Confusion stamped his features. "A lot. Don't you remember? We talked about it over coffee a few days ago."

"I don't mean recently. I mean right after I left town, when I lived with my aunt."

He scratched his head, taking a maddeningly long time to answer. "Only what your mother told me. That you met a guy and got pregnant and that he died in a car accident. I didn't ask you about Jaye's father because I thought it still might be a sore spot."

"It is," she verified, but for a different reason than Chris suspected. Jaye's father wasn't dead, but very much alive—and quite possibly sure he hadn't gotten Diana pregnant.

Chris anchored both hands on the counter, obviously believing she'd cued him to change the subject. "How's the job going, Diana?"

"Great," she said, the wheels in her head spinning madly as the pieces of the past clicked into place. It had never occurred to her that Tyler wouldn't have figured out she was pregnant when she left town.

"I'm glad everything's working out," Chris said with genuine enthusiasm. "I got the feeling you weren't too keen on manning the welcome desk."

She hadn't been, fearing the people who recognized her would try to figure out who in Bentonsville had fathered Jaye. Because of the story her mother had concocted and spread, that wouldn't be the case.

"You got me there," Diana admitted. "I'll have to put on my tin-foil hat the next time I see you coming."

He laughed. "I don't have to be a mind reader to tell you were nervous about running into people you used to know. Don't forget, I knew you way back when."

But he didn't know her secret. Apparently nobody except her immediate family members were aware that the father of Diana's child was from Bentonsville.

"I need you to do something for me," Chris announced, drawing her attention back to the present. She'd think about Tyler and the implications of what she'd learned later. Chris might be her friend, but first and foremost he was her boss. "Remember how I mentioned the turnout for the teen program has been disappointing? Tyler Benton is planning some fund-raising so we can equip the study lounge with computers."

Surprise jolted through her even though she'd seen

Tyler in the community center only a few hours before. "I didn't know Tyler was involved with the center."

"People as ambitious as Benton get involved with places like this all the time," Chris said, then remarked, "It looks good on their resumes."

Even as a teenager, Tyler had talked about surpassing the accomplishments of his very successful father and grandfather and one day becoming a judge. To that end, he'd taken the most advanced classes at Bentonsville High, read incessantly and applied to the best colleges. He poured himself into whatever he did, whether it was playing on the basketball team or taking an exam. Or kissing her. But something inside Diana rebelled at Chris's comment.

"Tyler wouldn't use the community center to make himself look good," she said. "He's not like that."

Chris squinted at her. "I thought you said you didn't know him that well."

"I don't. I mean, I only know what I remember about him."

"People change, Diana. You'd do well to remember that. But I'm not going to question Benton's motives. What I need you to do is let me know if he makes any progress on getting those computers."

"Okay," she said, her heart beating harder at the prospect of seeing Tyler again. "I'll see what I can do."

"You won't need to try too hard. Benton's a semi-regular at the basketball games that go on here at night. He mentioned he's about to start a trial, so you might not see him for a couple days. But believe me, he'll be around."

Diana's stomach jumped with anticipation at seeing Tyler again now that she was armed with her newfound knowledge. A bitterness she hadn't realized she harbored seemed to melt away from her heart as her mind formulated a plan.

Maybe she could ask Tyler out for coffee, possibly at the same Starbucks where Chris had taken her. The establishment had an outside seating area, where they could talk in relative privacy.

"Diana, are you listening to me?"

Her head snapped up. "Sorry. What did you say?"

"I asked if you figured out the filing system and familiarized yourself with the types of programs the center offers?"

"I did," she said.

He lightly rapped the desk. "Great. Let me know if you need anything else, including the number of the Realtor who's renting that place I told you about."

He'd mentioned the apartment enough times that she'd devised a tactful reply about being careful not to act in haste and repent in leisure. But that was before she'd learned the story her mother had invented about her pregnancy. Before she realized nobody would gossip about Jaye after her daughter moved in with her.

"Actually," she said, "I would like that number."

He grinned, reached into his wallet, pulled out a business card decorated with a Realtor's logo and slapped it on the counter. "Hot damn. That's good news. It means my newest hire is here to stay."

She smiled at his enthusiasm. "How do you figure that?"

"You wouldn't consider living in Bentonsville if you didn't think things would work out here."

She rested her hands on her hips. "I'll have to get out that tin-foil hat after all."

His good-natured laughter lingered in her ears even after he was gone. The sound traveled through her and stirred up the hope bubbling inside her.

Mere days ago, the thought of returning to Bentonsville had terrified her. Now with a little luck she'd be able to move out of the lonely hotel room in the next few days. Then she'd have the fast-approaching weekend to fix her new place up to her liking. She could spend part of it decorating the second bedroom in shades of pink, Jaye's favorite color.

She still had some major hurdles to overcome before she could get Jaye back—including dealing with her mother—but the biggest obstacle no longer seemed so high.

To think that for all these years she'd harbored an unfounded grudge against Tyler for not at least trying to find out whether he was Jaye's father.

The hope that everything would work out rose in her like the helium in a balloon. She picked up the colorful stone from the surface of the desk, tossed it into the air and caught it.

For the first time since she'd set foot in Bentonsville again, she truly believed the town where her daughter's father lived represented the perfect place to start over.

TO MOLLY JACOBY, anywhere was better than home. Even the community center, with the funny old ladies playing cards and the little kids squealing on the playground.

Besides, she'd catch hell if she got home before school let out. If there was anybody home to catch her. Her dad had moved in with his girlfriend after the divorce and still lived in Virginia, which Molly liked better than this nothing little town. Her mom was a nurse who was always around except when she needed her.

Not that Molly had needed her in a very long time. Not like her younger brothers and sister did. Jeremy and Jason, the twins, were second-graders. Little Rosie had just started kindergarten.

Molly was sixteen, as her mom constantly reminded her. Old enough to chip in now that her dad was gone. So how come Molly didn't help around the house more, babysit the kids and make better grades while she was at it?

Nag, nag, nag.

It had gotten so bad Molly invented lies so she didn't have to come home. Her mom actually believed she was on the technical crew for the school play. As if Molly would have anything to do with a production as lame as *Peter Pan*.

Although the center was one of her daytime hangouts, she seldom showed up after dark. The past couple nights, she'd hung with the crowd that snuck into the county park after closing. She'd made few friends since moving to town a month ago so she'd jumped when Bobby Martinelli told her she should come. She'd almost died on the spot that a boy as good looking as Bobby had noticed her at all.

He and his friends mostly drank beer at one of the picnic shelters. It tasted gross, so Molly didn't take more than a swallow or two even though Bobby urged her to drink more. Bobby had been pushing her to do a lot of other things, too, but so far she hadn't let him past second base.

Her mom would throw a fit if she knew where Molly had been spending her nights. And who she'd been spending them with. But her mom was so busy with the little kids and so bitter about the divorce, she didn't have the energy to keep tabs on Molly.

She sure could muster the strength to yell at her, though.

The teen study lounge was deserted, pretty much its usual state. Molly had lurked outside the center until Valerie, the usual receptionist, had left her post, then slipped inside, minimizing the chance that anybody would give her the third degree.

Molly dropped her backpack beside an armchair, then dug around for her CD player. Most of the other kids had iPods, but not Molly. Her mom claimed they were an "unnecessary extravagance."

She put in a CD by a loud rock band, plugged in her earphones and curled up on the chair with a book she'd lifted from the school library just to see if she could.

She tucked her legs up under her and soon lost herself in a Terry Pratchett book set in a make-believe land with trolls and elves and lots of other cool stuff. Just when she was getting to the epic battle, a shadow fell over her.

A woman she'd never seen before wearing a name

tag that identified herself as a center employee stood over her. Younger than most of the people at the center, she was still a good ten years older than Molly. An adult. Rolling her eyes, Molly took out her earphones, cutting off a heavy metal riff.

"You surprised me, too," the woman said. "I didn't know anyone was in here."

Molly said nothing, hoping the woman would take the hint and go away. She looked nervous enough. Instead, the woman asked, "Good book?"

Molly shrugged. "It's okay."

The woman angled her head, reading the author's name on the back cover. "Oh, I love Terry Pratchett. Have you read the one where the Grim Reaper takes an apprentice? That's my favorite."

Molly loved that book most, too, but she only grunted.

The woman's smile faltered, but she stuck out a hand. "I'm Diana Smith. I started working here a couple days ago."

Molly ignored her hand, but enough manners had been drilled into her that she grudgingly said, "I'm Molly."

"So, Molly," she said, her voice wavering a little, "what brings you here at this time of day?"

So that was what this was all about. Goody Two-shoes obviously knew school was still in session. Molly went on the defensive. "They don't care if you leave early if you have study hall last period."

Diana squirmed, as though talking to Molly made her uncomfortable. But that couldn't be. She was very pretty with great skin, clear and pale. Molly used tons of zit cream to ensure she didn't scare young children.

"How'd you do it?" Diana asked. "Forge a note about a doctor's appointment or slip out that back door by the gym?"

"How'd you know about the back door?"

"I went to Bentonsville High," she said. "If you go out that door and cross a road, the woods are right there. Then you're home free."

"*You* used that escape route?" Molly injected heavy skepticism into her voice.

"All the time." Diana's words carried a ring of truth, although she seemed ashamed of the admission.

Well, Molly didn't feel guilty. "I went out the back door. It was easy because I have PE last period. The teacher loses track of who's there and who's not."

Molly had forged her mom's signature before, too. She'd never leave school without covering her tracks. A terrible thought occurred to her, and her heart raced. "You're not going to tell my mom, are you?"

"Why would I do that?"

Molly's heart rate returned to normal. "Because I shouldn't be skipping school."

"Then why are you?"

"Why did you?" Molly shot back.

Diana didn't answer for a moment. "I guess because I didn't want to be there."

"That's my reason, too."

"Okay," Diana said, as though she actually accepted that. "I've got to get back to work."

She'd almost reached the door when she turned

around. "If you ever want to talk about anything—Terry Pratchett books, school, anything—just come find me. I'll be around."

Then she left.

Molly frowned, wondering what had possessed her to admit she'd skated out of her last class. How could she be sure Diana wouldn't rat her out?

Diana had seemed okay. She wasn't too old and she hadn't lectured Molly about doing the right thing. But Diana was one of them. An adult.

Molly snorted, disgusted with herself for revealing anything at all to Diana. She put her headphones back on and opened her book, wondering how long it would be until she caught hell for skipping school.

THE APPLE-CHEEKED KID on the stand looked about fifteen years old, although Tyler's court documents stated his age as nineteen.

Unlucky for the kid.

The juries in adult cases usually came down harder on offenders than juvenile court judges, a bad thing for Grant Livingstone. Because Tyler was about to prove without a reasonable doubt that the teenager had committed arson.

Nobody had died, but the owner of the single-family home that had burned to the ground suffered second-degree burns trying to contain the flames before the fire department arrived.

"I'd like to make sure I have some of the facts straight," Tyler said, sidling up to the young man. Up close, dressed in a too-big navy blue suit, Grant looked like a boy playing dress-up in his father's clothes. "Is that okay, Mr. Livingstone?"

"Uh, sure." The kid clearly wasn't used to being addressed formally.

"You say the empty gas can police found in your parents' garage is one you used to fill up the tank of the lawn mower. Is that correct?"

"Yeah," Grant said, then seemed to remember where he was. "I mean, yes, sir."

"You also maintain that you were seen in the vicinity of the fire shortly before it started because the house that burned down was along your running route. True?"

"Yes, sir." The teen straightened and spoke louder, more confidently. "I pass right by that house, I mean where that house used to be, when I go out for a run."

"How long have you been running that route?"

"Not long. I change my route all the time."

"I see," Tyler said.

And he did. Circumstantial evidence had been enough to bring Grant to trial, but not enough to convict him. Without a motive, the odds of the teenager walking free were sky high.

Grant knew that. That's why he'd refused to plea bargain and why his wealthy father had shelled out big bucks to hire a defense attorney. However, they were unaware of what Tyler knew.

"Mr. Livingstone, do you know a Dr. Millicent Osgood?"

Shock flashed across the kid's face, which he quickly masked. But Tyler had seen it and knew the case was as good as won.

"Objection," Grant's defense attorney called, clearly not recognizing the name. "Irrelevant."

Tyler glanced back at the young lawyer, a junior associate at a legal firm that counted one of Tyler's neighbors as a partner.

The attorney had mounted a fairly impressive defense but erred when he let Livingstone take the stand. The law didn't require defendants to testify, a marked advantage if your client was guilty. A prosecutor who'd done his homework could almost always get a guilty man to incriminate himself. The younger the defendant, Tyler found, the more likely he was to slip up.

All of which meant that the very young lawyer from Ernst, Cooper and Pettinger must actually believe his even younger client wasn't guilty.

"If the court will bear with me," Tyler told the judge, a statuesque woman in her sixties. "I'll show how Dr. Osgood relates to this case."

"Overruled," the judge said. "The defendant will answer the question."

"Dr. Osgood was my twelfth-grade biology teacher at Bentonsville High."

Tyler waited a moment for that fact to sink in with the jury. "Mr. Livingstone, do you have a high school diploma?"

Grant squirmed in his seat. "No."

"Why not? You were supposed to graduate with your high school class last year, weren't you?"

"I, uh, didn't pass all my subjects."

"Isn't it true that the subject you flunked was biology and Dr. Osgood was the teacher who flunked you?"

The pause before Grant answered stretched longer than before. "Yeah."

"Where do you go to school now, Mr. Livingstone?"

"Rockville Prep."

"If not for that grade in biology, you'd be in college, correct?"

"Objection, Your Honor," the defense attorney interrupted, not without a touch of panic. "I fail to see how any of this is relevant."

Before the judge could rule, Tyler said, "I'd like to submit a phone book into evidence, Your Honor. It goes directly to relevance."

"Don't try my patience, counselor," the judge told Tyler. "Connect the dots in the next minute or you'll have to move on from this line of questioning."

"Understood." Tyler strode to the prosecutor's table and picked up the community phone book he'd placed there. While walking back to Grant, he flipped it open to a bookmarked page, then handed it to the defendant.

"Mr. Livingstone, would you please read the address listed next to Dr. Millicent Osgood's phone number?"

The kid reminded him of a caged animal, his eyes frantically searching for a means of escape. After a moment, he cleared his throat and read, "9926 Fairmont Road."

"Do you know the address of the place that burned down?" Tyler asked.

"No, I don't," Grant said, but his eyes and his manner said otherwise.

"Let the record show that address is 9962 Fairmont Road."

Tyler didn't relish the gasps and shocked murmurs that reverberated throughout the courtroom. Despite the arrogance that shined through in his manner, Grant seemed more like a misguided kid than a bad one. He'd set the fire in a trash can, probably only intending to frighten. But the wind had been gusty that day, spreading the flames to the branches of a nearby tree that butted up against the house. The resulting inferno had happened very fast.

Tyler spent a good chunk of time trying to get Grant to admit to arson, with no success. But by the time the judge adjourned for lunch, the damage was done. Tyler had furnished the jury with a motive and a defendant who couldn't meet his eyes when he lied.

The defense attorney would probably spend the lunch break talking to his client about trying to make a deal, but it was too late for that now that Tyler had the case won. Tyler's boss, the state's attorney, took pride in his office's high conviction rate and would never approve a plea bargain at this late stage.

Tyler gathered his papers, placed them in the expensive calfskin leather briefcase his father had bought him last Christmas and headed for the exit.

"Impressive job in there, Tyler." Jon Pettinger, the neighbor who lived a few doors from him, separated himself from the crowd and shook his hand. Jon kept himself in such good shape that he could have passed for a man a few decades younger if not for his gray hair.

"Thanks, Jon. That's big of you to say, considering it was your colleague sitting at the defense table. I'm lucky you weren't there beside him."

"I'm working another case or I might have been. I was only present today because I happened to be at the courthouse and thought I'd check up on him. I didn't see much, just the fireworks at the end. You caught my guy unawares, which is a good lesson for him."

"It's all about gaining experience and putting in the time. Next time your associate will be better prepared so the prosecution doesn't surprise him again."

"You're right. But next time he won't be up against an opponent who might become the youngest circuit court judge ever appointed in Maryland."

"I take it you heard I put in an application for the vacancy."

"I heard more than that. I heard the judicial nominating commission is very impressed with you. Unless you blow the interview, they'll recommend the governor appoint you to the bench for sure."

The thirteen-member commission, armed with background information and statements from local bar associations and interested citizens, would soon meet to interview all the candidates. Tyler had every intention of sailing through the interview, the same way he'd aced his tests in college and law school.

"That's only the first step," Tyler said. "The commission can recommend up to seven candidates."

"I still wouldn't bet against a guy as accomplished as you, although I'd go nuts if I put in the time you do," he said with a laugh, then lowered his voice as though they were coconspirators. "Just tell me one thing. Did you get the idea to cross check the addresses because of what happened on Labor Day weekend?"

Tyler cocked his head, trying to remember back to last weekend. He'd spent most of it working, although Lauren Fairchild had stopped by his house in an unsuccessful attempt to persuade him to come to her family's cookout. "I don't follow."

"With that woman who transposed our house numbers. She stopped at my place on Saturday by mistake, but I pointed her in the right direction. Don't tell me she never found you."

"I was at the office most of the day Saturday," Tyler said, then quickly asked, "What did this woman look like?"

"Very attractive. Brown hair a little longer than shoulder length. Big hazel eyes. Oh, and a tiny mole to the left of her mouth, like the one that supermodel has."

The woman he'd described was Diana Smith.

If his neighbor hadn't pointed out the mole, Tyler never would have come up with her name.

What could she possibly have come to his house to say after all these years? And why hadn't she said it when he'd run into her at the community center?

A number of hackneyed expressions ran through his head: water under the bridge. Let bygones by bygones. What's done is done.

He didn't listen to any of them. What Diana had to say shouldn't matter and probably wouldn't in the long run. But one way or the other, he intended to find out what it was.

CHAPTER FOUR

THE TRIAL KEEPING Tyler away from the community center had entered the second day of its second week. Diana knew this, because the front page of the *Laurel County Times* had faithfully reported each day's events. Speculation was that the judge would hand over the case to the jury today.

The last time Diana had read the *Times* in any detail had been years ago when the prosecuting attorney had been Tyler's father and the boy on trial the one who'd murdered her brother.

This trial also had a teenage defendant and sensationalist elements, but there the similarities ended. A different Benton was prosecuting this case, the teenager's weapon had been a gas can instead of a knife and nobody had died.

Diana relegated J.D. to the back of her mind, from where he never left, and put aside the stack of registrations she'd been inputting into a computer spreadsheet. She stood up and stretched her arms overhead.

The hour hand on the wall clock had passed seven, meaning the pickup basketball game on the outside court was well underway. Since Tyler had finished presenting his side of the case, maybe he'd joined the game.

She reached into the pocket of her slacks, fingering the good-luck stone. For the first time in forever, it seemed as though things would work out. She enjoyed her job, and she was doing well in her classes. She'd also moved into the perfect place over the weekend: an affordable two-bedroom garage apartment in a neighborhood filled with children.

She'd yet to make contact with her mother but had tried calling twice, both times getting her answering machine and both times failing to leave a message. Baby steps, she reminded herself, even though she was poised to take a giant one.

All the ingredients had come together for her to tell Tyler about Jaye: tonight. Call her crazy, but she even looked forward to it.

She expected him to be angry at first, but he'd always been reasonable. Once she explained her belief that a baby would have dimmed his bright future, he'd come to understand why she'd lied.

She ventured into the twilight, following the sounds of young men chattering and a basketball bouncing until she reached the lighted court behind the community center. She kept close to the building, bracing herself for the sight of Tyler.

Ten males in baggy shorts and loose-fitting T-shirts raced up and down the court while another five or six sat courtside on a metal bleacher. Aside from Chris Coleman, who was dressed in street clothes and watching, nobody was out of their teens.

When her shoulders slumped, her heart actually felt as though it dropped, too.

"Looking for me?"

She whirled to see Tyler, and the old feelings came crashing over her.

His suit was similar to the one he'd worn last week, except he didn't appear nearly as pulled together. His hair was mussed, his mouth turned down at the corners and his blue eyes seemed tired. She itched to reach out and comfort him, the way he used to console her years ago, but kept her hands at her side.

"Is everything all right?" she asked.

A shutter descended over his face. "Why wouldn't it be?"

She checked herself, remembering that he still viewed her as the teenage sweetheart who'd cheated on him, and gestured to his suit. "I heard you get out there with the kids, but you're not dressed for basketball."

"I came by to watch. I had trial today and the jury reached a verdict rather quickly."

Understanding dawned at the reason for his haggard appearance, followed by surprise. The newspaper accounts had pointed out the evidence was circumstantial and the motive non-existent but also relayed that Tyler had never lost a case.

"I'm sorry the trial didn't go your way," she said.

"Actually, I won," he said softly.

She started. "You don't look like you won."

He didn't answer immediately, then said with a sigh in his voice, "Sometimes you feel like you lost even when you won."

Before she could ask him to expand on his enigmatic statement, he continued, "But you didn't answer my question. Were you looking for me?"

Not a single reason existed to issue a denial, but her throat suddenly felt dry. She couldn't blurt out her motive for seeking him out. She needed to build up to it.

"Yes, I was." She dredged her mind for the secondary reason she needed to talk to him. "Chris asked if I'd keep him informed of your progress to get those computers for the teen study lounge."

"I'm not talking about today. I meant were you looking for me on Labor Day weekend?" His eyes fastened on hers, holding her captive. "One of my neighbors directed a woman fitting your description to my place."

Her heart thundered like the hoofs of a racehorse. He'd provided the perfect opening to explain the real reason she'd returned to Bentonsville. Still, she hedged, "I'm surprised you heard about that."

"Neighbors talk. Especially about someone who looks like you." He delivered the compliment with a deadpan expression so it didn't seem like flattery at all. "Now suppose you tell me what is it you came to see me about."

She wet her dry lips. There was no need to ask him out for coffee. They were alone. The time and the place to tell him about Jaye had come.

"Tyler. There you are." The woman Diana had seen at Tyler's house appeared like an apparition, the short skirt of her stylish print dress swirling around her shapely legs. "I hoped I'd find you here. I heard the most wonderful rumor and couldn't wait to find out if it was true."

Diana blinked, both at the way the woman launched into conversation and at her appearance. The woman had approached from behind Tyler, but Diana should have seen her coming.

"Hello, Lauren," Tyler said smoothly, as though she hadn't interrupted anything of importance. "Lauren, this is Diana Smith. Diana, Lauren Fairchild."

Although Diana stood five feet six, she felt like an Amazon next to Lauren. The other woman's eyes were as dark as her hair, but she had more going for her than stunning coloring. High cheekbones, pouty lips, a tiny nose and a perfect figure. This woman had it all. Including, possibly, Tyler.

"It's nice to meet you, Lauren." Diana spoke first, though she seemed to be forcing out the words.

Lauren moved imperceptibly closer to Tyler, her smile not reaching her eyes. "Likewise," Lauren said. "I haven't seen you around before."

"I started working at the center last week."

"Oh, you work here." The edge to Lauren's voice dissipated. "So you and Tyler were discussing center business?"

"Something like that." Tyler didn't bother to explain that he and Diana had known each other in high school. "What rumor did you hear, Lauren?"

Lauren pursed her lips and glanced from Tyler to Diana and back again, clearly signaling she'd rather talk to Tyler alone. Diana thought about granting Lauren's unspoken wish now that her window of opportunity to tell Tyler about Jaye had passed, but something kept her rooted to the spot.

Lauren unpursed her lips. "I heard you threw your name in the hat for a circuit court judgeship."

"That's not a rumor," Tyler said. "That's true."

"Are you old enough?" Diana asked in surprise. Tyler had never kept secret his goal of becoming a judge. Anybody who knew him in high school knew about the toy gavel in his locker. But Diana thought most judges were in their forties and older.

"I'm thirty," Tyler said. "By law, that's the minimum age for a judge in Maryland."

"Mother says you'll be the youngest man ever appointed to the state's circuit court." Lauren's eyes shone, like the finish on a shiny black onyx. Diana wondered if Mother was also a lawyer.

"*If* I get the appointment. I haven't even gotten the nomination yet."

"Who determines whether you'll be nominated?" Diana asked, at a loss as to how Maryland politics operated even as her stomach started to sink.

"Something called a judicial nominating commission," Lauren answered when Tyler didn't immediately respond. "Mother explained this to me. They take applications, then do background investigations and interviews before recommending candidates to the governor."

Lauren laid one of her delicate hands on Tyler's arm, the pink of her nails contrasting with the dark gray of his suit jacket. "Oh, Tyler. I know this will work out. You have an impressive record and a spotless reputation. What could possibly stop you from getting the judgeship?"

The answer came to Diana in a flash: the sudden appearance of an illegitimate child with a mother who was a recovering drug addict.

The implications of the secrets she still held close to her heart raced through Diana's mind. The process Lauren outlined sounded exhaustive, as though the entire point was to weed out any candidate who hadn't led an exemplary life.

Although society was more accepting of illegitimate children and reformed addicts than ever before, the hint of a scandal could call Tyler's character into question and doom his chances for the prestigious appointment.

"I hope you get the nomination," Diana murmured, then shouldered past him, inadvertently bumping him in the process. "Excuse me."

She had to get away to think. She picked up her pace, her stomach churning as she tried to escape the knowledge of what she already knew she needed to do.

It weighed her down, but she didn't stop moving her feet until she'd navigated through the community center to a seldom-used back room. She shut the door, then leaned her back against a wall for support.

The last time she'd made the decision not to tell Tyler about Jaye, she'd done so with stars in her eyes. She'd expected him to discover she was pregnant and conclude she'd lied to him about sleeping with other guys.

She'd spent the months leading up to Jaye's birth with half an ear cocked to the driveway of her aunt's house, waiting for a boy who never came.

The passage of ten years should have taught her that not all dreams came true, but she'd invented another far-fetched scenario since returning to Bentonsville and impulsively deciding to live and work in town.

Although she'd tried to tell herself since returning to Bentonsville that she'd gotten over Tyler long ago, the knowledge came crashing down on her that wasn't so. Tyler had done nothing to indicate he still had feelings for her, but a hidden, dreamy part of her had fantasized that the three of them would become a family once Tyler knew about Jaye. Even in spite of what had happened in the past.

That was before she'd seen him with the exquisite Lauren Fairchild, with whom she couldn't possibly compete. And before she'd found out about the political nature of judicial appointments. With sudden clarity, she realized that a hit to Tyler's reputation could affect not only his shot to become one of the youngest circuit court judges ever appointed but his chances of ever becoming a judge at all.

It was time to bring her flight of the imagination back to earth and face a harsh truth: her fantasies would never come true, but she couldn't be responsible for snatching away Tyler's dream.

She'd never told a soul who had fathered Jaye, and now knew she never could.

CHRIS COLEMAN SAT on the metal bleacher adjacent to the basketball court, watching Lauren Fairchild smile up at Tyler Benton.

He'd spotted her the instant she'd joined the conversation between Diana and Tyler, although as usual she hadn't noticed him. That was pretty much the way things had gone since Lauren had moved to Bentonsville during her senior year of high school.

Chris had already been out of college, working for the social services department. Their differences in age and circumstance had been the only things that had stopped him from asking her out then and there.

Hell, who was he kidding? Lauren's total lack of interest might have had something to do with it.

He'd almost managed to put her out of his mind during the four years she was away at college, but then she'd graduated and returned to Bentonsville.

Chris couldn't understand the reason for it at first. A town this size didn't have much to offer a bright young woman with a business degree. She worked in the billing department of her father's doctor's office, but could certainly have landed a better job in a bigger city.

As he noticed her showing up more and more anywhere Tyler Benton happened to be, her reason for sticking around became apparent. After he got up the courage to ask her to dinner and she shot him down, so did her disinterest in Chris.

"Hey, director, did you see that sweet move?"

Chris's attention swung back to the game and the tall, lanky kid strutting down the court.

"Not bad, Hot Shot," Chris called, reluctant to admit his attention had been elsewhere. "How 'bout you show me another one?"

Hot Shot, also known as Davey, shadowed the player he was defending. When the opposing point guard lofted a lazy pass to his teammate, Davey swooped in, stealing the ball and racing down court. He glanced over his shoulder, verified nobody was in fifteen feet and went up for the slam. The ball hit the rim, careening down court.

The other players erupted into good-natured laughter. "Man, where do you think you are? The NBA?" a kid in shorts that nearly reached his ankles asked.

"I'll dunk it next time," Davey vowed. "I got mad hops."

Chris smiled at the kid's braggadocio. Davey had a nice shot, but he'd barely risen off the court on his dunk attempt. When Chris looked back at the edge of the building, Diana and Lauren were gone. Benton approached the court to hoots and hollers from the players.

"What's the matter, old man?" Davey called. "You afraid to mix it up with us tonight?"

"I thought you guys could use the break," Benton said.

"You gonna pay for that next time you play."

Benton laughed and moved toward the bleachers. No time like the present to leave, Chris thought.

"Hey, Chris," Benton said as they passed each other. "You should join us one of these days."

"Football was my game, not basketball."

"Have you watched the kids under the basket? There's so much contact, they should be wearing pads."

"I'll think about it," Chris said, his mind not on the basketball game but on Lauren. Had she already left the center? He took the long way back, passing near enough to the parking lot to verify her blue Mazda Miata was still there.

Finding no sign of her outside the center, he headed

indoors. She stood beside the unmanned welcome counter, filling out a form. With her hourglass figure and the high heels that added definition to her calves, she looked as good from the back as she did straight on.

Drawing in a breath, he squared his shoulders and approached her. "Hey, Lauren."

She turned, her eyes growing wary. "Hello, Chris."

"Can I help you with anything? It seems my receptionist is AWOL."

"Valerie's already taken care of me. She's helping somebody with a vending machine problem, but she'll be back in a few minutes."

He nodded, noticing that Lauren was filling out a registration form. "You're taking a class?"

"Step aerobics," she said.

It figured. That class met at the same time the pickup basketball game went on. When Benton was at the center.

"It'll be nice to see you around here more often," he said before he thought better of it.

Her half smile disappeared and she moved a step backward. Idiot, Chris called himself.

"No need to worry." He leaned in to cross the invisible barrier she always carefully kept between them. "I promise not to ask you out again."

Before she could reply, he pivoted and left the registration desk. He typically worked until seven or eight, but might start cutting his very long days shorter.

He didn't relish the thought of being at the center at the same time as both Lauren and Benton. Because whereas Chris might only have eyes for Lauren, all Lauren could see was Benton.

NINE O'CLOCK. Closing time at the center. The basketball game had broken up, the ladies in the step aerobics class had gone home and so had Chris Coleman and his receptionist.

From the cars remaining in the parking lot, Tyler figured the only people left in the building were Willie the janitor and Diana. He slipped inside, grateful to discover Willie hadn't locked up early.

"Why you dressed in a suit tonight, Ty?" Willie, a small, wiry man near retirement age, paused in the process of emptying trash cans. "You trying to impress a lady?"

"I'm trying to find one," Tyler said.

"That pretty little gal?" Willie's already wrinkled brow creased. "Seems to me she'd find you if she was here."

"Not Lauren. Diana. She's the new employee."

"Oh, I like that one. No airs about her. Keeps to herself, though, as far as I can see. Don't even know if she's married."

Tyler had wondered the same thing himself, having heard little about Diana in years. He'd heard plenty about her after she left town to stay with her elderly aunt, though. She'd gotten engaged, become pregnant, lost her fiancé in a car accident and given birth to a daughter.

Where her little girl was now, Tyler didn't know. Neither could he say whether Diana's lack of a wedding ring meant she was divorced, single or not fond of jewelry.

"Do you know where Diana is?" he asked Willie.

"She's right there." The janitor nodded in the direction of a back room, from which Diana was emerging. "Hey, Diana, we were just talking about you."

Her step faltered, but she kept moving toward them. She wore dark slacks and a short-sleeved blouse in a muted shade of gray, almost as though trying not to draw attention to herself. "Good things, I hope."

"We were wondering if you was married," Willie said.

Diana's eyes widened.

"Willie was wondering," Tyler refuted. "I wondered where you were."

"Well. Are you?" Willie asked.

"No," she said. "Not married."

"See. If you want to find out something, all you gotta do is ask." Willie patted Tyler on the shoulder. To Diana, he said, "Ty's single, too, although I can think of one woman who's not happy 'bout that."

Willie dumped the contents of the small trash can into a larger receptacle, then pushed the big can down the hall, raising his hand in farewell. "Diana, you lock that door behind you when you leave. Take Ty with you. After nine, there shouldn't be nobody else in here besides me."

"Sure thing. G'night, Willie," Diana called.

Tyler remembered the young Diana being so filled with words that they spilled from her like water from a faucet, but this older Diana didn't say anything. He thought about explaining again that he hadn't been curious about her marital state, but that wasn't exactly true.

"I'm glad you haven't left yet," Diana said, the tense

set of her shoulders contradicting her statement. "I wanted you to know how happy I am for you."

"Happy about what?"

"Your win in court today. Your chance to get the judgeship. And, well, everything else."

He hadn't a clue what she meant by everything else, but felt disinclined to ask her to elaborate. Not when he still had no answer for why she'd sought him out Labor Day weekend. "Thank you," he said.

They walked together to the exit, with Diana successfully avoiding his eyes. She indicated that Tyler should precede her through the door, then waited for him to exit before following him outside, reaching around the lip of the door and locking it.

The song of the cicadas filled the night air and the warm wind swept over them, carrying the smell of evergreen. The rich, earthy scent reminded him of the long-ago nights when he met Diana at the playground near her parents' house.

For ten years, he'd wondered about her. And now here she was, walking with him down a sidewalk and through a parking lot in Bentonsville.

"I stuck around because you still haven't told me why you came to my house," he said.

They'd reached her car, an older model Chevy. The street lamp shone down, glistening off her hair and casting her face in light. It had been so long, yet she hardly seemed to have aged aside from her updated hairstyle. She even smelled the same, like the peach-scented moisturizer and shampoo she'd once told him were her favorites.

He noticed her throat move as she swallowed, a telltale sign of nerves. But what did she have to be nervous about? He could hardly breathe as he waited for her reply.

"I came to apologize for what I did to you," she said.

Time seemed to freeze and a wild hope burst in his chest. Years ago he hadn't been mature enough to consider that she'd turned to other boys because she was in a bad place in her life. All he'd felt was crushing betrayal.

But he was older now, wiser. He could look back and see that everything she'd done had been to escape the pain of her brother's murder. Drinking, skipping school, staying out late, shoplifting. Even sleeping with other guys.

He'd never gotten her out of his mind, maybe never exorcised her from his heart. If she proposed giving their relationship a second chance, he doubted he could refuse.

"You're probably wondering why I'm apologizing now, after all this time," she continued speaking. "The thing is I didn't like the direction my life was taking. I decided to start over, but found I couldn't erase the past. I've done a lot of things I'm not proud of, and I can't move forward until I own up to them. The way I treated you is the thing I'm least proud of. I'm sorry, Tyler. It was wrong of me to lead you on."

The air left his lungs. Lead him on? Not only had she no notion of getting back together, she'd never felt the same intense connection as he had. What kind of idiot was he to jump to the conclusion that a woman who'd slept around on him, then jilted him, would show up out of the blue with a request to get back together?

And why would he want such a woman back?

He remembered the night she'd dropped the verbal bomb that blew his world apart. Lovesick fool that he'd been, he'd looked forward the entire school day to meeting her after dark as she'd requested. He'd loved having her to himself, even when all they did was talk.

That night, with an acceptance letter from Harvard in hand, he'd had plenty to talk about. He'd been so excited about his news that he hadn't been able to wait for hers.

He'd picked her up and hugged her tight, babbling about getting accepted into one of the best schools in the country. He'd told her how hard he planned to work to accomplish his goal of being a lawyer and then a judge.

Buoyed by love and fueled by naïveté, he'd spoken his thoughts and dreams aloud. Nothing between them had to change. He'd call her every day, come home every break and spend his summers in Bentonsville. If she got accepted into a college in the northeast, that would be a bonus.

Then she'd told him she'd had a terrible argument with her mother and was leaving town the next day. Before he could persuade her to change her mind, she'd added that the rumors making the rounds at school about her, the ones he'd almost gotten into numerous fistfights refuting, were true. She'd been sleeping around on him, not with one other guy, but with several.

The pain lanced through him now, the same as it had then. But he was better able to camouflage it.

"Don't worry about it," he said. "It wasn't that big of a deal."

Her lower lip dropped, separating from the upper. "Do you mean that?"

"Sure," he lied, something he seldom did. "We were kids. I was hurt at the time, but everything seems like life and death when you're that young. I got over it pretty quickly."

She looked stricken, but it could have been a trick of the light because her lips curled upward a moment later. "Good. I'm glad we got that out of the way."

She opened the car door and got in, the interior light illuminating her. He braced a hand on the door, stopping her from shutting it.

"I heard about what happened after you moved away from Bentonsville." He paused, noticing the stark pain on her face and feeling like an ass for being jealous of a dead man. "I'm sorry about your little girl's father."

She stared at him, saying nothing.

"What's your daughter's name?" he asked.

An emotion he couldn't identify crossed her face, but then it was gone. "Jaye. I named her after my brother."

"It's a good name." He'd heard from one of the kids playing basketball tonight that Diana had rented an apartment in his neighborhood, but the boy said it seemed as though Diana was the only one living there.

The obvious next question was about where her daughter was, but he couldn't trust his voice to ask. He let his hand fall away from the door.

"Good night, Tyler," she said softly before pulling the door all the way shut, ensuring that neither of them would ask or answer any more questions tonight.

He stood in the darkness staring after her car a long

time after she'd driven away, wondering where Jaye was. He tried and failed to shake off the feeling that the girl should have been here, in Bentonsville.

And that Diana's daughter should have been his daughter, too.

CHAPTER FIVE

DIANA SETTLED HERSELF behind the welcome counter as the woman who regularly worked the desk bent down, retrieved her purse from a low storage shelf and surfaced smiling.

"Have I told you lately that I love you?" Valerie asked, eyes sparkling. She was a rail-thin woman about Diana's age with curly brown hair.

"Only about a dozen times today," Diana answered.

"Well, I do. If Chris hadn't hired you, I couldn't have changed my hours so I can be home when Chubs gets off work at seven."

Diana shook her head. "I still can't get over how you call your husband Chubs."

"Everybody does. He used to be really skinny growing up so the others kids nicknamed him Chubs as a joke, and it stuck. The people at work even refer to him as Dr. Chubs."

"Is he still thin?"

"Heck, no. The nickname fits him now. But he's such a good sport, he'll probably answer to Baldy when he loses his hair. Nothing bothers him. Except me working late." She lowered her voice. "We're trying to have a baby, you know."

Diana knew that, as she did most things about Valerie's life although she'd only been acquainted with Valerie for a few days. "Then why are you still here?"

Valerie, usually a whirlwind in motion, made no move to leave. "Because I've been waiting half the day for you to tell me what's bothering you."

Having my pipe dream of living happily ever after with Jaye and her father smashed into oblivion, she thought. Being forced to lie to Tyler about the reason she'd sought him out. "What makes you think something's bothering me?"

"Besides the dark circles under your eyes? I guess because you look unhappy."

"I didn't sleep well, is all," Diana said, which was only a partial lie. She'd lain awake for hours, thinking about what might have been. "It was hard to focus on my classes this morning. I'm afraid I missed most of the fine points of creating and using spreadsheets."

"Can't help you there," Valerie said. "But I can give you the rundown on working the welcome desk. I know you've filled in for me before, but tonight will be a little different. We make an exception to the sign-in rule because of the twelve-step meeting in the back room."

Diana felt her body tense. "What kind of twelve-step meeting?"

"Alcoholics Anonymous," Valerie said in a low voice. "It's not posted on the bulletin board because of the whole confidentiality thing so you can see why some of them don't want to sign in. Most are from out of town, but a few live in Bentonsville. They're the ones who don't seem to mind who knows their business."

Diana had minded. In Tennessee, she'd driven forty-five miles to Narcotics Anonymous meetings to minimize the possibility of running into anyone who knew her. Then, she'd sat silently in the back of the room, listening to others tell their stories but never mustering the strength to speak up.

"That about covers it. Oh, except the basketball players are supposed to sign in from now on so we know how many teens are using the facilities," Valerie said, then leaned toward her. "And one other thing. One of these days you'll trust me enough to tell me your secrets. You'll see."

She blew Diana a loud, theatrical kiss during her dash for the door, her eagerness to join her husband obvious.

Diana suppressed a sigh. She doubted she'd ever reveal her secrets to Valerie, either about Tyler or the addiction that had led to her separation from Jaye. Telling the truth could only lead to more problems, perhaps even jeopardizing her chance to get Jaye back.

And now she'd have to be especially strong, since she could no longer anticipate help from Tyler. She'd muddle through on her own, the same way she always had. Plenty of women raised fantastic children with no help from a man. When she got Jaye back, she'd be one of them.

The door banged open, and her heart bounced like a dropped rubber ball. But it was only a group of five teenagers arriving for the pickup basketball game, laughing and talking and jostling each other the way boys did.

"You're not scoring a point today," the tallest told the shortest. "So start your cryin' now."

"If anybody cries, it'll be you, Davey. Because somebody's gonna stuff the ball in your mouth to shut you up."

"I'll do it," a boy with red hair offered, and the rest of them laughed, including Davey.

Davey signed in first, winking good-naturedly at Diana over the counter. "Don't mind them. They're just jealous. Is Ty here yet? He said he was coming tonight."

"Not yet." Diana's foolish heart thudded at the prospect even though getting involved with Tyler was out of the question.

"Maybe he's not coming," the redhead speculated.

"Yeah, he is," Davey countered. "When he says he'll be here, he shows up."

After the boys exited the building as noisily as they'd entered, Diana nearly jumped out of her chair every time the door opened. Most of the people signed in, but the ones she assumed were AA members walked briskly by. They came in such varied sizes, shapes and ages that Diana would never have guessed they had a common problem.

The phone rang, the first time all night. The caller asked about the step-aerobics class, and Diana dug out a brochure, reading off the cost and the times the class met. She replaced the receiver on the cradle, the sensation of someone watching her pricking her neck.

Her mother stood motionless steps inside the front door of the center, her eyes riveted on Diana.

Diana's breath caught as she returned the stare. Time

seemed suspended, like a moment caught in a photograph. The years hadn't been kind to Elaine Smith. Her hair had turned shockingly gray and her shoulders stooped slightly. Lines etched her face, weighing down her features.

Without a word, she pivoted sharply and strode out the door. It felt like she was taking part of Diana's heart with her.

"Mom, wait!" Diana called, but her mother kept walking.

Diana hesitated only briefly before rounding the corner of the welcome desk in full pursuit. She burst through the exit into the early evening twilight, locating her mother already halfway down the sidewalk. "Please wait."

Her mother didn't slow. Diana sprinted after her, the backs of her slip-on sandals slapping against the soles of her feet. Desperate to stop her mother's retreat, Diana circled in front of her, effectively cutting off her escape route.

They faced off like competitors on opposite sides of a battle, the only sounds the sharp ins and outs of their breaths and the muffled hollers from the basketball game. The silence stretched, as it had for more than ten years, with Diana unsure how to break it.

The two most logical words—*I'm sorry*—wouldn't come. Her mother had failed Diana at the time she'd needed her most. Their long separation had been at least as much her mother's fault as Diana's.

But Diana had to say something. Anything.

"Hello, Mother."

Her greeting wasn't returned. Elaine Smith had recently passed her fiftieth birthday but appeared much older, perhaps because of the harshness with which she regarded Diana. Was this really the woman who'd read her bedtime stories and tucked her in at night? Who told her she loved her to pieces? Who screamed that she was a whore and an embarrassment to her family?

Diana blocked out the last memory and focused on the present. She'd mentally rehearsed this initial conversation a dozen times, but her mind had gone blank. There was so much to say, but what came out of her mouth was, "What are you doing here?"

"I'm here to see for myself that it's true my daughter is back in town," she said harshly.

"Who told you?" Diana asked. Connor might have alerted her mother she was in Maryland, but her brother didn't know about the community center job or her move back to Bentonsville.

"It doesn't matter who told me."

Yet they both knew Diana should have been the one to inform her. No matter what had passed between them, this firm-jawed stranger was still the woman who'd brought Diana into the world.

"I called you a few times but didn't get an answer," Diana said, the excuse sounding lame even to her own ears. "I figured you were out of town."

"I didn't get any messages," her mother said. "And you could have checked to see if I was home. I assume you remember the address."

"I was going to. Whenever I..." *Got my courage up,* Diana thought "...found the time."

"You're that busy you couldn't drive across town and tell me you were here?"

"You're one to talk," Diana retorted. "You never visited when I lived with Aunt Aggie. You never even called. Not after Jaye was born. Not after Aggie died. You didn't even come to Aggie's funeral."

Her mother's chin set in a stubborn line. "Her house was a seven-hour drive. You could get to mine in two minutes."

The teenage Diana wouldn't have backed down from the argument. But rehashing the past served no purpose, especially when Diana had returned to Maryland to build a better future.

"You're right," Diana said. "I should have told you."

Her mother seemed taken aback by Diana's capitulation, but that didn't stop her from adding, "I'm surprised you admit it."

Don't rise to the bait, Diana warned herself. "I'm not a teenager any more. I like to think I can admit when I'm wrong."

Owning up to your mistakes. One of the twelve steps to a successful recovery. The step about making amends flashed to the front of her mind. It wouldn't hurt to try.

"I moved into a garage apartment near the high school over the weekend," Diana offered. "If you like, I'll give you my phone number."

"If I want to get in touch with you, I'll call the center." Her mother's tone indicated she thought that unlikely. She glanced over Diana's shoulder toward the parking lot, her mind obviously on retreat.

But now that Diana was over the initial shock of seeing her mother, she could think more clearly. She couldn't let her mother go, not yet. Not until she tried to repair their torn relationship.

"Now that I'm here, I was hoping..." She cleared her dry throat and started again, forcing out the words. "I was hoping we could see each other now and then."

"Why?"

Diana clenched her teeth to prevent herself from blurting out something she'd regret. "Because we're mother and daughter."

Her mother remained silent for charged moments, during which Diana could hear ambient traffic noise, the faint buzz of insects and someone cutting grass nearby. "I hear you haven't seen your own daughter since February."

The comment hit Diana like a sucker punch. She reeled, then regained her voice. "I guess I'm repeating your mistakes then," she shot back.

"At least I didn't abandon you."

"No," Diana rejoined. "You just drove me away."

Her mother glared at her before turning on her heel.

This time, Diana let her go. She walked back to the center, her eyes misting and her stomach cramping with regret.

She could take the easy way out and blame her mother for their disastrous reunion, but Elaine Smith had made a justifiable point.

If Diana couldn't fix what was wrong between herself and her own daughter, how could she expect to reconcile with her mother?

TYLER REMINDED HIMSELF as he walked through the community center parking lot of the strategy he'd devised should he run into Diana.

Keep it light. Keep it impersonal.

He'd considered staying away from the center but quickly rejected the tactic. Playing basketball kept him connected to the youth of the community. If he could help Chris Coleman get the teen program on track, they might prevent some youngsters from ending up on the stand across from prosecutors like Tyler. Besides, he'd told the kids he'd come tonight.

He breathed deeply of the jasmine-scented night air, glad he'd turned down his father's invitation for dinner at the country club. Considering the VIPs they ran into whenever they dined there, that was work. Tyler usually accepted it as part of the gig, but tonight basketball held more allure. He headed for the center.

A gray-haired woman traveled in the opposite direction, her posture hunched and her eyes downcast. Tyler ducked between two parked cars, barely avoiding a collision.

"Hey, careful there," he warned.

Her head jerked up, tears falling freely down her anguished face. With a jolt, he recognized Diana's mother. Elaine Smith kept largely to herself, but he'd seen her a few months ago in front of the Safeway soliciting signatures for a petition to keep her son's killer in jail.

"Sorry," she mumbled, her expression starkly unhappy.

"Mrs. Smith? Are you okay?"

"I'm fine," she said brusquely. She brushed the tears

from her cheeks and continued on her path, fumbling with her car keys when she reached her vehicle.

Had she been to see Diana? Had mother and daughter argued?

Keep it light, he told himself. *Keep it impersonal.*

Whatever had happened between Diana and her mother didn't concern him. He continued to the center, perhaps at a slightly faster pace. He expected to see Valerie at the welcome desk, but Diana sat there, her expression as bleak as her mother's.

Ah, hell.

He approached the desk as if drawn by a giant magnet, growing more concerned when she didn't lift her head. "Diana, are you okay?"

Seeming to shake herself out of a trance, she focused on him, blinked, sniffled and nodded. "Everything's great."

A lie. Tears welled in her eyes, but didn't fall.

"Everything's not great," he said. "I saw your mother in the parking lot."

The reception area was empty except for the two of them. He circled behind the counter, pulling out one of the high stools and positioning it across from Diana. Battling the urge to gather her into his arms, he sat down. His inability to control his impulses had been what had gotten him in trouble with Diana the last time.

He found the combination of dark brown hair and hazel eyes so striking it seemed incredible that he hadn't really noticed her until her junior year of high school. Then attraction had poleaxed him, playing havoc with his customary confidence.

Before he could muster the nerve to ask her out, her brother had died. Then it became obvious she needed a friend more than a boyfriend, a role he gladly filled. He'd listened while she talked, held her when she cried and kissed her back, hoping when they made love for the first time that he wasn't taking advantage of her grief.

"If you don't talk to me about this, who will you talk to?" he coaxed, as powerless as he'd been ten years ago to walk away when she was hurting. "I was there. I remember what things were like between you and your mom."

One of her hands covered her mouth, as though trying to prevent words from escaping. But then it dropped to her side and she started talking. "Things haven't changed, but I shouldn't have expected them to. That was the first time I saw my mother since I left town. The first time I talked to her, too."

"You two haven't even spoken on the phone?"

Diana shook her head, her dark hair rustling. "We didn't exactly part on the best terms. She was screaming ugly things at me. The last thing she said was that I was a disappointment to the family. She obviously still feels that way."

"She told you that?"

"Not exactly, but it was pretty clear. I think she came to the center mainly to criticize me for not letting her know I was back in town. The thing is I meant to tell her. I guess I didn't because I was afraid she wouldn't be happy to see me. And she wasn't. When I proposed we get together, she asked why. As though a mother and daughter need a reason to be together. And then…"

Her voice trailed off, some unnamed emotion playing across her lovely face. He reached across the chasm between them and picked up her hand, the first time he'd touched her since she'd returned, instantly feeling a connection.

"Then what happened?" he asked gently.

Her chest rose and fell. Her eyes slid away, and he sensed that confession time was over. "Then everything disintegrated."

She brushed at the tears beneath her eyes, sent him a sad, watery smile and quite deliberately changed the subject. "This feels like old times. Me complaining about my mother, you listening."

He wondered what she hadn't told him, but didn't feel he had the right to pressure her to come clean. "You had a lot to complain about. When you last lived in Bentonsville, your mother was so wrapped up in what happened to your brother that she didn't pay much attention to you."

"Except to yell at," Diana said. "But to be fair, I gave her lots of reasons to be upset with me. I guess it's too much to expect that we could repair our relationship now."

"I don't think that's true."

She spoke her response softly. "You didn't see her, Tyler. There was no emotion on her face, as if seeing me again didn't affect her at all. She could have been talking to a stranger."

"Then why did I see her crying in the parking lot?"

"What?"

"She was upset, Diana. She looked miserable. She's probably as hurt by the rift as you are."

"Really?"

"Definitely," he said and smiled.

She smiled back, gently squeezing his hand. He glanced down at their linked hands, then back up at her. Her smile faded. Awareness shimmered between them....

The door to the center banged open. Davey strode inside, breathing hard, his hands on his hips. "Hey, Ty. There you are. Mango thought he spotted your car."

Tyler dropped Diana's hand, the moment between them gone. "I'm coming," he called, pushing himself up from the stool. To Diana, he said, "Let me know how it goes with your mom. Don't give up on her."

She nodded, as though accepting his advice. Now who was going to advise Tyler not to get involved with a woman who'd already broken his heart once?

Light and impersonal? Yeah, right.

"SURPRISE!" Valerie stood on the doorstep of Diana's apartment, toting a leafy green plant and wearing a grin. "I brought you a housewarming gift. A dieffenbachia. It's low-maintenance and hard to kill."

She didn't wait for an invitation to enter, but swept past Diana, locating an empty spot in the corner of the living room and setting down the plant.

"There." Valerie stood back and viewed the dieffenbachia with satisfaction. "That's the perfect spot, don't you think?"

Another woman might have rebelled at having her home invaded, but not Diana. After spending the afternoon alone, Diana welcomed the sight of a friendly face.

"I love it." Diana gave her a swift hug. "You're a doll for bringing it over."

"I can't stay long, because I'm working at the center until nine tonight since it's your day off. Did I tell you that Chubs decided to have late hours at the vet center on Thursdays so his hours would coincide with mine?" She had, several times. "But I did want to see your new place. Is that paint I smell?"

She sniffed, following the scent down the hall to the first bedroom, the walls of which Diana had painted a dusty rose. When they'd dried about an hour ago, Diana had placed a frilly pink spread on the bed and a pink lampshade on the bedside light.

"I feel like I'm stepping into a bottle of Pepto Bismol!" Valerie quipped. "Is this pink palace where you're going to sleep?"

Diana smiled. "No. It's my daughter's room. Pink's her favorite color."

"You have a daughter? Why didn't I know that? How old is she? What's her name?"

Diana bit her lip, inwardly cursing herself for speaking without thinking. "Jaye's nine."

"Nine! You must have been a baby when you gave birth."

"I was seventeen."

"Then is her father here in Bentonsville?"

"No. I didn't get pregnant until after I left town and moved in with my aunt," she said, the lie slipping easily off her tongue.

"What happened to your boyfriend?"

Diana crossed her arms over her chest, finding this

lie to be more difficult, but her mother had been the one who'd invented it. "Car accident."

"I'm sorry." Valerie's face filled with compassion Diana didn't deserve. Diana hugged herself, unsuccessfully trying to ward off a sick feeling she recognized as guilt.

"Where is Jaye now?"

"She's staying with my brother in Silver Spring until I get settled." Diana felt marginally better that she'd answered this question with the truth, even if the truth was misleading.

"You *are* settled. Look at this room. Slap up a couple posters, and your little girl will be in the pink." Valerie barely took a breath before she continued. "When is she coming to live with you? How about school? It started last week. Won't that be a problem?"

"We're still working out the details," Diana said vaguely, hoping Valerie wouldn't press.

"If she's nine, that means she's in fourth grade. Like Chub's niece."

"Fifth," Diana said. Jaye wouldn't be ten until after Christmas. "I started her in kindergarten early."

"Close enough. We'll have to get her together with Chub's niece just as soon as she gets to town. Jaye will love Brittany. Everyone does." Valerie shook her head. "I can't believe you didn't tell me you had a daughter."

After Valerie left, Diana sat on the pink bedspread in the newly painted room, breathing in the fumes and thinking about the guilt that had swept through her when she'd lied.

Not that she could have told Valerie the truth. Who'd

want to be friends with a woman who'd gotten hooked on pain pills and hadn't spoken to her abandoned daughter in going on seven months?

Diana had finally accepted that her mother's cutting remark reflected what had happened: Diana hadn't only left Jaye with Connor. She'd abandoned her.

That admission explained why Diana hadn't repeated her mother's accusation to Tyler. She hadn't wanted him to wonder what kind of mother abandoned her own daughter. She didn't want to be that sort of mother.

"Then what are you waiting for?" She spoke aloud, her voice resonating in the small, pink room. "Start making amends."

The decision made, she scrambled to a standing position, hurried through the apartment to the wall phone in the kitchen, picked up the receiver and dialed. She heard her heart beating above the ring of the phone before her brother answered. "Hello."

"Hi, Connor. It's Diana." Before she lost her nerve, she got straight to the point. "I'm calling to talk to Jaye."

Her words hung there, stark and vulnerable.

"First tell me why the number that came up on caller ID is different from the last one you gave me? What's going on with you, Diana?"

Now that she'd stated her intention, she longed to hear Jaye's sweet, young voice. She kept her update brief, but his questions came fast and furious. Why Bentonsville? Had she seen their mother? Did she know about the false story her mother had spread around town about her pregnancy?

She answered as patiently as she could while a question of her own ran through her head: why hadn't he jumped to comply with her request to speak to Jaye?

"Is Jaye there?" she asked, interrupting his interrogation.

"She's upstairs in her room."

"Can you tell her I'm on the phone?"

A pause. "Sure. Hold on."

Diana paced from one end of the kitchen to the other, stretching the telephone cord to near breaking point. Her gaze fell on a tablet lying on the kitchen table. She snatched it up and read the opening lines she'd scribbled the last time she'd intended to call Jaye.

Hi, honey. I've missed you so much.

I know I haven't called, but I think about you every hour.

I love you.

Feeling marginally more composed with the tablet in hand, she stopped pacing. Above the hum of the refrigerator, she heard her uneven breaths. The oven clock slowly turned over one minute, then two.

"Diana." Not Jaye's voice, but Connor's. "Jaye's not coming to the phone."

"Why?" The question tore from her.

The noise she heard next sounded like his throat clearing. "She says she doesn't want to talk to you."

Her heart plummeted, the rejection stinging all the way through to her bones. "You knew Jaye would refuse to talk to me," she said flatly. "That's why you dragged your heels about telling her I was on the phone."

"I didn't know how she'd react, but I suspected

something like this." Connor sounded distressed. "You leaving her like you did, without a word, it hurt her."

Diana's gut clenched. Leaving Jaye had hurt Diana, too. But at the time she'd felt as though she had no other option. She never dreamed the split would be permanent. Please God, don't let her have been wrong.

"It's going to take more than a phone call to get back in her life, Diana. You need to come see her. Just call ahead and let me know when."

Her throat thick with despair and regret, Diana couldn't keep up her side of the conversation any longer. "I've got to go, Connor. But I'll be in touch."

"Come see her soon, Diana. With every day that passes, it'll get harder," he said before he hung up.

Logically Diana knew Connor's assessment was on the mark, but the prospect of traveling to Silver Spring filled her with dread.

If Jaye refusing to come to the phone hurt this much, how much more painful would it be if her daughter rejected her in person?

THE LEAVES on the branches overhead grew thick and green, creating a canopy effect that blotted out the glow of the moon.

Molly held tight to Bobby Martinelli's hand, the voices of the group of teens gathered at the picnic shelter growing dimmer with each step they took.

"It won't be much longer now," he told her, stepping surely over the rough ground while Molly stumbled along behind him.

She might have been steadier on her feet if she

hadn't put aside her taste for beer long enough to drink a can and a half of it.

And why not? Today had sucked out loud. She'd gotten an F on her algebra test, which wouldn't have been so bad if she didn't need to return it tomorrow with a parent's signature.

Then the girl she'd been eating lunch with told Molly she'd been acting weird and went off to a table with only one empty seat. The snub had hurt so badly that, as pathetic as it was, Molly had actually considered taking that new employee at the center up on her offer to talk. Diana, the one who hadn't told her parents she'd skipped school.

But then Bobby had asked if she was hanging at the park tonight.

Bobby didn't think she was weird. When she'd told him about her F, he'd done a first-class job of duplicating her mom's signature. Then, right after slipping his arm around her shoulders, he'd whispered another descriptive word in her ear: sexy.

She giggled to think any guy, let alone one as hot as Bobby, would apply that term to her.

"What's so funny?" Bobby's voice drifted back to her in the darkness.

Not wanting to tell him, she blurted out the first thing that popped into her head. "My parents think I'm at school building sets for *Peter Pan.*"

"Mine don't ask where I've been," Bobby said. "I think they don't want to know."

"I'd rather know where we're going than where you've been," she joked.

"Right here." Bobby stopped abruptly. Molly careened into him. Laughing, he caught her in his arms.

She squinted, trying to make out where they were. A break in the tree branches allowed a sliver of moonlit sky to illuminate their location. The ground was flatter here, the grass softer, but otherwise this slice of woods looked no different from the one they'd just passed through.

"I don't get it," Molly said. "What's special about here?"

"It's where we are," Bobby said, his teeth flashing. She almost giggled again. He looked swarthy in the darkness, like one of the pirates in the school play.

He held her securely by her upper arms. A thrill ran up her spine. She could hardly believe that Bobby chose to be with her above all the other girls at school.

She got a whiff of beer on his breath before his mouth came down on hers, his tongue immediately parting her lips and thrusting inside her mouth. One of his big hands slipped under her shirt, skimming up her bare stomach and cupping her breast.

He'd kissed her before, but never this insistently. She thought about asking him to slow down but she wanted him to like her. She was old enough to know the score. If a girl didn't put out, a boy moved on to someone who would.

Still kissing her, one of his hands under her bra now, he lowered her to the soft grass under the tree. Then his hands were everywhere, pushing aside her clothes, groping her where no boy had ever touched her.

Panic raced over her but she tamped it down and

kissed him back the best she could. Bobby was the only good thing in her life right now. No way would she give him any reason to move on.

CHAPTER SIX

LESS THAN TWENTY-FOUR hours later, Tyler's father carefully considered the contents of the leather-bound menu before meeting the waiter's questioning gaze over the heavy wooden table.

"I'll have the roast beef sandwich, cooked medium well, with new potatoes on the side and a mug of root beer," Douglas Benton said.

Since his father always ordered the same thing, Tyler might have found the ritual amusing. Except Tyler had already requested that the waiter bring him a turkey club and unsweetened iced tea, his customary order.

"We should try a new restaurant next Friday," Tyler suggested after the waiter departed. "I hear the Italian place across town started serving lunch."

"You can't be serious?" His father lowered his voice. "Look around you, son. This place is a who's who in Laurel County politics on Friday afternoons."

As though to underscore his point, he raised a hand in greeting to the county manager, who was dining with the sheriff a few tables away.

A couple of lawyers from the public defender's office occupied a table near the entrance, and a top private-practice trial attorney had stopped to chat with the two judges who sat together in a nearby booth. Tyler and his father had already greeted all of them.

"It's not only what you know, it's who you know," his father said, repeating one of his mantras. In a whisper, he added, "That's why we come here every Friday."

That might be the reason his father frequented Custer's, but Tyler carved the time out of his schedule merely to spend it with his dad.

At age sixty, Douglas Benton remained as busy as a man half his age. Employed by one of the most powerful law firms in Maryland, he left Bentonsville at dawn Monday through Thursday mornings for the hour's commute to Bethesda. He packed his day with meetings, power lunches and business dinners, arriving home after dark. His weekday routine varied only on Fridays, when he worked from home in the mornings so he could lunch with Tyler. Most of the time, he went into the office on Saturdays to make up for the time lost.

"I'm just glad to be having lunch with you," Tyler said. "How have you been? I called last night, and Mom said you'd been around even less than usual this week."

"It's been a big week, with your nomination still up in the air. I've been spreading the word that you're up for consideration and that the commission accepts written comments. That's why it would have helped if you'd come to dinner at the country club Wednesday. The more people who recommend you, the better."

Tyler sipped from his glass of water, thinking about how to word his response without offending his well-meaning father. "I'd rather get the nomination on my own merits."

"You will, son. The people I know, they can merely point out what those merits are," his father said. "The committee can't help but nominate you. You're undefeated in court, and you're a board member of an impressive number of trade and civic organizations. In fact, you've never taken a wrong step in your life. None of us Bentons have."

Tyler arched his brows. "I thought Grandpa's dad made moonshine in his basement."

He scowled, lines appearing on a face that looked too youthful for his head of gray hair. "Your mother never should have told you that. But since she did, you've got to take the times into consideration. During the Depression, everybody made moonshine."

"You always told me trying to fit in with the crowd was the world's worst excuse, that the last thing you wanted me to be was like everybody else."

"And thankfully you listened," his father said. "Look around. Do you see any other men your age in prime position to become a circuit court judge? No, you don't."

Pride laced every one of his father's syllables, which both pleased Tyler and caused a vague uneasiness. His father had always heaped an undue amount of attention on Tyler, both the blessing and the curse of being an only child.

Between colleagues and acquaintances stopping by to say hello and their plates of food arriving, father and son didn't share another private word until halfway through lunch.

"I've been thinking that you need to be as visible as possible these next few weeks," his father said after polishing off his sandwich. "It wouldn't be a bad idea to appear in public more often with Lauren Fairchild."

Tyler nearly choked on a piece of turkey. He took a healthy swig of water before asking, "You're joking, right?"

"Absolutely not. To achieve your goal of becoming a judge, you've got to understand that appearances matter. A lovely young woman from a fine family can only help you further your career."

"I'd prefer to date a woman for my sake rather than the sake of my career," Tyler said, his mind inadvertently turning to Diana.

"Why can't the same woman fulfill both roles? Your mother does. She always has."

Tyler's parents had been married for thirty-five years and treated each other with respectful cordiality. His mother never got upset over the long hours his father worked, and his father never rushed home to be with his mother. They greeted each other with chaste kisses and polite words.

Tyler hadn't consciously examined the dynamics of his parents' relationship, but spending time together didn't seem to be one of their priorities. Not the way Tyler would rearrange his life if he and Diana stood a chance of making things work.

"I can't see myself married to Lauren, Dad," Tyler said.

"Why not? Have you taken a look at that little lady? I wouldn't suggest spending more time with her if it would be a hardship. But she's a—what do you young people call it?—a babe."

"She is a babe," Tyler confirmed.

His father nodded in satisfaction, then finished the last of his root beer. "The Bentonsville Rotary Club's annual spaghetti dinner is this Sunday. You should ask Lauren to go with you."

Tyler refrained from rolling his eyes at his father's stubbornness, but just barely. "It's an all-you-can-eat buffet, Dad. Not dinner and dancing at the country club."

"It wouldn't hurt to take a date, but I guess it'd be okay not to. I'm sure Lauren and her parents will be there, anyway. Everybody who's anybody in Bentonsville will be."

His father was right. The Rotary Club consisted of a diverse group of professionals who worked together to address various community and international service needs.

"What are you thinking, son?"

"That I might be able to persuade somebody at the buffet to donate computers to the community center's teen program." He also thought it couldn't hurt to persuade Chris Coleman to come along.

"Good idea, son. Have I mentioned what a good move getting involved in that teen program is? The commission is impressed with civic-mindedness."

"I didn't get involved to impress anybody, Dad. I believe it's important to keep teenagers off the street so they don't end up in front of prosecutors like me."

His father stabbed the last potato on his plate with

his fork. "Excellent reasoning. But if you do manage to get those computers donated, let the commission know about it when they interview you."

Tyler didn't dare tell his father about the pool tables he'd donated to the center. His father might suggest he snap a photo to show the commission.

"Thanks for the advice, Dad," he said, even though he probably wouldn't take it. His father nodded and smiled. Tyler smiled back, although his mind was no longer on the judgeship he'd dreamed about since he was a young boy.

He could phone Chris about the buffet, especially because the forecast called for rain, which would wash out tonight's basketball. Not that he had time to join in a game. He planned to spend tonight going over the legal briefs one of the law clerks had prepared for his next case.

But it couldn't hurt to stop by the center. That way, he could check to see if the pool tables had been delivered as scheduled.

Satisfied with the plan, he picked up the check the waiter brought by their table before his father could reach for it. The legal briefs, for once, could wait.

"WAIT 'TIL YOU SEE what arrived today," Valerie said when Diana walked into the community center Friday afternoon. "I'll give you a hint. It came compliments of Tyler Benton."

Flowers? Tyler used to present her with bunches of wildflowers when they were teens, inventing silly reasons to give them to her. Because Friday was almost the weekend, because summer break was a mere five weeks away, because their beauty made him think of her.

Diana's throat closed up. Had Tyler sent her flowers to encourage her to repair her relationship with her mother?

She searched the immediate vicinity, locating a florist's bouquet of red roses on the counter behind Valerie. Red roses symbolized love.

"He sent me roses?"

Only when Valerie's gaze followed Diana's, then whipped back around, did Diana realize she'd spoken aloud.

"Chubs sent me roses for our anniversary, which isn't until Sunday, but he's smart enough to know I like to show them off," Valerie said. "What I'm trying to figure out is why you thought Tyler sent you flowers."

"I didn't think that," Diana denied, feeling incredibly stupid. She'd all but assured Tyler she had no romantic interest in him by apologizing for leading him on when they were teenagers. He had no reason to send her roses.

"Then why is your face flushed? And what's going on between you and Tyler that you won't tell me?"

"Nothing," Diana said, but from Valerie's face it was clear she wasn't buying that. "I knew him when I was a teenager, that's all. Okay?"

"I am such an idiot." Valerie smacked her forehead. "Of course it's okay."

Diana couldn't keep up with her train of thought. "Why are you an idiot?"

"Because I'm prying. All my friends will tell you it's

a terrible but endearing tendency I have. And, well, I was hoping you were starting to be. My friend, I mean."

She looked so adorably chastened that for a moment Diana actually felt as though she could confide the whole embarrassing mess. Then reality intruded. The fewer people who knew her history with Tyler, the slimmer the chances it would occur to anyone that he could be Jaye's father.

"I'd like for us to be friends." It had been far too long since Diana had one.

Valerie grinned. "Pool tables."

"Excuse me?"

"That's what arrived today compliments of Tyler Benton, esquire. The workmen were here this morning setting them up. The tables are in the room where Chris and Tyler are trying to get the teens to hang out."

Interesting. Chris had mentioned Tyler's plan to obtain computers for the center but hadn't said anything about him providing pool tables.

"You should take a look," Valerie said. "They're beauties."

Although not quite new, the sleek pool tables were exactly as Valerie had advertised, serving as centerpieces in the large room. Diana envisioned a couple of dartboards on one wall, maybe a video-game system in the corner and a stereo playing the latest CDs.

She heard something that sounded out of place. A sniffling. Identifying where the sound had come from, she rounded the pool table. A girl sat on the floor with her back braced against the wall.

"Molly! I didn't know you were in here," Diana said.

With one of the pool tables positioned between Molly and the door, that had probably been the girl's intention. Anybody walking by would think the room was empty.

Molly looked up from her book, another in a series by Terry Pratchett. "It's quiet in here."

As well it should be. Everybody else Molly's age had yet to finish the school day. Diana could have kicked herself for not handling the situation better the last time she'd run across Molly's truancy. She'd feared coming down on the girl too hard would frighten her away from the center for good, but doing nothing had been the wrong move.

"I can't condone you skipping school like this. You have to..." Her voice trailed off when she noticed something she should have seen before. The girl's red-rimmed, bloodshot eyes. "Have you been crying?"

"No." Molly sniffed and swiped the back of her hand under her nose.

Diana chewed on her lower lip, unsure how to help. She glanced down at the khaki skirt she'd worn today instead of her customary slacks and shrugged, then sat on the floor a foot from Molly.

The girl glanced at her. "Aren't you afraid somebody will see up your skirt?"

"Not with that pool table there," Diana said.

"It's not going to help, you know."

"Help what?"

"Bring more kids to the center. The kids at school think this place is lame."

"What would help?"

"I don't know." Molly's mind was obviously on

something else. Diana longed to grill the girl to find out what it was, but harnessed herself. When Valerie had given Diana the third degree not fifteen minutes ago, Diana had shut down.

The book lay open on Molly's lap, but Molly made no move to pick it up. Without looking at Diana, Molly asked, "Aren't you going to say anything?"

"Like what?"

"Like you'll have to tell somebody if I keep skipping school."

"If you already know that, why do I need to tell you?"

Molly slanted her a defiant look. "You would have left school, too, if your day sucked as bad as mine."

"What sucked about it?"

Diana listened to Molly's ragged breathing, feeling like a fraud. The psychologists she'd seen on television shows used silence as a tactic to get their subjects to talk. Diana didn't speak because she didn't know what to say.

"I'm failing algebra," Molly finally announced.

"Then maybe you should ask the teacher for extra help."

"My teacher sucks. I don't understand her explanations. Some of the other kids don't either, but they're doing better than me."

The sense of helplessness swept through Diana again. She'd offer to lend a hand, but algebra had been her worst subject. "Can you ask your parents to get you a tutor?"

"No way. I hardly talk to my dad, and my mom would say we didn't have the money."

Something in Molly's voice alerted Diana that a bad

grade in algebra wasn't the girl's only problem. "Why don't you talk to your dad?"

Molly sniffled. "He lives in Virginia with his girlfriend. We moved here last month after my parents got divorced."

That explained some things. "I called my dad a few weeks ago, but before then I hadn't spoken to him in years. He lives in Virginia, too, with a new wife and son. But I was never close to him growing up, not like I was to my mom."

Denny Smith's focus had been J.D. and the games he played so splendidly, something they'd all been proud of. Diana had loved her brother so much she didn't remember resenting the attention, possibly because her mother hadn't played favorites.

"Are you still close to your mom?" Molly asked.

"No." The admission hurt.

"Me, neither." A tear slid down Molly's smooth, unlined cheek. She closed the book on her lap and stood up. "I've got to get going."

"Going where?"

"Home," she said. "One of the little kids didn't go to school today because he was sick, and Mom said I had to watch him when I got back. If I don't come home, she'll notice."

She picked up her backpack, slipped her book into it and was on the other side of the pool table by the time Diana rose. Molly hesitated, turned and said, "Diana, do you think…"

"Do I think what, Molly?"

"Never mind," Molly mumbled. "See you around, Diana."

Then she was gone. Diana stared after her. She'd missed something between the lines of Molly's story, she was sure of it. Not only that, she hadn't gotten across the point sternly enough that Molly had to stop skipping school.

She should have hunted down Chris and turned the matter over to him. He would have gotten Molly to tell him her real problem. Diana couldn't even get her own daughter to come to the phone.

She could do one thing for Molly, however. She went off in search of Chris to ask if the center could hire a tutor to be on hand after school.

ON THE OTHER OCCASIONS Tyler had stepped inside the Bentonsville Community Center, he'd awarded Chris Coleman silent kudos for recognizing the importance of first impressions and staffing the welcome desk with personable young women.

"No offense, Willie," he told the janitor who greeted him Friday night. "But you're not nearly pretty enough to be sitting there."

Willie threw back his head and laughed, displaying an impressive set of teeth. "No offense taken. I wouldn't want to see me sitting here, either."

Tyler smiled. "Then what gives?"

"It's awful slow tonight so I told Diana I'd sit here so she could take a turn at a pool table."

"The tables are here?"

"Arrived today. Tried one of them out myself. The balls don't always go in the pockets, but it sure is nice."

The basketball court had been dark when Tyler pulled

up, the rain shower that had fallen earlier soaking the hard surface and eliminating the need to turn on the outdoor lights.

Tyler had been worried about what the boys who usually played basketball were doing tonight, but now he knew. Playing pool. With Diana.

Willie peered at him. "Now that you know she ain't married, did you stop by to see Diana?"

"No, Willie." Tyler reminded himself that his reasons for staying away from Diana still existed. "I stopped by to see Chris."

Willie waved a hand toward the back of the building. "He's in his office, I think doing paperwork."

Tyler picked up the pen sitting beside the sign-in sheet and scribbled his name. "I'll head on back there then."

"If you stop by to see the pool tables, could you tell Diana to take her time?" Willie picked up a dog-eared book and leaned as far back as the stool would allow. "I'm in no hurry to get back to my regularly scheduled duties."

Tyler wondered at the lack of noisy chatter as he walked down the hall and heard only the smack of ball against ball. With a message to deliver and the room containing the pool tables on the way to Chris's office, he might as well view his donation.

But at the mouth of the room, he checked out not the pool table but Diana. She leaned over the table, carefully lining up a shot meant to sink the eight ball in a corner pocket. The material of her khaki skirt stretched over her rear end, nicely outlining its shape.

Tyler's mouth went dry. He stared, paying little attention to whether the eight ball dropped until she straightened and blew on the top of her pool cue like it was a smoking gun.

"Nice shot, ace," she said aloud.

Grinning, Tyler paid her homage with loud, evenly spaced claps that resonated in the large room.

A becoming flush instantly spread over her face. Wearing a red short-sleeved shirt and that blush, she reminded him of the girl who'd captured his heart. "Please tell me you haven't been standing there long."

"Long enough to determine that Annie Oakley can shoot." He walked toward her, admiring the glow her natural blush lent her skin. "I didn't know you were a pool shark."

"Ha." She punctuated her comment with a genuine laugh. "Now I know you just got here. It took me three tries to get the eight ball to disappear into a pocket."

"To fall, you mean."

"I didn't fall."

"Not you, the eight ball." A corner of her mouth twitched and he crossed his arms over his chest. "You're teasing me, aren't you?"

"Just a little. I'm really not that familiar with the lingo."

"So you didn't hang out in pool halls and bars when you lived in Tennessee?" His question sounded casual, but the answer interested him more than he cared to admit.

"Hardly. When I went out at night, it was usually to a restaurant, and only because I was working there. But I've got to tell you something." Her hand ran over the smooth green felt of the pool table. "I really like these tables."

He remembered what it felt like to have that hand glide over his skin, the kind of thought that could lead to trouble. He wouldn't let it, he decided.

"Looks like you're the only one who does like the table," he remarked. "I thought the basketball players would be here, especially with the court wet."

"Six or seven of the boys played some pool when it started raining but left after about an hour. Along with everybody else, it seems. Nobody's here tonight besides me, Chris, Willie and a half dozen women in a book club."

She snapped her fingers. "Speaking of Willie. I should get back to the welcome desk to relieve him."

Tyler should find Chris Coleman, say what he had to say, then get home so he could put in a couple more hours of work. The state's attorney had assigned him another difficult case, this one involving an armed robbery and a defendant claiming mistaken identity.

"Willie told me to tell you to take your time. So why not play me a game of pool first?"

She blinked a few times, alerting him that his suggestion had surprised her. It startled the hell out of him, too.

Her head shook back and forth almost imperceptibly, but before she could refuse, he added, "It would be a kindness. I need someone to cheer me up."

An indentation appeared between her brows. "Why?"

"I'm bummed that the pool tables weren't enough to get kids to stick around. Teenagers would be better off if they hung out at the center at night, especially on weekends. Otherwise, who knows what they're off doing."

A charged look passed between them, and he knew they were both remembering what the two of them used to do. But then she broke eye contact, and he figured maybe he'd only imagined the shared memory.

"It seems like you feel strongly about the teens of Bentonsville having a refuge," she said.

"I'm a prosecuting attorney. I know what trouble idle hands can make. So do you. Things might have turned out differently for your brother if there had been a teen center for Drew Galloway to hang out in."

She winced.

"I'm sorry," he said. "I didn't mean to hit a nerve."

"It's okay. You're right. But not only about Galloway. J.D. could have used a hangout, too." She set down her pool cue and started transferring the balls onto the top of the table. "Except now that we have a teen center, the trick is getting kids to hang out here."

He used the rack to arrange the striped and solid balls in a triangular shape. "Computers might help."

"Possibly," she said thoughtfully, "but not enough."

Tyler picked out a pool cue and chalked its tip before setting down the cue ball at a slight angle across from the arranged balls. "You can break," he told her.

"No, I can't. If I try, I might miss the clump entirely."

"The rack," he corrected, laughing. "Okay, I'll break. You tell me what the teen program needs to attract students besides computers."

"A tutor to help with homework," she said. "A girl who's flunking algebra was here today. Molly's her name. I ran it by her, and she thought it was a good idea."

He sent the cue ball crashing into the colored balls

with a resounding crack, pocketing two of the striped ones.

"I've got stripes," he said while he examined the table for his next shot. "I like the idea of a tutor. Did you ask Chris about it?"

"He said the center doesn't have the money to pay one and suggested I find a volunteer."

"Not a bad idea. You could place a classified ad in the newspaper. Or, better yet, appeal directly to someone who's qualified."

"The trick is finding someone to fit that description."

He looked up from the table. "How about your mother? If I remember correctly, she used to substitute at the high school. Usually in the math classes, right?"

She took her time in answering. "Well, yeah. She has a degree in education but chose to stay home and take care of us."

"Then it can't hurt to ask her. Especially because it'll give you the excuse you're looking for to talk to her." He cleared two more of the striped balls from the table before missing. "Your turn."

She barely glanced at the layout of the balls on the table before shooting and missing wildly. "She'll say no."

"You can't know that until you ask." He sank two more balls, missed, then watched her get ready to take a shot she had no prayer of making.

"Hold on," he said. "You've got the angle all wrong, and your bridge is a disaster."

"Bridge?"

"The way you hold the shaft of the cue."

He positioned himself behind her, placed his larger hands on top of hers and leaned over. His body came into full contact with hers. He smelled her peach shampoo, felt her softness and couldn't regret the colossal mistake touching her represented.

"Grip the butt of the stick with your right hand and put the palm of your other hand down on the surface," he said near her ear, moving her hand about ten inches from the cue ball and resisting the urge to kiss that little mole of hers. "Now lift your thumb and lay the shaft of the stick between your thumb and forefinger. Got it?"

"Got it," she said, her voice as breathy as his.

"Slide the stick back and forth. When I let go, you're going to pull the stick back and strike the cue ball at its center. Do you think you can do that?"

She nodded, but didn't reply. *Let her go,* Tyler told himself. The trick was gathering the resolve, as impossible now as it had been ten years ago. His body remembered what it was like to be inside her. God help him, he wanted that again.

The sound of a throat clearing gave Tyler the impetus he needed to move back from Diana. Chris Coleman regarded them, his expression unreadable.

"Chris. I was just instructing Diana in the fine points of playing pool," Tyler said calmly.

"I see that." He practically oozed disapproval, and Tyler wondered at the reason.

"I'm not a very good pool player," Diana said, her voice still husky.

"You're good at things that matter a lot more than

pool," Chris said, like a big brother. Was that it? Had Chris, who'd once been J.D. Smith's best friend, taken on his pal's role?

"I'm glad to hear you say that, considering you're my boss." She sounded more like herself now, the breathiness gone from her voice. "Speaking of the job, I hope it's okay that Willie's filling in for me for a few minutes."

Tyler interpreted the look Chris sent her as indulgent. "Of course it's okay. Hardly anybody's here tonight, and everybody who is likes Willie."

"I should still be getting back." She returned her cue stick to the contraption mounted on the wall, then looked at Tyler. "Thanks for the pointers, Tyler."

"Any time," he answered, wondering if he imagined the heat shimmering in her eyes. He didn't think so. His gaze lingered on her as she left the room.

"Willie said you were looking for me," Chris said.

Tyler pulled his attention from Diana with difficulty. "That's right. The Rotary Club's spaghetti buffet is on Sunday. I thought it would be a good place to spread the word that the teen program needs computers and wanted to make sure you were going."

"I'm a member," Chris said, a fact of which Tyler was aware. "Of course I'll be there."

"Good," Tyler said.

"That's all you wanted to talk to me about?" He looked faintly suspicious.

"That's it."

"Then I'll be getting back to work. I have more paperwork to finish before I can leave."

Tyler walked with Chris into the hallway, nodded a farewell and watched the director head back to his office.

"Hey, Chris," Tyler said before Chris had taken ten steps. The other man turned. "You should ask Diana to come to the buffet, too. I think Sunday's her day off. Between the three of us, we could hit up every business-man in Bentonsville."

Chris nodded slowly. "Maybe I will."

Tyler fought the impulse to push for a stronger commitment. "Okay, then. Guess I'll see you Sunday."

"Yeah. I guess you will." Chris headed off to finish his work, leaving Tyler to face an uncomfortable truth.

His father's lunchtime conversation about bringing a date to the dinner had gotten his thoughts spinning in a direction that had led him straight to the community center.

He hadn't come here tonight to assure that Chris would be at the buffet on Sunday.

He'd come to talk the director into bringing Diana, because Tyler couldn't ask her himself without seeming like the chump of the universe. Which he was starting to believe he was.

CHAPTER SEVEN

THE HALL LOCATED on the basement floor of the sprawling Methodist church built from the generous donations of parishioners was the only place in Bentonsville large enough to house the popular spaghetti buffet.

Pastor Richardson weaved between the long tables that dominated the hall, shaking hands and agreeing that it was indeed fortunate that he was a member of the Rotary Club.

The chairs on either side of the tables were filling up fast with town residents carrying plates of spaghetti, salad and garlic bread.

The portion of the table in front of Lauren Fairchild and her parents held no plates, although Lauren had poured herself a diet soda before letting her mother direct her to a chair with a clear view of the entrance.

"When Tyler gets in line, I want you to go to the buffet table." Her mother smoothed her already perfect dark hair into place. She looked lovely, as usual, in an aqua-colored, scoop-necked designer dress that suited her skin tones. "If you're in line together, you'll sit together."

"Shouldn't I sit with you and Dad?"

"That's a sweet thought, but sitting with your parents is not the way a young woman gets what she wants out of life."

"And what does a young woman want out of life, Marie?" Lauren's father asked with a typical levity that seemed at odds with his distinguished appearance. A family practice physician with salt-and-pepper hair, he already had enough money that he didn't need to work at all. "No, don't tell me. I'll take a stab at this one. She wants a husband. Preferably one who's successful, handsome and wealthy."

"Don't joke, Peter," her mother said crossly. "You know that Lauren is interested in Tyler Benton."

"Ah, the judge-to-be. Quite an impressive young man. But, if you ask me, he'd be lucky to capture Lauren's fancy rather than the other way around."

Lauren smiled at him, appreciative of the compliments he regularly tossed her way even if they were outrageous.

"You are wonderful for my ego, Daddy," she told him, omitting that her self-confidence had taken a hit lately.

As overbearing as her mother could be, she'd readily and correctly identified Tyler as one of the most eligible bachelors in the state.

Lauren had gone along with her mother's suggestion of subtle pursuit. Although Lauren enjoyed working at her father's office, she aspired to be a wife and mother. Why not try to attract the most accomplished bachelor around, especially one as handsome and charming as Tyler?

"If a man doesn't notice how lovely you are, Lauren,

then he's blind," her father said. "You get more stares than the fake skeleton in my office wearing the Yale sweatshirt."

Lauren grinned at him. "For a different reason, I hope."

"I wish you'd get rid of that thing, Peter," her mother interjected. "What possible purpose does it serve?"

The feeling that she was indeed being stared at struck Lauren. Only half paying attention to her father's defense of his overdressed skeleton, she swung her eyes forward and encountered Chris Coleman's dark gaze.

Dressed head to foot in shades of gray that somehow made him appear taller and leaner, he looked…sexy. A word she'd never applied to him before. Industrious, socially conscious and intelligent, yes. But never sexy.

Uncomfortable with the label, she abruptly looked away from him. And found her mother regarding her intently. "Who's that, Lauren?"

"It's nobody," she said, an answer she quickly realized would never satisfy her mother. "Just Chris Coleman, the director at the community center."

"Not him. The woman with him."

Lauren's gaze zoomed back to Chris, who was no longer staring at her but talking to some people while his hand lightly rested on the back of the woman at his side.

"Her name's Diana Smith," Lauren recited in an emotionless voice, disguising the dislike pulsating through her. First Tyler, now Chris. Diana seemed to have captivated both of them. "She works at the center. Why do you ask?"

"Because it seems to me you have some competition."

Lauren directed her a sharp look. How did her mother know Chris had asked her out? She'd never mentioned it.

"Your Tyler can't seem to take his eyes off her," her mother added.

Tyler was here? She searched Diana Smith's immediate vicinity, only to discover that Tyler was one of the people Chris and Diana were talking to. For the life of her, Lauren didn't understand how she'd missed him.

"They're moving for the buffet table," her mother said. "Hurry and get in line, Lauren. And make it seem like a coincidence. You don't want Tyler to think you're chasing him."

"If he calls you on it, Lauren, tell him your mother made you do it," her father remarked.

"Peter!" her mother admonished. "Must you?"

Leaving them to their disagreement, Lauren stood up and smoothed the skirt of the casually chic ice-blue dress with the peekaboo styling at the bodice that she'd bought precisely for this occasion.

The buffet line had stretched from a few people to a dozen or more since she'd arrived, but now it had dwindled to nothing and Tyler's party was moving through the line at an alarming rate. Already the men dishing out the spaghetti had filled up the plates Tyler and Diana held out.

Lauren hurried over to the serving table on her high heels, arriving at the stack of plates at the end just as Chris reached for one. A few other people had somehow gotten in line between him and the people he'd been talking to.

"You can have my plate," he said, offering it to her. His eyes held hers, making it impossible to look away. "I'll even let you cut in front of me."

She didn't want to be anywhere near him, let alone beside him in line. But the place he indicated was a couple spaces closer to Tyler.

"Okay." She practically whipped the plate from his hand, hyperaware of Chris picking up another from the stack and following her.

The middle-aged woman in front of her bent over the salad bowl, using tongs to transfer some of the romaine and iceberg blend onto her plate. Chris stood so close behind that Lauren imagined she felt his warm breath on her neck.

"I hope you don't mind if I pass," Lauren remarked to the woman, even though it meant skipping the salad, which she loved. She moved quickly around the woman, her momentum carrying her too close to the next man in line.

Holding a plate already brimming with spaghetti generously topped with fragrant tomato sauce, he turned to see what was happening. The plate tilted, and the pile of spaghetti slid downhill like the snow in an avalanche.

Lauren recognized imminent disaster, but she couldn't move backward quickly enough to avoid the spaghetti shower. It rained down on her new blue dress in stunning color.

She stared down at the ruined garment, thinking the saleswoman who'd insisted it would get her noticed couldn't have known how right she'd be. Mortification burst inside her as the man who'd spilled the spaghetti apologized profusely.

"That's okay. I know you didn't mean to do it," Lauren muttered, trying to smile at him through threatening tears. She hadn't envisioned she'd be stained with spaghetti when Tyler saw her.

She looked down the line, expecting to meet his pitying gaze, but amazingly he had his back to her. The noise level inside the church hall, in fact, had reached such an advanced stage that not many people seemed to have noticed her mishap.

If she could get out of here fast, she might be able to face the Bentonsville citizenry with her dignity intact. The problem was that she'd driven to the buffet with her parents, whose table suddenly seemed a mile away.

The tears pricked her eyes again, because she was stuck.

Chris appeared in front of her, holding out a dish towel he'd magically procured and shielded her from curious looks with his body. She eagerly took the towel and patted at the front of her dress.

"What do you say I take you home so you can change?" he asked, his eyes no longer reflecting heat but understanding.

"Oh, yes. Please," she said gratefully and let him lead her out of the church hall.

BE FRIENDLY BUT DISTANT, Diana told herself as she preceded Tyler through the buffet line.

Shifting her plate of spaghetti and garlic bread to her left hand, she grabbed a cup of coffee with her right.

Do not let him guess you haven't stopped thinking about his body pressed against yours since his impromptu pool lesson. Do not reveal that the guilty pleasure of being around him was the buffet's main attraction. Think about the needs of the teen center.

She waited until Tyler had chosen his own drink, a cup of unsweetened iced tea, then told him, "We'll be able to talk to more people about those computers if we don't eat together, so Chris and I will catch you later."

She glanced behind her, expecting Chris to be moving through the line, but instead saw volunteers cleaning up a spot where someone had spilled spaghetti.

"Where's Chris?" she asked Tyler. "He was right behind us a minute ago."

Tyler's head swiveled as he searched the area behind them. "I have no clue."

"Are you Diana Smith?" An older man who didn't look familiar hurried up to them. Wondering where she knew him from, Diana nodded.

"Chris Coleman asked me to tell you he'll be back soon. He said you should go ahead and eat without him."

"Where did he go?" Diana asked.

The man's face reddened slightly. "I accidentally spilled my spaghetti on the woman with him. He took her home so she could change clothes."

Diana frowned. She'd thought she was the woman with Chris. After Chris invited her to accompany him to the buffet so they could network, he'd picked her up en route to the church hall.

"Thanks for telling me," she said in a shaky voice.

She'd initially balked at attending a gathering filled with people she used to know but convinced herself she'd weather it just fine with Chris by her side. Now she felt as though her safety net had been yanked away.

"Guess you're stuck sitting with me," Tyler said. "I see some empty chairs on the right side of the hall."

She didn't allow the relief surging through her to take hold, because dining with Tyler did not qualify as keeping her distance. "Wouldn't it be smarter to split up?"

He cocked an eyebrow and said in a low voice, "It's okay with me if you go your own way, but I got the impression you were a little nervous about being here."

A little? That was an understatement. At the consideration in his eyes, something inside her softened.

"I'm more than a little nervous," she whispered back. "But I don't want to cramp your style."

"Are you kidding me?" He smiled, revealing the dimple in his left cheek that always seemed so incongruous on his face. "It's harder to say no to two persuasive people than one."

"I don't know about that. I always found it difficult to say no to you."

His smile disappeared, his eyes darkening as he gazed at her. The mood between them changed, the air becoming as charged as it had been at the pool table.

She swallowed, mentally calling herself a fool for speaking before thinking. No matter how attractive she found him, she couldn't get involved with him again.

"Tyler, my man. Good to see you." An older gentleman with a ruddy complexion patted Tyler on the back as he passed by.

"Hey, Ty. Good job on the arson case," another man called from the head of a nearby table.

The connection between them broken, Tyler indicated Diana should precede him to the empty seats. A half dozen others greeted him along the way, serving as a powerful reminder of Tyler's respected position in the community—and of Diana's determination not to compromise it.

Those same people greeted Diana, too, but she couldn't be sure if it was because they recognized her or because she was with Tyler. Nodding and smiling, she didn't notice the two women at the table where they were headed until it was almost too late.

"Tyler, stop."

The panic in her voice must have communicated itself because he halted and regarded her with concern. "What's wrong?"

"We can't sit at that table. My mother's there. See? With Mrs. Wilson."

His gaze followed hers, locating the gray-haired woman with her back to them. If she had been facing forward, Diana knew no sign of welcome would be on her face.

"Then now would be a perfect time to talk her into volunteering to tutor at the center," he said.

Diana shook her head vehemently. "No. I can't do that."

"Sure you can," he said, his voice reassuring. "Remember what I just said about two people being stronger than one? You don't have to do this alone. I'll be with you."

He exuded calm confidence, as though he really believed she could talk her mother into anything. With Tyler by her side, maybe she could.

"Okay," she said softly.

"Atta girl," he said, smiling at her encouragingly.

She drew in a deep, ragged breath and steeled herself to face the mother who had become a stranger. Her legs felt leaden as she moved forward, her voice failing her when she and Tyler arrived at the table. She sent him a panicked glance.

"Mrs. Wilson, Mrs. Smith, it's good to see you," Tyler said heartily. "Do you mind if Diana and I join you?"

Elaine Smith had yet to turn, but Diana noticed her hand tighten on her fork.

"Not at all, Tyler." Mrs. Wilson beamed at them. "We'd love to have you sit with us. Wouldn't we, Elaine?"

"Of course." Her mother's face creased in a semblance of a smile, apparently unwilling to snub Diana in front of friends and neighbors. Appearances had always been important to Elaine Smith. Obviously, they still were.

Not wishing to sit next to her mother, Diana set her plate down across from Tyler's and circled around the table before she sat. The strategy backfired. With a direct view of her mother's disapproving face, the positioning couldn't have been worse.

Diana swallowed, relieved to discover her vocal cords once more in working condition. "Hello, Mrs. Wilson. Mother. I'm surprised to see you here."

"Didn't she tell you she was coming?" Mrs. Wilson didn't wait for an answer. "After I ran into you last week, Diana, I called up Elaine, just like I said I would. My Harry's a member of the Rotary Club, but he serves food at these things and I'm always left by myself. So I persuaded Elaine to come with me."

"We're glad you did." Tyler aimed a warm, charming smile at her mother. "Diana had a wonderful idea about how to get more teens into the community center. This will give her the perfect opportunity to run it by you."

"By me?" The words squeaked with surprise.

"It involves you, but I'll let Diana tell you about it." Tyler transferred his attention to Diana, his gaze as steady and encouraging as her mother's was not.

"I'm looking for volunteer tutors to be available at the center after school," Diana said, drawing strength from Tyler's silent support. "Naturally, we thought of you."

"We?" her mother asked.

"Tyler and I. He remembered you substituted at the high school." Diana paused to gather her courage. "So will you do it? It doesn't have to be every day. We'd be grateful for any time you could spare, even if it was only once or twice a week."

Mrs. Wilson clapped her hands. "You simply must say yes, Elaine. Wasn't I just saying you need to get out of the house more? You have so much to offer the community."

Her mother didn't meet Diana's eyes. "I don't know if it's the right situation."

"Of course it is," Mrs. Wilson said. "It's perfect. Not only can you help teenagers, you'll be working in the same place as your daughter."

"Mrs. Wilson's right," Tyler said. "After all the years Diana spent away from Bentonsville, it'll be nice for you two to be in the same building."

Mrs. Wilson was in the dark about Diana's relationship with her mother, but Tyler must realize Diana's presence would be more of a detriment than a draw. He winked at her, confirming the method to his madness.

The wink gave Diana the impetus to add, "Please, Mother."

With Mrs. Wilson and Tyler waiting for her reply, both part of the community where appearances did matter, her mother could only give one response.

"Okay. I'll do it."

HIS FEET SINKING into the plush carpeting, Chris wandered through the exquisitely furnished living room in the house where the Fairchilds lived while Lauren changed clothes in an upstairs bedroom.

House seemed like the wrong term. Palace was more accurate. Built on a rise with at least five acres surrounding it and a long driveway leading up to it, the three-storey monstrosity featured angular construction, oversized windows and an upstairs balcony.

Chris hated it, as he did the living room with the overstuffed kid leather furniture and original artwork that screamed wealth and privilege.

He liked the family photos, though, because nearly every one showed Lauren in another stage of her development.

As an adorable toddler filling a sand bucket at the beach, a leggy adolescent with a mouthful of braces and a frilly ballet costume, an airbrushed beauty posing for her senior photo and a poised young woman whose loveliness took his breath away.

He recognized that last woman as the one he'd spirited away from the church hall, but the self-assurance had been missing. Lauren didn't seem to recognize that she was as gorgeous wearing a tomato-stained dress as she'd be without it.

He groaned. Okay, that wasn't quite true. She'd be much more beautiful without the dress.

In an effort to get his mind off the woman who occupied far too much of it, he moved from the photos to a plaque on the wall.

He recognized her father's name, Dr. Peter Fairchild. *Chief of Surgery,* the plaque read, *Philadelphia Memorial Hospital.*

"Wow." The exclamation escaped from him. He hadn't known Lauren's father had been such a bigwig.

"Okay, I'm ready." Lauren entered the room looking much more cool and collected than when she'd gone upstairs, but no less beautiful. This dress was a burnt orange, perhaps to minimize the embarrassment factor if someone else should target it with tomato sauce.

She seemed impatient to leave, but now that he was inside the Fairchild residence, where he'd most likely never be again, he wasn't ready to go.

"I hadn't realized your father had such impressive credentials." He indicated the plaque. "Tell me something. Why would a powerful man like him move to a small town like Bentonsville?"

She stayed where she was, a good ten paces away, far out of the range of optimum conversational distance.

She shuffled her feet, conveying her unwillingness to linger. "To get out of the rat race. It was always his dream to run a family practice in a small town where things are simpler."

"Simple?" He gestured around him with a sweep of his hand. "That's not the term I'd use to describe this house."

"Daddy didn't have anything to do with the design. That was all my mother. She wasn't crazy about moving. This house was their compromise. He got the family practice. She got the big house."

"How about you? What did you get?"

Her shoulders moved up and down in a delicate shrug. "I got to live in a nice town full of nice people. That's why I didn't move away after I graduated from college. I like it here."

He had a different take on why she remained in Bentonsville. She liked the thought of a future with Tyler Benton.

"There would be more opportunities for you in a bigger city," he said, playing devil's advocate.

"Maybe, but I'm not career minded. As long as I enjoy my job and get off work at a reasonable hour, I'm happy."

"Really?" He injected doubt into the question. "An enjoyable job and some free time are all you want out of life?"

"Of course not." She crossed her arms over her chest, and he wondered if she felt threatened by the question. "I want the usual."

"And what is that?"

She didn't immediately answer and for a moment he thought she might not, but then she said, "In a nutshell, a husband who loves me and children I can love."

He took a couple paces toward her. She moved a few steps back. "And you think you'll get those things from Benton?"

Her posture became rigid. He'd briefly imagined the wall she had erected between them had gotten lower, so he could see over it to who she was. Now it had risen with a vengeance.

"That's none of your business," she retorted.

He'd usually take a remark like that as a clue to shut up, but not today. Today he was feeling frustrated and perhaps a little sorry for himself.

"Maybe it is none of my business, but I've known Benton for years. You might want my take on the situation."

"Why would you possibly think that?" She sounded haughty, like the princess her parents had no doubt raised her to be. But underneath the haughtiness, he sensed curiosity.

"Because you don't know him like I do. Benton's ultra ambitious. Has been since high school. His job will always be more important to him than a woman. So if you have your sights set on him, you might want to take some music lessons so you can learn to play second fiddle."

Her chin tipped up, and her eyes blazed. "You sound jealous."

The filter Chris used in normal conversation disappeared, and the truth burst free. "You're right. I am jealous."

"Why do you say these things to me?" she asked.

"Because they're true." He didn't attempt to move closer but held her immobile with his gaze. "I don't want Benton to have you, because I want you for myself."

"You said you wouldn't ask me out again."

"I won't," he confirmed.

"Then why tell me that?" She sounded not so much miffed as...threatened?

He shrugged, wanting to put her mind at rest, angry at himself for raising even a kernel of fear in her.

"Because I don't seem to be able to hide the truth from you," he said. "But don't worry. I won't call you every fifteen minutes or lurk outside your home or office or anything like that. I fully intend to leave you alone."

From her troubled expression his assurances didn't seem to assuage her, but he couldn't do anything about that now.

"Come on," he said. "I should get you back to the buffet."

They walked to the front door, with her keeping her distance, but his arm inadvertently brushed hers when he passed through the door.

She shied away as though she'd been burned, but in the instant before she did their eyes met. What he saw in them surprised the hell out of him.

Because he could swear it wasn't fear but awareness.

Not that it meant much. A pampered princess who lived in a palace didn't end up with a working-class stiff. If she gave him a second look, that's all it would be: a look.

Benton had the inside track, even if he was as wrong for her as Lauren Fairchild seemed to be for him.

TYLER SUPPRESSED the urge to stomp on the gas pedal and tear out of the church parking lot, which had seemed a lot like hell for such a holy setting.

He motioned instead for Mr. Burlington, the CPA who did his taxes, and his wife to cross in front of his car. Then he drove slowly to the exit and flicked on his turn signal before pulling onto the main street. And, finally, salvation.

He slanted a sideways look at Diana. Slumped in the passenger seat with her head leaning on the backrest, she looked utterly spent.

"Am I glad to get out of there," Tyler told her. "The muscles holding up my smile actually ache."

She turned her head toward him, satisfaction written on her features. "It worked. That smile got the teen program the computers it needs."

"No way. *Your* smile did it. Once you warmed it up, the wattage was dazzling. The unsuspecting souls we approached didn't stand a chance."

"Then why did we talk to two dozen people before we got the donations?"

"Because nothing worthwhile comes easily." Realizing he'd reiterated one of his father's favorite sayings, he laughed. "If I had a dollar for every time my dad told me that one, I'd be a millionaire. But it's true. Good things come to those who work hard."

He pulled up to a stoplight and let her direct him to the neighborhood where she was renting her apartment, even though he already knew the location.

"The apartment really isn't that far from the church hall," she said. "In a pinch, I could have walked home."

"Chris would have stuck around if he thought you couldn't get a ride home," Tyler remarked. "Did he give a reason for leaving early?"

"Just that he'd mingled enough for one night."

"I say amen to that." Tyler often felt that way, but his father had drilled home the importance of fulfilling the social obligations associated with club memberships. Few successful men, he pointed out, lived in a vacuum.

Diana indicated a single family Colonial on the right side of the road and, beyond it, a detached three-car garage with a simple design and a shingled front dormer window.

He pulled into the driveway and cut the engine, then got out of the car. She emerged from the passenger side before he could open the door for her.

"It's up those stairs." She indicated metal steps that ascended to a small porch and second-storey entrance, but made no move to climb them.

The moon shone down on her, spotlighting her wholesome beauty. Simply clad in a short-waisted navy blue jacket over a white blouse and khaki slacks, she hadn't dressed to draw attention to herself. But Tyler couldn't take his eyes off her.

She regarded him through her clear hazel eyes,

chewing on her lower lip. "There's something I should have said when we were talking earlier. You know, about the work we had to accomplish tonight. Lauren seemed unhappy that I was spending so much time with you. I hope she realizes it was because of work."

Tyler hadn't spent more than ten minutes in Lauren's company all night, during which she'd seemed more preoccupied than unhappy. Tyler's father, conversely, had made his displeasure known. He'd pulled Tyler aside, warning him that town residents might get the idea he was interested in the wrong woman.

A strand of hair had fallen in Diana's face. He brushed it back, letting his fingers linger. "Are you sure about that?"

Confusion flitted across her features. "Well, um, yes. Lauren was definitely unhappy we spent so much time together."

"Not about Lauren." Tyler moved his hand to her cheek, enjoying the soft feel of her skin against his palm. "About tonight being only about work?"

Her eyes seemed to darken while her breaths grew uneven. "What else would tonight be about?"

He placed his hands on either side of her soft cheeks, saw himself reflected in her pupils and lowered his mouth inch by slow inch, watching for a sign that she didn't want him to kiss her. A flinch, a shake of her head, a word from her lips.

She didn't speak, neither did she move, giving him the green light to claim her lips. He kissed them softly, reacquainting himself with the feel of them, the feel of her. Only she was no longer merely a girl, and he surely didn't feel like a boy. His left hand left her face to trail down the elegant slope of her neck, the plane of her shoulder, the length of her arm.

Oh, how he'd missed her. He'd repressed what he felt for so long that he hadn't realized how strong the sensations were until this moment, when he finally had her in his arms again.

He buried his right hand in the soft hair at her nape and kissed her more fully, coaxing her to open her mouth to him. But he wasn't the only one participating in the kiss. It was her tongue, soft and moist, that ventured forward to mate with his, her hand that skimmed down the front of his chest.

And then they were kissing the way they used to, with a passion that could have ignited a blaze. It certainly felt like fire raging inside him as he drew her more closely against him, as he felt himself grow hard against her softness.

It was crazy, but it seemed like she filled up a part of him he hadn't known was empty until this moment.

He angled his head, deepening the kiss, delighting in her eager response. When he cupped her bottom, she pressed more fully against him, the friction of their bodies driving him wild. He longed to strip off her clothes and make love to her, but this wasn't the place. They were around the side of the garage, in a spot not visible from the street but not completely private.

With difficultly he pulled back from her mouth, trailing a line of kisses from her tiny mole to the side of her neck. He felt a shiver go through her as he kissed her in a particularly vulnerable spot under her chin.

"Invite me in, Diana," he said, his voice raspy and barely recognizable.

He felt her grow still. "I can't," she said, her words barely above a whisper.

Had he heard her correctly? He drew back, searching her face. Her lips looked well kissed, her cheeks abraded where his five-o'clock shadow had come into contact with her skin. But her eyes looked miserable. A possible reason occurred to him.

"If this is about Lauren, I wouldn't be cheating on her," he rushed to reassure her, chastising himself for not putting her mind at ease before he kissed her. "We dated casually a few times, but that's it. I swear it."

"It's not Lauren," she said. "At least, not entirely."

"Then I don't understand." He kept her close, feeling their hearts pound in tandem. "It's obvious we both want this."

"I'm different now, Tyler. I don't always take what I want." She moistened her lips, the gesture shooting heat to his groin. "Please understand. I can't leap before I look. I have responsibilities, somebody else to think about other than myself."

He drew back, feeling as though he'd collided with a wall, the same way he did every time Diana mentioned the daughter she'd had with another man. He'd been under the impression that Jaye didn't live with Diana, but since he never asked about her he couldn't be sure that hadn't changed.

"Is your daughter inside your apartment with a babysitter? Is that why you won't invite me in?"

"No." She put an arm's length of distance between

them, straightening her clothes. "Jaye is staying with Connor until I get settled."

He dragged a hand through his hair, frustration rising inside him like a live thing. He tried to conceal it. "If she's not in Bentonsville, I don't see what the problem is."

"It's not only Jaye." She seemed to have a hard time forming her words, a more difficult time meeting his eyes. "It's me. Like I said, I don't feel settled. And you don't know me any more, Tyler. Not really. Since I left Bentonsville, well, let's just say I made a lot of bad decisions. I'm more careful now."

He swallowed the urge to argue that making love to him wouldn't constitute a bad decision and shoved his hands in his pockets so he wouldn't drag her into his arms and convince her of that.

"Okay," he said.

"Okay?" She looked as though she'd expected an argument.

"I get it. You need time." With great difficulty, he managed to smile at her. "I'll see you around. It's not like I don't know where to find you."

Unwilling to take the chance that she'd maintain the time to make love would never be right, he said an abrupt good-night and headed for his car.

Now that he'd determined what used to be between them still existed, his goal became clear: to get into both Diana's bed and her heart.

It hardly mattered that she'd devastated him once and might well do so again. They were older and wiser than they'd been in their teens. She no longer actively grieved a murdered brother, which had clouded every decision she made.

And he was no longer the crushed, lovesick kid who didn't know how to get what he wanted.

CHAPTER EIGHT

HER LUNGS BURNING while she tried not to gasp for air, Lauren struggled to keep pace with the freakishly fit instructor and her minions.

"You're doing great, ladies," the instructor extolled. A bubbly redhead in her forties who favored country music with titles like "Redneck Woman," Patsy's sculpted body advertised the benefits of step aerobics.

Everybody else was doing great. Lauren, the beginner relegated to the back of the class so she could follow the moves, kept starting off on the wrong foot. She'd find herself on top of the step while the other ladies had their feet on the ground.

What had possessed her to sign up for this class? When her mother suggested it, did she not realize that Tyler hung out at the basketball court outside the center while the class took place in the aerobics room with the mirrored walls that caught every mistake Lauren made?

Patsy, named for the famous country singer who'd died young, sang along with the music while executing an intricate combination of moves.

Lauren kicked when she should have jumped, shuffled instead of shimmied and once again ended up alone on top of the step. She shuddered to think how much worse it would be if she'd dared add the arm movements.

At least she didn't look amateurish. She'd bought some seriously cute exercise clothes in that clingy material that wicked sweat away from the body. This ensemble featured black capri pants and a hot-pink top with black piping that bared her toned stomach. Even a closet klutz like her could do sit-ups.

Not that anyone had noticed her outfit aside from a few classmates who'd taken pity on her and told her she looked cute.

Chris Coleman, who'd made it such a point to tell her how much she attracted him a mere five days ago, had barely glanced at her. What kind of man says something like that, then ignores the supposed object of his fascination?

A movement caught her eye through the glass windows that extended the length of one wall.

Lauren craned her neck, still trying to keep up with the music, which had changed to a tune with the catchy title "Save a Horse, Ride a Cowboy."

Was that Chris passing by? Yes, it was. From a distance, he vaguely resembled Tyler but his hair was much darker and his movements more leisurely.

His back was to the aerobics room, as though he had no special interest in anyone taking the class, while he talked to somebody. Lauren peeked around a high-kicking classmate for a better look at who it was. Diana Smith, Miss-I-Attract-Men-Without-Half-

Trying. Had the traitorous Chris changed his allegiance so quickly?

"Don't forget to step up, ladies," Patsy called, a comment obviously directed at Lauren.

Careful not to flex her leg beyond a ninety-degree angle, Lauren climbed the four-inch step.

Chris seemed awfully chummy with a woman who was supposed to be his employee, smiling and laughing through a conversation that seemed to be about more than business.

"Now step down," Patsy called.

Oh, yeah. Stepping down. Her eyes still on Chris, Lauren lowered her foot and caught the heel of her tennis shoe on the edge of the step.

Her balance hopelessly lost, her foot shot out from under her in an awkward position. She went sprawling backward, landing hard on her butt.

"Lauren, are you all right?" The instructor's voice, rising above a twangy lyric.

Everybody in the class turned to stare. She offered up a silent prayer that wasn't answered. Outside the windowed wall, Chris Coleman had finally noticed her.

Her face feeling lit by flames, she called cheerily, "I'm fine," then gave a thumbs-up signal.

"Let me help you up, honey." A woman clad entirely in black who'd confided she was trying to lose her baby weight offered Lauren a hand. Lauren took it, hiding a grimace when she put weight on her ankle.

"Go ahead," she called to Patsy. "I'll just sit the rest of this one out."

Thanking the woman who helped her, she walked

gingerly to a back wall and leaned against it. First the incident with the spaghetti and now this. He must think her the biggest klutz in the world.

The song ended. Chris and Diana were no longer visible through the window so she begged off from the rest of the class, telling Patsy her ankle was vaguely sore.

Amid well wishes, she walked gingerly into the guts of the community center. She'd half hoped and half feared Chris would wait around to see how she'd fared, but he was gone.

Tyler, however, leaned over the welcome desk talking to Diana Smith, the two of them totally absorbed in each other. How had she missed seeing him enter the building?

Diana laughed at something Tyler said, giving Lauren the opening she thought she needed to slip out of the center without being seen. She limped toward the door.

"Lauren. Are you all right?" Diana called, sounding genuinely concerned, which Lauren found hard to believe. Hadn't the other woman recognized they were rivals? "That was a nasty spill you took."

Great. Now Tyler knew, too. Lauren met Diana's gaze head on, searching for ill will but finding none. "Everything's fine but my dignity, thanks."

Diana appeared chagrined. "You think that was embarrassing? I once slipped while walking past one of those decorative water fountains and fell in."

"Did you really?" Tyler asked.

"Broke a heel, too. I limped to my car, wetter than a seal." She paused. "You're limping, too, Lauren. You sure you're all right?"

Try as she might, Lauren could discover no ulterior motive in the question. "Yes, thanks. I think I just tweaked it."

"Do you want me to take a look at it?" Tyler asked.

"No," Lauren said, surprising herself. "I'm fine."

"Then at least let me walk you to your car." He started toward her, no less tall or gorgeous than he'd been last week when she'd signed up for the exercise class to get him to pay attention to her. It had taken an embarrassing fall, but it was working.

"I'm fine, really." She waved a hand in their direction. "Don't let me interrupt."

She left them together in the reception area, where she'd bet Tyler had been a number of times during the past week. It didn't take a genius to figure out that Tyler had developed a thing for Diana, but it would take a lot more brain power than Lauren possessed to figure out why that didn't bother her.

And why Chris Coleman's interest in Diana did.

DIANA'S GAZE FOLLOWED Lauren's limping, retreating form before focusing once again on Tyler. "Do you really think she's okay?"

"She can put weight on her ankle, so it's not serious. It's probably a little sore but she'll be as good as new in no time."

"Did you think she acted a little strange?"

"How so?" he asked, but didn't seem overly interested. As though he truly didn't care that Lauren, with her combination of beauty and class, could help further his ambitions in a way Diana never could.

"Until just now, I had the strong impression Lauren was interested in you," Diana said. "But she didn't seem at all put out that you were talking to me."

Tyler digested the comment, nodding slowly. "I noticed that, too, but Lauren must have figured out my interest lies elsewhere."

His eyes never leaving her face, his hand covered the one she rested on the counter. He turned her hand over, tracing gentle circles on her palm, his meaning unmistakable.

Her insides went haywire, tying up her tongue and preventing her, as it had after the spaghetti buffet, from telling him outright that she wouldn't get involved with him.

Before she could regain her poise, he released her hand. He grinned at her, not lasciviously, but like a friend would. "I never finished my story about the juror who lied and said she didn't know the defendant."

"Go on," Diana said, the moment when she could have discouraged him lost.

"Turns out she figured she could squeeze him for cash in exchange for persuading the rest of the jury he wasn't guilty."

"Really?" Diana asked, her interest captured. "How'd you find out about her scheme? Did the defendant tattle on her?"

"No way. He was all for it. She went to the police to file charges against him after he stiffed her."

Diana laughed. "That's almost unbelievable."

"I couldn't make this stuff up. I've learned since becoming a lawyer that the rarest of creatures is the criminal mastermind. Most bad guys get caught because they're not very bright. But enough about me. Tell me about your business classes."

She looked pointedly toward the door. "If you don't get back to your basketball game, those boys will come hunting for you."

"Nah, we've got extra players tonight. They won't mind if I sit out a game."

This marked the fourth night this week he'd said the same thing. The days since the spaghetti buffet, in fact, had settled into a pattern.

They started slowly when Diana, cappuccino at the ready, drove to the career center in Gaithersburg for her morning classes.

They gathered steam when she arrived at the center at lunchtime. Carrying the sandwich she'd picked up at the corner deli, usually a turkey club without mayo, she typically ate with a group of senior citizens who hung out at the center.

They really got rolling as she fulfilled her community center duties, helping out at the day care, inputting records into the computer and interacting with the still-meager number of teens who trickled in while she worked the welcome desk.

But the highlight of the day arrived at about seven o'clock, dressed in basketball shorts, looking tall and lean and handsome and checking back in with her every water break. Although she knew she should discourage him, all she could come up with were halfhearted attempts.

"You say every night those boys won't come looking

for you, and every night they do," Diana said, which she knew full well wouldn't get rid of him.

"Then talk fast and tell me about your classes before they get here."

Talk. She could do that, as long as she remembered talking was all they should do together. "There's not much to tell except we're learning how to use the computer for record-keeping, payroll, stuff like that."

"Are you enjoying it?"

"Enjoy isn't the word I'd use." Two of her fingers flew to her lips. She hadn't admitted that to anyone. Not even herself.

An indentation appeared between his brows. "What word would you use?"

"I can't believe I'm going to say this aloud." She grimaced, then let her true feeling escape. "Boring. The classes are boring."

"Then maybe you should study something else."

She shook her head. "No. It's probably not the classes. All the changes going on in my life have made it hard to focus."

"But what if it is the classes? You might not want to be in business administration."

"I'm not like you, Tyler. I haven't known what I wanted to do since I was a kid. I need a career path, and the school's providing one." She sounded like she was trying to convince herself as much as him, an uncomfortable realization. "Like I said, I'm probably only bored because I've been having trouble concentrating, what with the move back to town and dealing with...everything."

By "everything," she mostly meant her complicated new relationship with Tyler. She held her breath, hoping he hadn't picked up on her verbal slip.

"You're talking about your mother, aren't you?" He zeroed in on another of her concerns. "Have you talked to her since we saw her at the buffet?"

"I called and left a message asking when she could start tutoring, but she didn't call back." She glossed over her mother's failure to acknowledge her as though it hadn't hurt, although in reality it felt like a wound had reopened. "I…"

The door opened, and what she had been about to say died on her lips.

"Oh, my gosh," Diana breathed, "there she is."

ELAINE STRODE to the welcome desk, wearing the emotionless expression she'd perfected in the car. She couldn't let anybody guess it had taken a good five minutes after finding a parking spot to get her hands to stop shaking.

"Hey, Mrs. Smith," said the man in gym shorts and T-shirt standing beside the desk. "It's nice to see you again."

Elaine did a double take, belatedly recognizing Tyler Benton, the boy wonder who'd grown up to be a first-class lawyer. Tyler hadn't hung out with her J.D. in high school, but the two boys had been in the same graduating class and the people of Bentonsville had spoken of him with nearly the same awe. While J.D. had won acclaim on the football field, Tyler had earned it on the basketball court and in the classroom.

"Hello, Tyler." Her gaze flicked to Diana, but didn't hold. Being able to look at her daughter again after so many years without her produced a physical ache. "Diana."

"Hello, Mother."

The resulting silence was so absolute Elaine could hear the faint murmur of voices from a back meeting room. Tyler finally broke it.

"Sorry to say hello and run, but I've got to be getting back to the basketball game." Addressing Diana, he said, "I can't let those boys think I'm afraid to play them."

Tyler squeezed Diana's hand, gently and encouragingly, and Elaine wondered if he knew what had gone on between mother and daughter in the past.

She searched her memory, trying to recall if the teenage Diana had ever mentioned Tyler. But most of what she remembered of the terrible time before Diana left Bentonsville was the wrenching pain over losing her younger son, followed by the shock of learning Diana was pregnant.

She'd initially rejected the rumors that Diana was sleeping around as ugly gossip, but then started thinking about Diana's late nights and failing grades. Fear had caused her to be more accusatory than inquisitive when she'd finally confronted Diana. After angrily confirming her pregnancy, Diana had shattered what was left of Elaine's heart by adding she'd been with so many boys she had no idea who the father was.

Had Tyler been one of the boys Diana slept with? Elaine rejected the thought almost as soon as it occurred to her. Tyler, who hailed from a fine Bentonsville family, hadn't been the type to get a girl in trouble.

"Nice seeing you again, Mrs. Smith," Tyler said politely, then he was gone. The door closing behind him made a soft sound, then once again silence reigned. Elaine had things to say, but absolutely no idea how to say them.

"I called you Monday to see when you could start tutoring," Diana abruptly announced.

Elaine meant to phone her back, but it had taken her this long to put aside her disappointment that the call hadn't been personal. Or maybe she needed an excuse to come to the center in person to fulfill her longing for another look at Diana.

"That's what I'm here to talk about." Elaine launched into the spiel she'd come up with on the way to the center. "You should find someone else. I haven't taught for years and you of all people know I don't have a particularly good rapport with teenagers."

"But the whole thing will fall apart if you back out," Diana cried, her distress visible.

"How can that be? I'm only one woman. You need more than that to start a tutorial program."

"My goal is to have at least one tutor here every weekday."

"Where will you find these volunteers?"

Diana picked up a painted stone from her desk and palmed it before she answered. "I was hoping to talk you into heading up the program. You taught in Bentonsville. You must know some retired teachers who wouldn't mind donating their time."

Elaine bit down on her lower lip, fighting feelings of inadequacy. She'd poured so much energy these past ten years into getting justice for her dead son that she'd kept in only superficial contact with people in the community.

"Please, Mom," Diana implored, her eyes wide and pleading, reminding Elaine of the little girl who'd come begging for a cookie before dinner. The little girl she hadn't been able to resist.

Feeling herself weakening, Elaine countered with, "I find it interesting that you're going to great lengths to help other people's children when you neglect your own."

She watched the hurt come over Diana's face and wanted to soften the harshness of her comment. To apologize for flinging salt in an open gash. But Elaine's own unhealed wounds felt too raw.

Diana's jaw flexed, but she didn't raise her voice. "How do you know anything about Jaye?"

Elaine knew less than she would have liked, including the reason Diana and her daughter were estranged, but she took the opening and ran with it.

"I know Jaye's playing soccer at ten o'clock Saturday at the recreation complex in Silver Spring. I went to her last two games but can't go to this one, which will be disappointing for her. She likes to have people who love her come watch."

Diana remained silent, telling Elaine more loudly than words she hadn't been aware Jaye played soccer. Refusing to take the chance Diana would ask why Elaine wouldn't be at the game, Elaine changed the subject.

"You were right. I do know some people I can ask about becoming volunteer tutors. I'll let you know what they say when I come in on Monday."

"Monday?" Diana parroted.

"To tutor. I'll be here as soon as school lets out."

Elaine noticed Diana's fingers tighten around the stone in her hand before she said, "Thanks, Mom. That means a lot."

Elaine nodded shortly, then left the center without saying goodbye, her mission accomplished.

She knew firsthand that a mother's time with her children was finite. Death had stolen J.D. from her, but she'd lost valuable years with Diana through her own foolishness.

It might be too late for Elaine to repair her relationship with Diana, but she could do her best to prevent Diana from losing any more time with her own precious child.

THE SUN BEAT DOWN on the green grass, bathing in bright light a field where girls wearing either brilliant blue or vivid yellow shirts chased a soccer ball with youthful abandon.

Diana approached from behind the bleachers where parents and other family members sat, glad her sunglasses hid the nervousness that must surely be in her eyes.

Sweat dampened her palms and her heart beat hard as her gaze eagerly panned up and down the field, then over the substitutes on the sidelines. She didn't see Jaye. Could her mother have been wrong about the time and location of the game?

Her stomach seemed to sink to the earth beneath her tennis shoes a moment before the crowd emitted a roar.

A girl in blue had broken away from the pack and rushed toward one of the goals, dribbling the ball in front of her, the other players in mad pursuit. Just when it looked to be a sure score, a goalie wearing red lightning bolts on her shirt rushed recklessly forward, cutting off the angle of the shot.

The field player reared back her right leg and kicked the ball hard. It slammed into the onrushing goalie's midsection, taking Diana's breath away. But the still-breathing goalie tumbled to the ground and smothered the rebound.

"Great save, Jaye," one of the parents yelled amid cheers from the yellow team's section and groans from the supporters of the blue team.

Jaye?

Diana squinted. Still holding the ball, the goalie stood up. The sun caught her ponytailed hair, causing it to shimmer like gold. With both thin arms outstretched, she dropped the ball and punted it downfield.

Oh, my gosh. The kamikaze goalie *was* Jaye.

"Diana. Over here." Connor sat in the bleachers, not five yards away, motioning to an empty space next to him.

Diana started. She'd anticipated her brother would be among the spectators, but she'd planned to deliberately hang back until she figured out how to approach him. She must have ventured forward in her eagerness to get a better look at Jaye.

Wearing shorts, a T-shirt and sunglasses, he looked

like the doting big brother she remembered but she reminded herself she'd given him plenty of reasons to disapprove of her. Taking a bracing breath, she went to join him.

"Hi, Connor. I hope it's okay that I came."

"Okay's an understatement." A corner of his mouth lifted, and his hand briefly covered hers. "I'm thrilled that you're here."

A wave of warmth swept over her, and she leaned over and kissed his cheek.

"Is this that fiancée you were telling us about, Connor?" A heavyset woman wearing tiny glasses peered at Diana with undisguised interest from two rows behind them.

"Nope, this is my sister Diana." Connor introduced Diana first to the inquisitive woman, whose name was Marlene, and then to the coach's wife and a married couple who looked barely old enough to have a child.

"Jaye is a great addition to the team," Marlene remarked. "She's so good, it's hard to believe she only just started playing."

"Athletic genes run in the family," Connor said, causing Diana's mind to veer to Tyler's talent with a basketball. Her breath caught. Did Connor know Tyler was Jaye's father? "Our brother was a football star, but he excelled in whatever sport he played."

Diana breathed again. Of course Connor had been referring to J.D. and not Tyler. Like their mother, he believed Diana couldn't pick Jaye's father out of a crowd. She bit down on her lower lip, wishing circumstances were different. Wishing Tyler was here with her so they could marvel at their daughter's athletic prowess together.

"Your niece is lucky your family's athletic. My Kelly, bless her heart, keeps tripping over the ball. But then she comes from a long line of uncoordinated folks." Marlene suddenly leapt to her feet, her eyes on the game. "Come on, Kelly. You can do it."

Oblivious to whether Kelly managed to stay upright, Diana couldn't reconcile what she'd heard. Connor didn't lie. That was Diana's forte.

"I didn't tell her Jaye was my daughter," Connor said in a quiet voice. "A lot of people assume she's mine, and sometimes it's easier to let them keep thinking that."

"I understand," Diana said, barely able to choke out the words. And she did understand. Connor couldn't have been more wonderful, taking care of Jaye when she hadn't been able to. She owed him a debt of gratitude she'd never be able to repay. "When did Jaye start playing soccer?"

"A couple weeks ago. She's always cooped up in her room with her violin so Abby and I figured it would be good exercise."

Abby, his wife to be. Shame pricked Diana, like a needle piercing her skin. How could Diana have yet to meet the woman who made decisions about her child?

"Is Abby coming to the game?" Diana asked.

"She was going to before she got sucked into giving a makeup violin lesson. She still thought she'd make some of it, but it's starting to look unlikely."

"That's too bad. I'd really like to meet her."

"The door to my place is open whenever you feel like walking through it," Connor said meaningfully. When Diana didn't reply, he continued, "But, like I said, it's great you're here. How'd you hear about the game anyway?"

"From Mom."

That seemed to surprise him. "Did she say whether she'd be here?"

"She said she couldn't make it."

A look crossed his face that Diana couldn't read, but then he nodded toward the field. "The ball's in front of our goal again."

The players in blue fanned out in front of Jaye, outnumbering the girls in yellow. One of the blue-clad players kicked the ball to a teammate, who sent it careening toward a corner of the goal cage.

Jaye took two quick steps to her left, barely managing to deflect the ball with a gloved hand. It skittered harmlessly to the side of the net.

"Wow, she really is good," Diana said, her comment lost amid more cheers.

After Jaye's teammates worked the ball to the opponent's side of the field, Jaye gazed directly into the stands.

"She knows she's having a good game and wants her props," Connor said, laughter in his voice as he gave her a thumbs-up.

Jaye's posture suddenly changed, the hint of cockiness leaving her body as her shoulders slumped.

"She's seen me," Diana said.

"Then smile and wave," Connor said.

Diana took her brother's advice, making her smile wide and her wave big but Jaye turned away without acknowledging her. Even though she'd expected the reaction, Diana's throat thickened.

Connor patted her shoulder. "It's not going to happen overnight, Diana. It'll take a while."

Not trusting herself to speak, Diana kept her attention on the game. But Jaye seemed distracted, standing flatfooted as the next shot on goal whizzed by her into the net.

"Too bad," Connor said. "Her team hasn't scored, and that's the first goal she let in all day."

"All day? I thought the game started at ten."

"They pushed the time up," Connor explained, a moment before the referee blew his whistle in three short bursts. "So it's over."

Showing up late to the game, Diana thought. Yet another transgression to feel guilty about.

After a short talk with their coach, Jaye and her teammates crossed the field to their waiting parents, most of them upbeat despite the loss. Diana overheard excited chatter about the coach's offer to treat the team to ice cream.

Another girl and Jaye, her head down and her steps slow, brought up the rear. Diana had long ago memorized every angle and plane of her daughter's face, so the subtle differences struck her. Not so much in the shape of Jaye's features, but in her expression. A wariness around the eyes. A tightness to the lips.

The other girl veered off, but Jaye kept coming until she finally reached them. Because her arms itched to fold her daughter in a tight embrace, Diana wrapped them around her midsection.

"Hello, Jaye." Diana's insides shook so hard she was surprised her voice didn't follow suit. "It's great to see you."

Jaye said nothing.

Connor filled in the silence. "You played a good game. A couple of those saves in the first half were fantastic."

"Yeah, but we lost." Jaye stared down at her feet, scuffing the toes of her shoes in the grass. "And I gave up that goal at the end."

Diana swallowed hard and tried to remember what she knew about soccer. "The ball had to get past eight other girls before it got to you."

"Ten." Jaye still didn't look at Diana. "There are eleven players on a soccer team, not nine."

Diana hugged herself harder. She didn't want to talk about soccer when there were so many more important things to discuss. Like her move to a town not even an hour's drive from Silver Spring.

"Did your uncle tell you I'm living in Bentonsville now?" she asked with forced brightness. "It would be wonderful if you came to visit."

Jaye's mouth trembled. She blinked hard a couple times, then looked straight at Connor. "Uncle Connor, can I please go to the ice cream place with Becky? She said her mom could drive me home."

Connor moved closer to Diana, silently lending his support. "Your mother's here, Jaye. You can go for ice cream another time."

"No. It's okay," Diana forced out the words past the lump in her throat. "I have to work today, anyway."

Jaye didn't have to be told twice, but Diana thought she saw the sheen of tears in her eyes before her daughter ran off. Behind her sunglasses, her own eyes had grown watery.

"You shouldn't have told her to go," Connor said.

"I can't force her to let me back into her life."

"Yes, you can. She's nine years old and you're her mother."

"You're the one who said rebuilding our relationship would take time. As long as you don't mind having her live with you, I can give her time."

"Of course I don't mind." He made a frustrated movement with his hand. "But I want what's best for you, too, Diana. And that would be having Jaye with you."

Touched by his concern, Diana didn't trust herself to speak. How could she have let so many years go by without contact with her brother?

"Don't tell me I missed the entire game." The woman Diana had seen in front of Connor's town house with Jaye rushed up to them, her short dark hair bobbing and her face flushed. "What happened?"

"Jaye's team lost 1-0, but she made some fantastic saves in goal," Connor said.

"Darn it. I wanted to see her."

"I know you did." Connor put an arm around the woman's shoulders, gathering her close. "But you're here in time to meet my sister. Abby, this is Diana. Diana, my fiancée, Abby Reed."

Recognition struck Diana so hard she swayed.

Abby's hair no longer fell to her waist and her body had filled out, but she saw the girl in the woman's face.

"You're Drew Galloway's half sister," she choked out, emotions churning inside her. How could this be? How could Connor be engaged to a woman who had blood ties to their brother's killer?

She noticed Connor's arm tighten protectively around Abby. Connor had been in college when Abby's family moved to Bentonsville, so he wouldn't have known her in high school. Diana, a year ahead of Abby, had only made it a point to find out who she was after the crime.

"That's right. I'm Drew's sister." Abby looked straight at Diana, her voice strong and steady. "I'm also your brother's fiancée and somebody who loves your daughter."

"I don't understand," Diana murmured. "How could you two have gotten together?"

"It's a long story," Connor said. "The short version is we ran into each other by chance and didn't realize our connection until we were already involved."

Diana gazed from Connor back to Abby, her mind rebelling against the impossible.

"You're the reason my mother skipped today's soccer game," Diana said with sudden insight, easily envisioning how her mother would react to the other woman.

Abby visibly winced. "Unfortunately, I think you're right about that. She's upset that I'm still in touch with my brother. She doesn't understand how I can still love him. So I don't imagine she'll come to the wedding, either."

"It's two weeks from today," Connor said, hugging

Abby even tighter to his side. "If I had your new address, Diana, we would have mailed you an invitation."

"We hope you'll be there," Abby added, both her manner and voice uncertain.

The realization that Abby expected Diana to snub her because her future sister-in-law couldn't hate her own brother cut through Diana's own anguish. "Of course I'll come."

Abby reached for her hand and pressed it. Diana blinked hard, battling tears. Having Abby in the family would take some getting used to, but Diana couldn't hold the innocent woman who'd captured Connor's heart even partially responsible for J.D.'s death. Especially because Diana didn't entirely blame Abby's half brother.

Diana hadn't been on the scene the night Drew stabbed J.D., but the person she held most accountable was herself.

CHAPTER NINE

SATURDAY NIGHT and every other teenager in Bentonsville had somewhere to be.

A girl in history class had informed the cute guys sitting in front of Molly that her parents were out of town before inviting them to a blow-out party at her house. The girl ignored Molly.

Some other students talked about meeting up at the pizza place. Molly considered trying to wrangle an invitation, but then one of the girls pointed at her and whispered something to the other.

That kind of thing had been happening a lot to Molly since the night in the park with Bobby Martinelli.

Bobby, who had probably snuck into the park with his friends tonight to drink, smoke and go all the way with some other stupid girl who wanted him to like her.

Giving Bobby what he wanted hadn't made him like Molly any better. He'd seemed preoccupied the first few times she'd approached him after that night. Now he didn't talk to her at all. Whenever she passed him in the hall, he stared right through her.

Molly struggled to hold back the tears stinging the backs of her eyes. She'd told her mom she had play practice even though the play's run ended last week. Her mom, who was bandaging her wailing little brother's skinned knee, told her to go ahead. She hadn't even asked when Molly would be home.

The lie had gotten Molly out of the house but she was such a loser she could think of only one place to go. In keeping with her continuing run of bad luck, it was somewhere that required checking in at the front desk.

Molly peered through the glass door to where Diana sat at the welcome desk. Surely Diana would step away from the desk sooner or later, giving Molly the opportunity to slip inside unnoticed.

What appeared to be a textbook lay open in front of Diana, but she stared into space, her expression sad. Then her body shook, as though she was trying to hold off a sob.

Molly ventured into the center. Molly had almost reached the desk before Diana looked up and pasted on a smile that seemed as false as Bobby's promises.

"Diana," Molly asked gently, "were you crying?"

"No." The single tear trickling down her face contradicted her denial. Diana wiped it away, then grimaced. "Maybe a little. I'm kind of upset today, that's all."

"About what?"

"Nothing you need to be concerned about," Diana said with false brightness. "Forget I mentioned it."

Molly's face fell. But why had she ever thought Diana would confide in her? She was just a stupid kid. "That's okay," Molly muttered. "You don't have to tell me."

"Oh, no, Molly. That's not it. It's just that..." Diana's voice trailed off. "Something that happened today got me thinking about my brother. His name was J.D. He died when I was your age. He was seventeen."

Molly's problems—the divorce, the move to a town where she had no friends, even sex with Bobby—suddenly seemed insignificant. As annoying as her little brothers and sister were, she couldn't bear to lose any of them. "He died? How?"

"Another boy stabbed him."

Molly gasped. "I'm sorry."

"It was a long time ago." Diana's voice sounded raw. "But I know what it's like to be sad, Molly."

"Is that why you used to skip school? Because you were sad about what happened to your brother?"

"I think it might have been why I did a lot of things I shouldn't have done."

"Now I feel stupid," Molly blurted out.

"About what?"

Without realizing what was about to happen, tears streamed down Molly's face like a freaking waterfall.

Diana was suddenly beside her, encircling Molly's shoulders with her arm and guiding her to a chair behind the desk. No one else, thankfully, was around to witness Molly's humiliation. "Molly, what's wrong?"

"I already told you," Molly choked out between sobs, "it's stupid."

"If it's making you cry, it's not stupid." Diana scooted her own chair forward and picked up one of Molly's trembling hands. "What is it, honey?"

The endearment was Molly's undoing. "There's this guy I like," she managed, then grew silent, her breaths sounding labored.

"What's his name?" Diana asked.

"Bobby." Molly squeezed her eyes tight, finding it easier not to look at Diana. "I thought he liked me, but ever since we were together he ignores me."

"What do you mean, since you were together?"

Molly's cheeks burned. She couldn't tell anyone, even Diana, she'd gone all the way with Bobby. "After we made out. I think he's telling people at school about it."

Diana rubbed her shoulder. "Oh, honey. I know how that feels. When I was in high school, I kissed a couple boys who turned out to be loud mouths. Before I knew it, everyone was talking about how easy I was."

Kissed? If only that was all Molly had done.

"As hard as it is, you have to hold your head high and wait for the kids at school to start talking about something else." Diana kept up the comforting shoulder rub. "And don't blame yourself. It's not always easy to figure out which boy is worth spending time with."

"Did you find a boy who was?"

"Yeah, I did." Diana's smile was the saddest Molly had ever seen, clueing Molly in that Diana's story hadn't ended happily. "But it doesn't sound like Bobby falls into that category."

Molly sniffled, but tears still fell down her cheeks. "I just wanted him to like me."

Diana grasped both of her hands. "Oh, Molly. This

is Bobby's loss, not yours. You're beautiful and smart and kind. You have lots going for you."

Molly drew back to look into her face. "You really think those things about me?"

"Absolutely." Diana smiled, smoothing the hair back from Molly's wet face. "I can see you're beautiful because I have eyes. And I know you're smart because you read my favorite author."

Molly smiled back, tremulously at first, then a little bit wider. Because for the first time since she'd moved to Bentonsville, the dense fog of loneliness seemed to lift and she felt as though she'd made a true friend.

DIANA CLOSED THE CENTER up tight behind her, the click of the lock signaling the end of a trying day.

The pickup basketball game still raged, but she resolved to ignore the temptation to stop by the lighted court. Watching Tyler play could only lead to problems, and she already had enough of those.

This morning she'd botched an attempt to reconnect with her daughter and discovered Connor was engaged to the sister of their brother's murderer. This evening she'd nearly unburdened her problems on a teenager beset with her own.

Molly didn't need to hear about how Diana had failed J.D. Or how she deceived Tyler and alienated Jaye. Not that Diana knew exactly what Molly—or any other teenager—needed.

Unless she asked.

The thought stopped Diana in midstride. Of course. She'd been tasking her brain to come up with ideas to improve the teen program while ignoring the obvious one. Heading home, pulling the covers over her head and praying for sleep suddenly didn't seem nearly as attractive as it had a moment ago.

She'd much rather run her idea by somebody who cared as much about Bentonsville's teens as she did.

Chris had authorized Willie to keep the lights blazing when the basketball court was in use, but the slight chill in the air portended that it would soon be too cold to play basketball after dark. Yet another reason to devise new ways to keep the teens at the center.

Wrapping her light jacket more securely around herself, she walked around the building to the bleacher adjacent to the court and sat down on the cold metal. She counted ten players: nine teenage boys and Tyler.

She'd gotten used to seeing him in workout clothes, but still appreciated the sight. His shorts, not quite as long as those of his teenage counterparts, left a length of his leanly muscular, hair-sprinkled legs bare. His gray T-shirt hugged well-developed abs.

He leaped for an offensive rebound, pulled the ball down with both hands, dribbled to his left, pump faked, then executed a perfect jump shot that sent the basketball swishing through the net.

The shot transported Diana into the past, before J.D. had died, when she'd sit in the bleachers at the high school games crushing on the dark-haired boy with the perfect form. Coaches from a few small colleges had also noticed how good he was, but Tyler had passed up their scholarship offers for Harvard.

"I think Ty's trying to impress someone," Davey yelled. "Aren't you, Ty?"

"Guilty as charged." Tyler shot Diana a grin as he ran down the court to set up on defense. "So how about you boys help an old guy out by taking it easy on me?"

They erupted into laughter, giving answers that roughly translated to "no way."

Tyler didn't need their help. He finished the game off strong, scoring seven of his team's last nine points, including a deep three-pointer that sealed the win.

"That's it for me," Tyler said. "I can't run the way I used to."

"Are you kidding?" The admonition came from a teammate of Tyler's. "You could run most of us into the ground. I'm drenched, and you're barely sweating."

"Let him go, Jimmy," Davey called. "He has more important things to do than play with us."

Tyler walked straight for Diana, comically wagging his eyebrows. "I'm hoping that's true. Diana, please say you're here because of me."

She laughed at his silliness. "I do have to talk to you."

"Then it's my lucky night."

Davey picked up a water bottle and took a swig from it. "I've been wondering why Ty's been here so much. He's never showed up on Saturday until tonight. I should have figured out he was sweet on you."

"You've got it wrong," Diana quickly refuted. "We're just friends. I need to talk business with him."

Davey laughed. "No disrespect intended, Miss Smith. But if you was Pinocchio, your nose would extend clear into the next county."

The teenager's remark robbed Diana of speech as she silently acknowledged that what she had to discuss with Tyler could have waited until Monday. Had she become so accustomed to lying to others that she'd started to lie to herself?

"You're just jealous because you don't have a pretty woman waiting around for you," Tyler told Davey.

"True, true," Davey said, laughing.

The game broken up, the teenagers gathered their stuff and left, calling goodbyes over their shoulders.

"I really do have business to discuss." Diana sounded as though she was trying to convince herself as much as Tyler. "I have an idea about the teen center."

"I'd love to hear it." He pulled on a crimson Harvard sweatshirt, picked up his water bottle and drank. "But I'm open to talking about anything else on your mind, too." He sat down next to her on the bleachers and rested his forearms on his thighs, turning his head sideways to look at her. "I heard earlier today that Connor's marrying Drew Galloway's sister."

"I just found out myself," Diana said. "This morning, in fact. I can't say I wasn't shocked, but despite everything I like her. More importantly, it's pretty obvious she makes Connor happy."

"Then you're okay with it?"

Her feelings about the subject were still new, especially because finding out about her mother's unfair treatment of Abby had resurrected Diana's own guilt. Abby, she reminded herself, wasn't guilty of anything.

"I'm as okay with it as I can be," she answered.

"You're a good person, Diana Smith," Tyler told her,

praise she didn't deserve. A good person wouldn't have her brother's death on her conscience. "So what's your idea about the teen program?"

Grateful for the change of subject, she did her best to switch mental gears and resurrect her former enthusiasm. "To stop trying to think of ideas and let the teens think of them for us."

He snapped his fingers. "You mean poll them on what they want out of the center?"

"Exactly. We could contact the Bentonsville High principal and ask her to assemble a group we could meet with."

"Or better yet, we could—"

The lights cut off, plunging the court and the bleachers into darkness. Diana blinked, barely able to distinguish the outline of Tyler's shape. She hadn't realized until that moment that no moon shone out from the overcast sky.

"What just happened?" Diana asked.

"Willie must have seen the other players leaving and not realized we were still out here."

"If I could make out what was two feet in front of my face, I'd suggest we leave, too," she said.

"Hold on to me and I'll get you out of here." He grasped her hand, his warm grip immediately reassuring. "Remember, we're sitting two rows up and be careful you don't trip."

He descended the bleachers first, with Diana following closely behind. "I can't tell how big of a step to take."

"Don't worry. I've got you." He hooked his hands

under her arms, lifting her to the ground as though she weighed almost nothing. Then he simply held her.

Her eyes hadn't fully adjusted to the darkness, but she could make out the square shape of his jaw and lushness of his lips. Her memory filled in the rest, because she'd never forgotten anything about him.

She raised her hand and touched his slightly scratchy cheek, then ran her fingertips over the softness of his lips. She couldn't see into his eyes, but knew that whatever blazed there was reflected in her own.

He lowered his head slowly, blotting out what little light there was. And then she didn't need to see, because everything was about feel. The softness of his hair underneath her fingers. The firmness of his lips. The excitement of his tongue stroking hers. The strength of his body pressed against hers.

She'd kissed other men since leaving Bentonsville and had even made love with a few of them, but none of the experiences approached the excitement of Tyler's kiss. She felt more alive in his arms than she'd been in years, maybe even since she'd last kissed him.

The intimacy of the night closed around them, wrapping them in a cocoon where only the two of them existed.

But even as Diana had the thought, she realized it wasn't so. Other people had always impacted their relationship. Her brother, whose death had driven her into Tyler's arms. The boys of Bentonsville, whose gossip had wrenched her out of them. And now the members of the judicial nominating commission, who could deny Tyler the judgeship if they discovered that a former drug addict was the mother of his child.

She anchored her hands against Tyler's chest, pushing weakly against it but he got the message. He lifted his head.

"I'm sorry. I wasn't supposed to do that, was I?" he asked, his voice slightly raspy, the fact that he still held her counteracting his apology.

"No, you weren't." She made a valiant effort to ignore the electric sensations skittering over her skin. "Tell you what, walk me to my car and we'll forget about it."

"Unless someone strikes me on the head and I get amnesia, I'm not forgetting a kiss like that," he said.

"Don't joke."

"Believe me, it's no joke."

A thrill ran through her at his words, but she tried to suppress it. "I still think I should go home."

"I don't."

She wet her lips, trying to gather her weakening resistance. "Tyler, we've talked about this. I can't go home with you."

"I'm not asking you to. I'm asking you to go to Angelo's."

"The pizza place?" Her insides tightened, but this time her reaction had little to do with Tyler. She stepped back until he no longer touched her. "Why there?"

"Because the local teenage hangout will give us a better cross-section of teens to talk to. Principals tend to pick only the top students when they're asked to get a group together."

She didn't dispute Tyler's logic, but her dread couldn't

have been more acute if she'd been compelled to go to a dentist's office to have a tooth pulled.

"You're with me, right?" Tyler asked.

"Yeah, I'm with you," she finally said.

Her eyes had adjusted to the gloom, but she held on tight to Tyler's hand as they navigated the distance to their cars. She felt like she was walking to her doom.

Once they got to Angelo's, she needed to right an old wrong. If she could raise the courage to do it.

TYLER CLAIMED the only empty table at Angelo's Pizza and glanced around at the groups of teens guzzling soft drinks, devouring fragrant-smelling pies and creating enough noise to distress his eardrums.

He recognized a few of the teens from his neighborhood and others from church, but the rest were strangers. One dark-haired girl reminded him vividly of the young Diana, perhaps because of the seriousness of her expression.

His Diana stood at the long, wooden counter where patrons had the option of ordering. Tyler had suggested table service, but Diana offered to place their order if he saved a table. So why wasn't she ordering?

She positioned herself at the very end of the counter, then motioned a teenage couple in front of her, perhaps unaware that Tyler's stomach growled with hunger.

"Can I get you anything, Mr. Benton?" asked Meg Humphries, a harried-looking teenage girl who lived across the street from him. "Although to be honest, it's so crowded tonight that you'd be helping me out if you ordered at the counter."

"Sure, Meg. No problem."

Had he told Diana he preferred mushrooms on his pizza? Armed with an excuse to join her, he vacated the table even though it probably meant losing it.

Before Tyler reached the counter, a small man with gray hair, eyebrows that resembled twin caterpillars and a big voice bustled over to Diana. Angelo Spinelli, the owner.

"I hear you're waiting for me," Angelo said. "You want Angelo to make you a special pizza?"

Diana shifted her weight from one foot to the other, as though she was...nervous? Tyler couldn't hear her reply, but he didn't have the same problem with Angelo's loudly voiced response. "Apology for what?"

Before Diana could answer, Angelo spotted Tyler and raised a hand. "Hey, Ty. What you doing in here tonight with all the teenagers?"

"I'm not with them, Angelo." Sensing Diana growing tenser by the second and hoping to put her at ease, he placed a hand on her rigid back. "I'm with Diana and feeling mighty lucky about that."

Angelo's gaze swung back to Diana. "Now I recognize you. You're Elaine Smith's daughter. Haven't seen you in years. So what is it you have to apologize about?"

Diana's gaze swung to Tyler, her eyes appearing trapped. He gently rubbed her back, silently conveying he was on her side. He felt her draw in a breath before she looked Angelo straight in the eyes.

"I did something ten years ago I still regret," she said. "I walked on a check. Even though my father found out and paid the bill, I never apologized. That's what I'd like to do now. I'm sorry, Angelo."

The simple eloquence of her apology, which she delivered in a steady voice despite her obvious anxiety, touched a chord deep inside Tyler.

"Ah, forget about it." Angelo, too, seemed affected. He lowered his voice to a loud whisper. "But don't let any of the kids in here know I said that. I don't even remember it. What I remember is that terrible business with your brother. A tragedy, that was. Now what can I get you?"

After taking their order for a medium mushroom and extra cheese pizza with a couple of Cokes, Angelo relayed the order to a cook and went off to help another customer.

"I'm sorry you heard that," Diana said in a voice so low Tyler could hardly hear it above the din. "It's embarrassing to think I was ever that girl who'd cheat a nice man like Angelo."

"Hey, I liked that girl." He leaned close, getting a whiff of peaches and warm skin. "I like this one even better. Not everybody could do what you just did."

A blush stained her cheeks. "That was nothing."

He held her gaze. "That was amazing. That took courage."

"Then it's your turn to be courageous."

"I don't follow."

She nodded toward a group of rowdy teenagers who'd pushed some tables together. "You lost our table, so you can be the one who asks those teenagers if we can join them."

"Done," he said, taking her by the hand and leading her to the table. Three pieces of pizza and half a Coke later, he listened in amazement as one teenager after another opened up to her.

"A hip-hop club. I love that idea," Diana told a boy with dyed black hair and a nose ring. "But what would get a guy like you to come to the center at night? Would a dance do it?"

The boy rolled eyes fringed with black liner. "Dances are lame."

"I'd come to listen to a band," said a pretty girl with curly blond hair and too much makeup.

"Another good idea," Diana said. "But we don't have the money for that."

"I know some bands that wouldn't charge," the girl said. "They're always looking for a place to jam."

"I'd come to hear that," said the boy with the nose ring.

"And you could host an open mike night," another boy suggested. "Those are always fun. Plus a talent show so the hip-hop group can perform."

"I'd come if you showed free movies," a girl with a squeaky voice chipped in, "as long as they weren't G-rated."

The ideas flowed like soda refills after that, with Tyler content to let Diana act as a funnel. Before the teenagers left the restaurant, she had promises from three of them to help implement the ideas.

Diana beamed at Tyler when they were finally alone at the table, causing him to wish she'd smile more. That he could be the one to make her smile.

"That went very well, if I say so myself," she said.

"I say it, too. You have a way of getting kids to open up to you." The next observation sprang from him before he could stop it. "You must be a wonderful mother."

Her smile vanished, like the bulb in a lamp that had been switched off. Her eyes shifted. "I know a little girl who would disagree with you."

"What do you mean by that?"

"Nothing." She checked her watch, and picked her purse off an adjacent chair. "It's getting late. We really should be going."

She half rose, but he remained seated. Now that he'd finally asked about her daughter, he couldn't contain his curiosity. No, his *need* to know more about the girl who was a part of her. "I'm a good listener."

She sighed heavily and sat back down, her expression pained. "You won't like what you hear."

"Try me."

Her shoulders rose and fell. "Remember how I said I'd just found out about Abby being Connor's fiancée? That's because I was at Jaye's soccer game this morning. But meeting Abby wasn't the most traumatic thing that happened. Jaye was so angry at me she barely acknowledged my existence."

Tyler had subconsciously known something was amiss between Diana and her daughter, but he hadn't let himself wonder about it. He did now. "What is she angry about?"

"It was the first time I'd seen her since I left her with Connor in February."

He tried to make sense of what she said and couldn't. "Why did you leave her?"

Her eyes slid away and he knew with complete certainty that she wouldn't give him a straight answer.

"I was having financial trouble and thought Jaye would be better off with Connor until I got back on my feet."

Something about the explanation struck a wrong note, but he couldn't put his finger on what. "So that's why you went back to school?"

"I'm trying to build a better future for her."

"I take it she doesn't understand that?"

Again she wouldn't look at him. "It's a little more complicated than that, but that's close enough."

He longed to hear about the complications but she obviously had no intention of sharing them. "Then she'll come around."

She nodded, but the triumphant mood of a few moments ago was gone. She suggested they leave, and this time he agreed. He walked with her to her Chevy, so preoccupied he didn't even try to kiss her goodnight.

Something was going on with her daughter she hadn't told him about, something he very badly wanted her to confide. Jaye was so inexorably linked to Diana it was imperative he let go of his jealousy for her dead father.

No longer would Tyler be satisfied with only one of the Smith females in his life. He wanted both the mother he'd never stopped loving and the daughter he'd find it in his heart to treat as his very own.

CHAPTER TEN

CHRIS COLEMAN quickly discovered he couldn't count on his willpower when it concerned Lauren Fairchild.

He'd vowed to either remain sequestered in his office or be gone for the day when she showed up for step aerobics class, a strategy that had worked well the first two weeks after the benefit dinner.

Yet here it was only Wednesday of the third week and he was already walking by the exercise room and stealing glances at the women moving to the music, none of whom were Lauren.

Because, he belatedly realized, she was rushing from the direction of the ladies' room. She stopped when she saw him but didn't smile the way he'd seen her smile countless times at Tyler Benton.

"Hi, Chris."

"Lauren." He nodded in acknowledgement, trying without success not to notice how delectable she looked in her tight-fitting, stomach-baring exercise outfit. Tried not to dwell on how his fingers itched to trace the inches of visible bare skin under her shirt. He started to move past her.

"Wait." She extended her arm, laying a delicate hand

on his forearm. He looked down at the spot where she touched him, then up at her, relatively sure he hadn't banked the desire in his eyes. She removed her hand.

"I wanted to thank you again for rescuing me at the spaghetti buffet," she said. "It was very gallant."

Yeah, right. That was him. Sir Gallahad. Barely able to keep from sweeping the fair Lauren into his arms and ravishing her.

"It was nothing." He shrugged, hating that she looked so nervous around him. She'd called him gallant. She had to realize he respected her right to reject him. "How's your ankle?"

She stuck out one shapely leg and flexed her ankle. "Good as new."

"Great," he said gruffly, keeping his eyes on her face so his gaze didn't travel lasciviously up her leg. "Then you better get to exercise class. It's already started."

He walked away, unable to resist glancing back. She stood staring after him, looking so tempting it was all he could do not to rush back to her and forget about gallantry. Or good sense.

He desperately needed something to take his mind off Lauren—and Tyler Benton, who'd made the center his second home. There Benton was again, hanging around the welcome desk. He was leaning forward, his forearms on the counter, flirting with Diana.

He wondered if Lauren had noticed that the man she was set on having had developed a new fixation. Chris unashamedly eavesdropped as he passed the welcome desk.

"I'm sorry. You're right. I do have Thursdays off, but

I already have plans," he overheard Diana tell Benton, a brush-off if he'd ever heard one.

Chris's anger started slowly but burned bright by the time he reached his office. He firmly believed Benton was the wrong man for the domestic-minded Lauren, but it incensed him that Benton's pursuit of Diana might hurt Lauren. Now how twisted was that?

A sane guy would encourage a romance between Diana and Benton in the hopes that he could pick up the pieces of Lauren's broken heart. Except that Chris was rational enough to realize Lauren wouldn't look his way no matter how shattered she was.

Chris slammed the door to his office, plopped down into his desk chair and cradled his head in his hands.

DIANA RUBBED the space between her brows, wondering how to get the message across to Tyler that she wasn't interested when he'd picked up on the fact that she very definitely was.

She'd blown yet another chance to discourage him when he'd asked her to dinner, inventing an excuse instead of outright telling him to leave her alone.

She hadn't thought of herself as weak willed. After all, she'd kicked her earlier addiction like the people who were there meeting tonight for Alcoholics Anonymous.

Spying the pamphlets an AA member had spread on the counter in a fan shape, she picked one up. Her breath caught at the sight of the Narcotics Anonymous logo, the realization hitting her that the leaflets advertised a variety of support groups. The back of this one listed times and locations of area NA meetings.

It might not hurt to attend one, although she couldn't expect an NA meeting to help her overcome her addiction to Tyler.

"Is everything okay, Diana?" Chris Coleman joined her at the desk, his features pinched with concern.

Diana quickly covered the pamphlet and placed it on her lap. But from the way Chris peered at her, he could already have seen the NA heading and guessed at the source of her interest.

"Oh, hey, Chris. Yeah, everything's fine." Unwilling to provide him the opening to ask a pointed follow-up question, she kept talking. "Entries are coming in for the talent show the teens suggested we host. And I did tell you that my mother got commitments from two more retired teachers to help with the tutoring program, right? In the three days she's been here, attendance has tripled. Of course, the computers arriving could have had something to do with that. And we did only start with one student. But, still, that's a pretty good rate."

"Yes, it is. And, yes, you did tell me. But you're changing the subject." He came around to her side of the desk, leaning a hip against the counter. She tensed. "You didn't look fine just now. I'm all ears if you want to talk about it."

She stared down at the NA brochure, shame filling every inch of her. "You wouldn't understand."

"Oh, no? Then why am I pretty sure this has something to do with Tyler Benton?"

Tyler? "Why would you think that?"

With his coal-dark hair and eyes, it struck her that Chris rivaled Tyler in the looks department. More importantly, she'd always liked him. So why couldn't she have had the good sense to fall in love with him instead of the far more complicated Tyler?

"I've seen Benton more since you started working here than I did all summer. I also overheard you brush him off." Chris's stare seemed to bore into her mind. "That *was* a brush-off, right?"

"Right," she conceded, then figured she might benefit from a man's perspective. "Don't get me wrong. I definitely want Tyler as a friend, but I can't seem to get across that I'm not in the market for romance."

"Why don't you just come out and say that?"

Diana frowned. "It sounds pretty simple when you put it that way, but I don't seem to be able to."

"Then tell him you and me are dating. That should do it."

A laugh started deep inside Diana but stuck when he didn't crack a smile. "You're not joking, are you?"

"Nope. Use me as the reason you can't go out with Benton and that'll solve your problem."

"But won't Tyler notice we're not actually dating?"

"I don't see how. We're friends, we work together, we know a lot of the same people. Besides, once you tell him you're dating me, he'll stop hanging around here so much."

The less frequently Diana saw Tyler, the more likely she'd be to keep from doing something stupid. Like sleeping with him.

"Maybe it could work." Diana didn't speak above a murmur, but Chris heard her and took her comment as tacit agreement.

"That's settled, then. The next time anybody asks, we're dating."

Before she could question Chris about who he expected to be interested in their love lives besides Tyler, he was gone.

LAUREN JOGGED along the trail through the park in the opposite direction of the regular flow of runners.

Her physician father had checked out the ankle she'd tweaked in exercise class last week and pronounced it fine. She should have asked him to examine her mind.

Her common sense was pretty much gone.

Why else would she have rearranged her own noon break when she discovered Chris Coleman jogged on his lunch hour? She'd only been at it for five minutes and already her breaths came too fast. She was no athlete, that was for sure, even though she'd started to enjoy the step aerobics class.

Ironically the reason she'd signed up for class no longer applied. She still agreed with her mother's assertion that Tyler Benton was a spectacular catch, but Lauren was more interested in running into Chris.

She'd risen earlier than usual that morning to shave her legs and stuff a backpack with coordinating shorts, T-shirt and socks. She hadn't packed a lunch because she planned to grab a quick bite at the sandwich place around the corner from the park. With Chris.

True, Chris had vowed to leave her alone. He'd been doing a pretty good job of it, too, but he couldn't avoid her forever. If she kept arranging accidental meetings, he was bound to get the idea she'd changed her mind about dating him.

She supposed she could tell him that, but lately she got tongue-tied whenever he was near. Besides, her mother had drilled into her from an early age that she should never, ever ask out a man.

You chase him until he catches you, her mother always advised.

She instantly recognized the jogger with long, lean lines who turned onto the path in front of her as Chris. But he was heading, as she was, counterclockwise.

"Oh, no," she cried aloud. "You're supposed to be running toward me, where you can see me."

Determined that all the jogging she'd already done wouldn't be for naught, she lengthened her strides, running at what for her was a breakneck pace. She made up some ground, but she'd never catch him unless she did something fast.

"Chris, is that you?" she yelled, literally loud enough to wake whatever nocturnal animals might be having their daytime snoozes.

He turned, spotted her and jogged in place until she caught up to him. She attempted a smile but thought the sweat dripping down her face might have obscured it.

"Lauren. I didn't know you jogged."

"Oh, yeah...I'm...a jogger." She was so short of breath, she could barely get the words out. "Don't stop. I'll...keep up."

He sent her a skeptical look, but complied. She tried to match his longer strides as they ran side by side, their relative silence broken only by her labored breaths.

Oh, the hell with it. At this rate, the only way Chris would catch her was if she fell over from exhaustion.

"So…do you have…any plans this weekend?" She paused to catch her wind and prepare for the second of her two questions, the one where she defied everything her mother had taught her and asked him out.

"We probably will, but we haven't talked about it yet."

"We?" She had no trouble getting that question out.

"Diana Smith and I. You know Diana, right? We're dating."

She gaped at him and almost tripped over an exposed root.

"How…nice," she said when she recovered her balance, almost choking on the word.

"I think so."

Her pace had slowed considerably since she'd caught up to him, and he was obviously holding himself back to match it. The futility of her quest suddenly struck her.

"You go on ahead." She made a supreme effort to sound light and breezy. "I'll see you around."

"Okay. Catch you later." He took off, his long legs eating up the ground.

Unable to maintain the fiction that she was in running shape a moment longer, Lauren bent over and anchored her hands above her knees. She gasped for breath, feeling utterly miserable.

She looked up, expecting to see Chris's retreating back. But he'd craned his neck to gaze back at her. Even from this distance, she read the concern in his expression.

She stood up straight, smiled and gave a cheery, I'm-okay wave. As though it wasn't eating her up inside that he was dating Diana Smith, the quintessential girl next door with sex appeal. His steps faltered, but then he turned and kept on going.

She couldn't blame him. Around him, she was a shell of her normal poised, assured self. Spilled spaghetti, a tweaked ankle and now labored breathing.

No wonder the attraction he'd admitted to was as long gone as he was.

TYLER LIFTED his right hand from the steering wheel and flexed it. It could have been his imagination, but his fingers felt a bit stiff from all the hand shaking he'd done tonight.

His father had invited Tyler to dine with him and Tyler's mother at the country club in lieu of their regularly scheduled Friday lunch. Douglas Benton claimed to have a busy day on tap tomorrow, but his father must have known in advance that the dining room would be crowded with people who could help Tyler's career.

Between bites of roasted duck and snippets of conversation with his parents, Tyler had talked to most of them.

He'd enjoyed visiting with his mother, whom he didn't see often enough, but he'd spent most of the evening wishing he'd been otherwise engaged. With Diana.

Diana hadn't specified what she had planned for her day off and Tyler hadn't pressed in case it involved repairing her relationship with her daughter. He wished she'd talk to him more in depth about the problem, but he obviously needed to work harder on gaining her confidence.

When he reached the Bentonsville town limits, the traffic light across from the new Safeway turned red and he slowed to a stop. He needed a carton of milk and a loaf of bread, now that he thought about it. Trying to decide whether he felt like stopping, he gazed over at the grocery store parking lot and spotted what looked to be Diana's dark gray Chevy.

A trip to the grocery store, he concluded as he switched on his turn signal, was an excellent idea.

He found Diana a short time later in the produce section between the navel oranges and the Granny Smith apples. Dressed in slim-fitting blue jeans topped by a navy blazer, with her dark hair loose, she looked no older than a teenager.

Her eyes lifted from the shiny green apple she held and brightened, her full lips curving into a smile. He smiled back, feeling happier than he had all night.

"If you passed up a date with me to do your grocery shopping," he remarked when he reached her, "I'm going to get a complex."

"But you haven't seen my cupboards. They're really bare. Mother Hubbard bare."

He laughed, but noted she didn't correct his joking assumption. He might conclude the attraction that nearly scalded him was one-sided if he hadn't felt an answering heat in her kiss.

She'd told him not quite two weeks ago that she needed time to settle into her new life. He'd intended to give her time, but he'd never been a patient man, which had turned out to be more of a virtue than a curse.

He forced issues, made things happen, got himself

in positions where he could excel. Just today, the defense for the armed robber claiming mistaken identity had been so convinced of the strength of his case that they'd jumped at a plea bargain.

Tyler couldn't succeed with Diana if he only interacted with her at the community center. He didn't intend to maneuver her into bed. Not yet, anyway. But in his opinion, it was possible to take things too slowly.

"You want me to steer your cart? It'll free up your hands to get your groceries. Or, and this is only a very strong suggestion, grope the cart driver."

She laughed, as he'd intended. "Thanks for the offer, but as soon as I bag these apples I'm finished with my shopping."

"Then I'll see you in the checkout line. I only need a couple things."

After a speedy trip to the bread aisle and refrigerated section, he managed to nab the spot in line directly behind Diana. Helping her place her groceries on the conveyor belt, he told her about his day, starting with the plea bargain and ending with his hand-shaking marathon.

After chatting with the grandmotherly clerk who knew both their families, Tyler wheeled Diana's shopping cart into the parking lot and lifted the bags of groceries into her trunk.

"I've been wondering about something," Diana said after he shut the trunk. "If you dislike having your dinner interrupted, why don't you avoid the country club?"

Tyler shrugged. "My father says a truly successful

man can't live in a vacuum. That no man gets to the top without help."

"So the top is where you're aiming?"

"If by the top you mean a judgeship, then yeah."

Something flashed across her features that resembled disappointment, but it vanished so quickly he thought he must have imagined it. She unlocked the car door and settled in the driver's seat. With her hand on the interior door handle, she said, "Thanks for the help, Tyler."

Before she could pull the door shut, he closed his hand over the top of the window, no longer able to hold back the question burning a hole in his mind. "Why didn't you go out with me tonight?"

She hesitated, then said, "Because I'm seeing someone else."

He felt as though he'd been slugged in the windpipe, but managed to croak, "Who?"

"Chris Coleman."

The shock of her revelation didn't start to wear off until after she'd driven away. Only then could he think clearly about what she'd said.

It didn't add up.

First off, a romance between Diana and Chris wasn't in keeping with her supposed unwillingness to jump into a relationship.

Second, Diana and Chris interacted like brother and sister.

Third, and most importantly, Diana wouldn't respond to Tyler so enthusiastically if she were involved with someone else.

All of which meant she'd lied.

The more Tyler thought about it, the more sure he was of his conclusion. He jumped in his car and turned on the ignition, following the path Diana had taken, intent on discovering the reason she'd fed him a load of bull.

When he pulled his Lexus into the driveway adjacent to her garage apartment, she'd already popped the trunk of her Chevy. The night was too dark and the street-lights too dim for him to read her expression, but the rigid way she held herself spoke of tension.

"I thought you might need help." He nodded toward her apartment. "That flight of steps is pretty steep."

Not giving her a chance to refuse, he grabbed the four heaviest grocery bags, repositioning them so he carried two in each hand.

He waited at the foot of the stairs until she'd unloaded the bag filled with bread and paper goods and slammed the trunk, then moved aside so she could precede him up the stairs.

Her hand shook slightly when she unlocked the door, pushed it open and flipped on a switch that partially illuminated the inside of the apartment. He followed her down a hall to a darkened kitchen and deposited the bags he carried onto a small, square table.

She turned on another light, which highlighted the slight worry lines between her brows and anxiety around her mouth. No. He wasn't wrong. She was nervous.

"You need any help putting this stuff away?" he asked.

"No, thanks. I can take it from here."

A not-so-subtle signal for him to leave. He ignored

it, leaning against the counter nearest the refrigerator, one of his hands resting on his thigh. He resisted the urge to clench his fingers.

She removed a quart of skim milk from one of the bags, started toward the refrigerator and hesitated. He held his ground, noticing how she avoided inadvertent contact while she put the milk away.

"Don't feel like you have to stick around and keep me company," she said.

Another attempt to chase him off. Another hint he ignored. "That's not why I'm here."

Her eyes flew to his, and he could see the pulse in her neck beating. She spoke in a tone barely above a whisper. "Why are you here?"

"To find out why you lied about dating Chris Coleman."

DIANA FELT LIKE A FOOL for going along with Chris's suggestion. She possessed a much more effective means for killing whatever rekindled feelings Tyler had for her: the truth.

Not the whole truth, but enough of it to make Tyler understand why a relationship with Diana would be poisonous for him.

"There's a lot about me you don't know," she said softly, "things you wouldn't like if you did."

He crossed his legs at the ankles, appearing cool and collected in gray slacks and a charcoal dress shirt that brought out the dark blond of his hair. Add a suit jacket, and she had a pretty good idea of the formidable image he presented to a defendant in court.

"I'm listening," he said.

Calling upon a reserve of internal strength she didn't know she had, she took a deep, audible breath and met his gaze, knowing he'd never look at her in the same way again.

"Before I moved back to Maryland, I was so addicted to Vicodin I needed four or five pills to get through the day."

"Vicodin?" Nothing in his manner or voice betrayed what he thought of Diana's admission. "Isn't that a prescribed pain pill?"

"That's right. My doctor put me on it after I strained my back. I couldn't believe how fantastic the pills made me feel. Like I had enough energy to accomplish anything. But then I started needing more and more pills to achieve the same high until eventually I couldn't get the prescription refilled."

"What did you do?"

"By then, I was hooked. I found out later that the poppies used to produce heroin are the same ones found in Vicodin. I tried not taking them, but my body ached, my head pounded and I could barely function. So I went to another doctor. When the prescription he gave me ran out, I started buying pills on the street." She massaged her brow, trying to rub out the memories of that dark time. "It got so bad that the drugs were often the first thing I thought about when I woke up."

She couldn't look at him as she related the story. Neither could she tell him about her self-loathing that she hadn't been able to stay away from drugs.

"Things went on like that for five or six months until

I crashed head-on into a tree. I was barely hurt, but it scared me that Jaye could easily have been in the car with me." She inhaled deeply, aware she had to confess how low she'd sunk. "I left Jaye with my brother because I didn't trust myself to be around her."

Her bravado faded. Embarrassment saturated her, so thick it came as a jolt that her skin didn't turn red. She steeled herself for his disapproval, telling herself she deserved it.

"It sounds like leaving Jaye with Connor was the responsible thing to do."

She swung her gaze to him and searched his face, finding not condemnation, but acceptance and…understanding.

"That's not all of it, Tyler. I didn't just leave her there." She forced out the rest of the admission, the shame rising in her like the ocean at high tide. "I *abandoned* her. I snuck out of my brother's house in the middle of the night while she was asleep."

His brows pinched. "Are you trying to shock me?"

"I'm trying to get you to understand what kind of person I am. I'm a drug addict."

He straightened from the counter and moved toward her, not stopping until he was barely a hand's width away. "Are you still on drugs?"

"No, but—"

"Then you're a recovered addict who managed to kick your habit. To go back to school. To get a job. To start over." He touched her cheek. "Why would I think less of you after you accomplished all that?"

His words wrapped around her heart, encasing it in

a warmth she needed to fight. Common sense told her Tyler couldn't afford a connection with a recovering addict. Not to mention one with an illegitimate child. No one would know as long as Diana kept her mouth shut and stuck to the fiction her mother had invented.

"If you get involved with me, I could be the skeleton in your closet," she said. "What if this committee investigating you finds out I've been in detox?"

"What if they do?"

"You know better than I do that politics are unforgiving. I keep hearing about how your squeaky clean reputation and flawless character will help you get the judgeship. A relationship with a drug addict wouldn't."

"*Former* drug addict," he corrected. "And I'm not so sure I accept that. Haven't you ever heard of the Betty Ford clinic?"

"Betty Ford publicly admitted her addiction *after* she and her husband left the White House."

He stroked his chin, clueing Diana in that she was getting through to him. "Let's assume for argument's sake that what you say is true. How will anyone find out about your addiction? Detox records are private."

"People talk, Tyler. After I crashed my car, the boss at the warehouse where I worked insisted I take a random drug test. I failed it, and he fired me. What if the committee tracked him down?"

"I'm willing to risk that."

"What if I'm not? Did it occur to you that I might not want anybody looking into *my* background?" she asked. "That I don't want your selection committee or anyone in Bentonsville to know I was on drugs."

"It's nothing to be ashamed of."

"Yes, it is. Nobody knows. Not Connor, not Jaye, no one. Why do you think I didn't come straight out and admit I was a drug addict instead of telling you I was dating Chris?"

"There's something about that I don't understand," he said. "Why tell me either of those things? Why not just tell me you weren't interested?"

She lowered her eyes, and he tipped up her chin, forcing her to look at him. The impulse to lie died before she could invent a believable excuse. She felt as though she balanced on the side of an abyss, with one foot hovering over the edge, but she couldn't pull it back.

"I needed to give you a reason to avoid me," she said truthfully, "because I don't have the strength of will to stay away from you."

She shouldn't have made the admission, not when there was so much she couldn't tell him, so much that was unresolved. But the old feelings rose up and invaded her heart, as though they'd never died but had been lying dormant, waiting for a moment like this.

Comprehension dawned in his eyes. His hand moved from her cheek to her nape, his fingers burying in her hair to cradle the base of her skull. She smoothed her hands over the broadness of his shoulders before hooking them around his neck, holding on to something she thought she'd lost. To this volatile passion that erupted whenever they touched.

Only inches separated their lips and a mile of reasons not to kiss him, but Diana didn't heed any of them. The distance disappeared, and their mouths meshed, desperate to rejoin.

The highs Diana had experienced with Vicodin dimmed in comparison to this. Her blood flowed like a heated river through her veins, causing her entire body to come screamingly alive.

They kissed as though all the years and all the pain hadn't separated them. He seemed to know exactly when she needed for him to deepen the kiss, to stroke her tongue with his, to gather her closer so the thin layers of material separating them seemed like barriers instead of clothing.

How had she managed to get through all these years without him? Without this?

One of his hands left her hair to trail down her arm, then skimmed up her rib cage, cupping her breast. Her nipple pebbled and she pushed herself more fully into his hand, kissed him more desperately.

His lips broke off from her mouth. She threw her head back so he could skim the sensitive spot below her neck. Intense, mindless need spiraled inside her.

"Let me make love to you, Diana," he whispered, his voice raspy.

She knew there was a reason they shouldn't do this, but she couldn't focus, couldn't concentrate. All she could think of was Tyler.

His fingers glided up and down her arm, even that simple caress leaving a path of sensation. The only answer she was capable of giving hovered on her lips. "Yes."

His lips curved into a smile of pure joy, and the warning bells ringing in her head silenced. She smiled back, took him by the hand and led him to her bedroom. She should have smelled the vague scent of fairly fresh paint or the peach-scented lotion she'd smoothed on her body this morning, but when he flicked on the light she thought she smelled evergreen. The scent she'd breathed in on those long-ago nights at the park.

"I want to see you this time," he said, his eyes hot while he helped her remove her blazer and slip her shirt over her head. She understood. They'd made love the other times on a blanket with only the stars and the moon casting any light.

"Your turn," she said, raising her eyebrows.

He stripped out of his clothes so quickly, she laughed and kept on laughing when he gathered her to him, his hands warm on her naked back.

"I've never forgotten you, Diana," he said before his mouth descended once again. He must have maneuvered her nearer to the bed, because suddenly her feet weren't under her. They tumbled to the mattress, the same way her heart toppled in her chest.

They stripped off the rest of her clothes together with impatient hands until she finally felt his bare skin against hers and the hard, hot length of him. Heat pooled, moistening her center, driving her almost mad with need. She stroked him, enjoying the sound of his throaty groans.

"Can't wait," she said.

He tore his mouth from hers, reached over the side of the bed to where he'd tossed his clothes and from somewhere produced a foil package. It barely registered that it was a condom before he'd sheathed himself. And then she opened her legs and pulled him inside her, her last conscious thought that, after ten long years, she'd finally found her way home.

DIANA WOKE abruptly a few hours later to the faint barking of a neighborhood dog and the pangs of her conscience. Her eyes took a few moments to adjust to the darkness. Tyler lay next to her, his face relaxed in sleep, his muscular arm thrown over his head. The covers bunched around his waist, revealing his bare chest.

Even though they'd made love a second time before falling asleep, a wave of longing swept over her so intense she almost cried out. She checked her bedside alarm clock, which showed the time at just before midnight, and shrugged into a night shirt she removed from a dresser drawer.

Like Cinderella's, her fairy-tale evening was about to end. She disregarded the pain that sliced through her, the same way she'd ignored her physical symptoms when she left detox and fought her addition cold turkey.

Tyler, she reminded herself, was becoming even more of a weakness than Vicodin had been.

"Tyler." Getting no response except a soft sigh, she shook him slightly by the shoulder closest to her. "Tyler, wake up."

One of his eyes cracked opened. His lips curved in a sleepy smile and a warm hand traveled from her knee to her hip before dipping to the crease where her leg met her groin. Desire flared inside her and she cursed herself for not bothering to put on underwear. With great diffculty, she moved backward, out of reach of his questing hand.

His other eye snapped open. "Something wrong?" he asked in a voice thick with sleep.

She propped herself up on one elbow. "When is your interview with the judicial nominating committee?"

It took him a moment to answer, as though he had to dredge up the information from the recesses of his brain. "A week from Friday."

"When will the governor make the appointment?"

"Three or four weeks later." He blinked a few times, his eyes still bleary. "Why are you asking these questions?"

"Because it's nearly midnight, and you need to leave."

He sat up and ran a hand through his tousled hair, looking so good she barely stopped herself from reaching for him. "I was kind of hoping I could stay."

She sat up, too, being careful to keep enough distance between them that their bodies didn't touch. "If you do, people will see your car and they'll talk. We can't afford to have that happen."

"I thought we already went over this."

"We didn't resolve anything. I still don't want anybody to find out I had a drug problem, and you shouldn't risk losing your chance at becoming a judge by getting involved with me."

He indicated her and the tangled bedcovers with a sweep of his hand. "I'm already involved with you."

The guilt hit her hard. After what they'd just shared, could she really say this?

"It was just one night." She tried to sound blasé, but her voice cracked. "We don't need to keep seeing each other."

"That's where you're wrong." He tugged on her hand, and then, once more, she was in his arms. Exactly where she wanted to be. "I lost you once. I'm not about to lose you again."

"But the commission is investigating you. I don't want them to investigate me, too."

"Then let's compromise. The commission will be through looking into my background by the day of the interview. If you agree to keep seeing me, I won't tell anybody about us until it's over."

She felt herself weakening. "It won't truly be over until the governor fills the position."

"I already told you. The chance of anyone finding out what you went through is slim. Besides, I can't promise to keep quiet about us for that long. A couple of weeks is the best I can do."

She knew she should protest, but before she could he covered her mouth with his, kissing her exactly the way she liked to be kissed, stroking her in the spots that made her sigh.

"Say you agree, Diana," he murmured against her mouth.

"You're not playing fair," she said breathlessly.

He drew back and placed his hands on either side of her face. "I'm not playing at all. Now that I know you feel something for me, I don't intend to give up. If I can't convince you tonight to keep on seeing me, I'll be back."

"So you won't try to convince me to let you stay the night?"

"Not if you don't want me to."

"I don't want you to." The light went out of his eyes, and he dropped his hands from her face. She caught one of them on the way down, then pressed it to her lips. "Yet."

A smile appeared in his eyes. "Then you agree?"

"I agree," she said softly.

It was the only thing she could say, because she was in love with him. All over again.

CHAPTER ELEVEN

"WHAT ARE YOU so happy about?" Valerie asked the following afternoon seconds after Diana arrived at the community center.

"How do you know I'm happy?"

"Besides the humming and the smiling and the skipping? Wild guess."

Diana laughed. "I was not skipping."

"Floating, then. So what gives? Did you get an A on a test? Convince another teenager the Bentonsville Community Center was the place to be? Had a series of screaming orgasms last night?"

"No, no and no." Diana justified the last no because she was relatively certain she hadn't screamed. "I guess I'm just happy to be back in Bentonsville. Happy and...hopeful."

Hopeful that her long-ago dreams that had resurrected themselves overnight would come true. Because she'd started to believe that she, Tyler and Jaye might become a family if Tyler got the judgeship. With Tyler's position on the bench secure, there would be no more reason for secrets. She'd be able to tell Tyler about Jaye and explain why she'd waited so long. Maybe, just maybe, he'd forgive her.

"How about you? How's it going on the baby front?"

"Still trying," Valerie said. "Although there's something to be said for that."

Diana laughed. "Is Chris in?"

"Yeah, he's in his office."

"Thanks." Diana hurried to the director's office and rapped on the door, needing to tell Chris at the earliest possible moment that Tyler had seen through her lie about them dating.

She opened the door at his invitation to enter.

"Chris, I..." The confession died on her lips when she caught sight of him sitting miserably at his desk. Redness covered the area around his right eye, which was puffy and nearly swollen shut. "What happened to your eye?"

"I'm not exactly sure," he said. "It felt irritated when I woke up this morning, but it's gotten worse since then."

"I'll say." She moved deeper into the office to get a better look. The eye didn't improve on closer inspection. "It's probably not allergies, because it's affecting just the one eye. Do you have discharge?"

"My lid's a little crusty."

"You need to see a doctor," she said decisively.

He shook his head. "I'm not going to a doctor."

"Unless you want to lose that eye and become a Cyclops, you're going to see somebody. Now who's your doctor?"

He harrumphed. "I haven't been to a doctor in Bentonsville since Dr. Stravidis retired."

"Didn't I hear somewhere that Lauren Fairchild's father took over his practice?" At Chris's nod, she marched straight to the phone book, flipped to the physicians listed in the Yellow Pages and found Dr. Fairchild's number. "I'll call and see if he can fit you in."

A friendly, professional-sounding receptionist answered the phone, her voice growing clipped after Diana identified herself and asked to speak to a nurse.

Diana figured the receptionist had merely reacted to the severity of the situation, then forgot about her as the nurse requested a description of Chris's symptoms.

"Get him over here as soon as you can, and don't let him drive," the nurse ordered, something Diana had to repeat to Chris twice before he surrendered and let her take him to the doctor's office.

"You don't have to stick around," Chris groused to Diana on the way into a bright, cheerful office with new furniture and berber carpeting. "I'm a big boy."

"Then who's going to drive you home, big boy?" Her voice reverberated in the quiet, empty waiting room.

She turned to face the receptionist and was shocked to find Lauren Fairchild staring at them. It hadn't occurred to her that the woman worked for her father. Lauren's eyes turned as icy as her voice had on the phone when they touched on Diana but clouded with concern when they focused on Chris.

"Are you okay, Chris? That eye looks awful."

"Yeah." He gestured at Diana. "Although Diana here tells me I look like a Cyclops."

Diana had meant for the Cyclops comment to convince Chris to see a doctor, but it sounded mean-spirited when put in that context. "I said you'd look like a Cyclops if you didn't take care of that eye."

"I think you look like you need my father," Lauren said without acknowledging Diana. "I'll tell him you're here and convince him to see you right away."

"Don't I have to fill out paperwork?"

"Not with your eye swollen like that, you don't. We can take care of all that later."

Lauren evidently was serious because a nurse appeared almost instantly and told Chris to follow.

Left alone in the waiting room, Diana checked her watch and looked at a few magazines. She approached the receptionist's desk, waiting silently for Lauren to finish an entry in the computer.

Lauren finally looked up, her lips unsmiling. "Can I help you with something?"

"How are you, Lauren?"

"I'm fine." Lauren returned to work, silently dismissing Diana. Searching her mind for what she might have done to incur Lauren's dislike, Diana returned to her seat. Before she reached it, Lauren added, "Although your boyfriend was right. You didn't need to stay. Someone in the office could have given him a ride."

The back of the seat hit her legs, and Diana practically fell into it.

Her boyfriend?

That was it. Lauren disliked her because she'd switched her interest from Tyler to Chris. But why hadn't Diana noticed something was going on between Lauren and Chris before now?

Diana observed plenty after Chris emerged from the doctor's office with a diagnosis of conjunctivitis and a prescription for antibiotic eye drops. Lauren stole glances at him when he insisted on filling out the necessary paperwork, and Chris's good eye lingered on Lauren when he thought she wasn't looking.

Diana waited until she and Chris had picked up his prescription from a local pharmacy to run her theory by him. "You're in love with Lauren Fairchild, aren't you?"

He probably would have bolted out of his seat if he hadn't been confined to a car. "What? Why would you say that?"

"Because it's true. And now your plan to help me out of a jam has only made Lauren jealous."

A soft thump sounded when Chris leaned back against the head rest. "Nice try, Einstein. But you're only half right. Women don't get jealous on account of men who don't interest them."

"Did you see Lauren staring daggers at me? Believe me, she's interested in you."

"She's interested in Benton. If she doesn't like you, it's because she figured out that Benton does."

"Maybe Lauren did have her eye on Tyler at one time, but I don't think she does any longer," Diana said thoughtfully.

"Then Lauren will find some other successful man who can provide for her in the manner to which she's become accustomed." Chris blew out a long breath. "She certainly won't settle for a lowly community center director like me."

"That's how you think of yourself?"

"That's how Lauren thinks of me. I love what I do. But I realize certain things are beyond my reach because of the profession I chose. Lauren's one of them."

"You're selling both yourself and Lauren short. If you don't seize the moment, it might never come again and you'll have to live the rest of your life with regrets."

Is that what she'd done last night? Diana wondered. Fought off future regrets—and her own good sense—by seizing a moment she was afraid wouldn't last?

"Seize the moment to get shot down?" Chris asked. "No thanks. It doesn't matter, anyway. I told Lauren you and me were dating."

They'd reached the community center. Diana pulled into a parking space and cut her car engine. "Then you'll have to tell her we broke up, because Tyler figured out pretty quickly I was lying about that."

Chris groaned. "You're kidding."

"Nope," Diana said. "About this, at least, I'm telling the truth."

AT LEAST THREE DOZEN teenagers crammed into a room at the community center that had been transformed into a makeshift recital hall.

Strobe lights flickered across the raised podium at the front of the room where Davey hammed it up every bit as much as he showed off on the basketball court. He wore a T-shirt and blue jeans, standard fare for him. Except he'd cut off the T-shirt to bare his stomach, covered his dark hair with a long, blond wig and donned the largest pair of high-heeled women's shoes Tyler had ever seen.

While prancing around the stage on these ridiculous shoes, Davey lip-synched the vocals to a pop song.

"Who's he supposed to be?" Tyler asked Diana.

She scrunched up her brows as she considered the teen, who had one hand on his heart and the other raised to the ceiling. "I don't recognize the song, so I'm not sure. Davey might not even know. He told me he was going to imitate a blonde teen queen singer."

"So I take it the community center's standards of what constitutes talent for this talent show aren't real high?" Tyler joked.

"Hey, look at the audience." Diana indicated the teens gathered around the stage, most of whom were laughing uproariously. "Making people laugh is a talent, and Davey's certainly succeeding at that."

On stage Davey executed a one-eighty, stood with his back to the audience and shook his rear end in tempo to the music. The laughter in the room grew more pronounced. Diana turned to Tyler, the mirth that had already been in her eyes spilling over into a hearty laugh.

Tyler extended his arm so he could hug her to him, then remembered their pact and pulled it back. Damn. Good thing he hadn't agreed to keep their relationship secret until the governor announced his choice for the vacated judgeship. A week or so was stretching it. A month would have been impossible.

Thankfully Diana stayed out of temptation's range for the next two hours, shuffling performers ranging from rap singers to break dancers on and off the stage until the talent show finally wound down to its inevitable conclusion.

"When's the next event?" a teenage boy asked on his way out.

"Next weekend. A band called Heat Wave. We're also planning a pool tournament," Diana answered. "You can pick up a flyer with a list of activities on the way out. Spread the word. Tell your friends."

"Will do," the boy said.

The teenagers continued to file out of the room, more than a few asking about upcoming events, until only Diana and Tyler remained. He made sure they were completely alone, then lifted her up and twirled her around until she was breathless with laughter.

"What was that for?" she asked when he set her down, her eyes shining.

"For breathing life into the teen program."

"The talent show wasn't my idea."

"It was your idea to ask the kids about what we should offer, so you're stuck with the credit."

She was still in his arms, fueling thoughts of last night and the time they'd spent in her bed. His body hardened against her softness. Neither of them moved, their eyes locked.

"We should really let go of each other." Diana made no attempt to get away from him.

"I agree." He didn't relax his hold on her.

"Anybody could come along and see us."

He dipped his head, his lips grazing her cheek. "That would not be ideal."

"No, it wouldn't." Her voice had lowered an octave, the way it did when she was turned on.

He rested his forehead against hers, wondering when his self-control had gone to hell. "Tell you what. Since neither of us seems to be able to let the other go, let's do it together on the count of three. Ready? One. Two. Three."

Neither of them moved, not a muscle. Her giggles resonated in the room, followed by his deeper laughter, and then their eyes met. Something in the very air around them changed, silencing the laughter and drawing them even closer until their lips merged.

And then they were kissing, as though nothing else mattered—not the past, not the pact and not the public setting—except each other.

TAKE THE HIGH ROAD, Lauren Fairchild's father always told her. In Lauren's case, unfortunately that lofty street was the road less traveled.

If Lauren didn't keep hearing her father's nagging little voice in her head, she'd be far from the Bentonsville Community Center.

She'd started off the night skipping her step aerobics class because it had been easier to not show up than risk running into Diana Smith, to whom she'd been unspeakably rude.

The woman couldn't help it that Chris Coleman had the good sense to prefer her over Lauren. Look at all the work Diana was doing with the teen program. Lauren might have beauty going for her, but Diana had both good looks and good character.

Diana hadn't been at the welcome desk when Lauren arrived, but another woman said Lauren could find her in the multi-purpose room cleaning up after the talent show.

The woman—Valerie was her name—directed Lauren to the back of the building. She walked into the room and stopped dead. Beside a microphone that had already been unplugged, Diana and Tyler stood enveloped in each other's arms, kissing as though a crowbar couldn't tear them apart.

Lauren gasped, but Tyler and the two-timing Diana were too engrossed in each other to notice. Well, Lauren would make herself heard.

"How dare you!" she cried out. Her presence finally communicated itself to Diana and Tyler, who turned at her advance but didn't have the decency to spring apart. Instead they sort of edged away from each other and gazed at Lauren like she was a lunatic.

Lauren ignored Tyler, who she'd thought had better morals, and addressed Diana. "I won't stand by and let you do this."

Tyler took a step sideways, partially shielding Diana. "Don't talk to Diana like that, Lauren. You and I only went on a few dates. We never had a commitment."

Lauren gaped at him, wondering what he was talking about. Then it hit her. Tyler thought she was jealous of Diana because of him, but Lauren was so over him.

"You've got it wrong. I'm angry because she—" Lauren pointed at Diana "—doesn't know a good thing when she has it. I can't let her hurt Chris this way."

"Chris? Diana's not involved with Chris," Tyler stated firmly.

"That's not true."

"Then ask her."

Lauren gazed past Tyler to Diana, who appeared more than a little guilty. "Are you or are you not dating Chris?" Lauren demanded.

"Not," Diana said, which could only mean one thing.

Diana wasn't the liar. Chris was.

"Where is he?" Lauren asked. Diana hesitated. "You might as well tell me because I *am* going to find him."

"His eye was still bothering him so he went home early."

Lauren had moved at least ten quick steps toward the door when she remembered the high road. She turned back with all the poise her mother had taught her.

"I'm sorry. I was out of line and hope you'll both forgive me. Especially you, Diana, although I'd understand if you didn't."

"Of course I forgive you," Diana said. "A woman in love isn't always rational."

The knowledge that Diana had read the situation correctly hit Lauren like a thunderbolt. She was in love with Chris Coleman. And she just might tell him that, after she got through giving him a piece of her mind.

THE THUMPS on his front door sounded like the work of a battering ram, albeit a small one.

Chris Coleman finished chewing a bite of grilled cheese sandwich and navigated his modest little house to the front door, wondering if his doorbell had malfunctioned.

He opened the door to a very angry Lauren Fairchild, temptingly dressed in low-rise blue jeans and a cropped red shirt that brought out the flaming color in her cheeks.

Before he could reconcile Lauren being at his door, she swept by him.

"Why did you lie to me about dating Diana Smith?" she demanded, eyes flashing.

He closed the door, then rubbed the back of his neck, not understanding why he had one hundred odd pounds of angry woman in his living room. "Why does it matter to you if I did?"

"Just answer the question."

"What if I'm not sure why I lied?" The pitch of his voice rose to match hers, the strain of wanting to scoop her into his arms but not being able to adding to his frustration. "I could tell you it was because I thought I was helping Diana, but maybe she's right. Maybe I did it to see if I could make you jealous."

Lauren stamped one of her small feet. "Well, it worked, you big jerk."

She barely resembled the poised creature she'd tried to convince the rest of the community she was. Around Chris, she'd always been herself.

"You were really jealous? Why?"

"Why wouldn't I be?" she snapped.

"Because you made it clear you were in the market for somebody with a bright future to marry and father your children. Somebody like Tyler Benton. Not somebody who works for peanuts at a community center."

"I've got news for you, buddy. I'm not stupid enough or shallow enough to pass over a kind, smart, handsome man who makes my heart pound harder than Tyler ever did. Even if that man is an idiot."

He pointed to his chest, where his own heart had started to lighten. "Are you talking about me?"

"Of course I'm talking about you. Why do you think I've been practically stalking you for the past few weeks?"

Amusement bubbled inside him. She was an absolute delight, part proper woman, part petulant girl. And he loved absolutely every facet of her.

"To make sure you knew where the enemy was at all times?" he teased.

"I've been trying to give you a chance to ask me out again," she retorted.

"Why didn't *you* ask *me* out?"

She put a hand on one hip, her brow furrowing. "Well, because...I'm not exactly sure why, okay? Maybe I was afraid you'd reject me."

He stopped himself from demonstrating what an impossibility that was and raised an issue with the potential to tear them apart. "Or maybe you were apprehensive about what your parents would say. Have you thought about how they'll react if we start dating?"

"My mother will be upset, but my father already likes you even though I gather you're not the most cooperative of patients. Eventually both of them will come to love you." She paused. "Just like I already do."

Lauren loved him. The news burst inside him like fireworks on a summer night, cutting off his ability to speak.

"Aren't you going to say anything?" she asked, looking small and vulnerable.

"Oh, yeah. That thing you said about being afraid I'd reject you. If you come over here, you'll find out that's not going to happen. Because I'm over the moon in love with you."

Laughing, she practically flew into his arms. Then, at long last, he captured her lips. The way he hadn't even realized he'd claimed her heart.

"YOU'RE DISTRACTING ME, lady."

At the sound of Tyler's throaty voice, Diana smiled into the phone and leaned back in the cushy chair behind the desk in Chris's office. She could hear the rustle of papers over the phone line. "Oh, yeah? How exactly am I accomplishing that, considering I'm at the community center and you're at work?"

"I am at work, on a Saturday yet, and getting nothing done because I keep thinking about what we did last night." His voice deepened. "And what I want to do again tonight."

Diana barely kept herself from sighing in remembered pleasure. After Lauren had caught them kissing in public, they'd continued what they'd started in the privacy of Diana's apartment. Since they'd taken the precaution of leaving Tyler's car at his place and driving together to hers, Diana had even agreed to Tyler spending the night.

Agreed? She'd practically salivated at the prospect, recklessly dismissing the possibility that anybody could have seen them leaving her place together this morning.

"When do you get off work?" Tyler asked.

"Nine o'clock, the same as usual."

"That's too long to wait. I'll come by during your break and take you to dinner."

Diana bit the inside of her lip so she wouldn't jump at his suggestion. "We agreed to keep this quiet, Tyler. Going out to dinner together now is not a good idea."

"How about two weeks from now? My boss invited me to dinner and said I could bring a guest. The nominations should have been announced by then."

But not the governor's choice to fill the judicial vacancy.

At the sound of footsteps, Diana turned and saw Chris entering the office, his eye nearly back to normal.

"Let's talk about it later," she said to Tyler. "Right now I need to explain to Chris why I commandeered his office chair."

"I'll take you up on the later, but I can promise you that I'll want to do a whole lot more than talk," Tyler said suggestively and rang off.

Smiling, Diana turned her attention to Chris. "I hope you don't mind that I'm using your computer, but the ones in the teen lounge are in use. I've been researching how to run a pool tournament with only two tables. What do you think of this idea? Depending on how many entries we get, we could hold the tournament during the week with the semifinals and final on Saturday night."

"Sounds great," Chris said, came around the desk and planted a resounding kiss full on her lips.

"It wasn't *that* good an idea," Diana said.

"That's not why I kissed you."

"You're not still trying to convince people we're dating, are you?" Diana angled her head to peer around him into the empty hallway. "Because if you are, nobody's around to see."

"Been there, done that, bombed spectacularly." He perched on the edge of his desk and grinned. "That kiss was for telling Lauren we weren't dating."

"Ah, so she must have found you last night."

"She did."

Diana made a circular motion with her index finger. "And?"

"And you were right. She loves me. She doesn't even have a problem with what I do for a living. I'm going to wait a couple months before I bring up what a perfect job it is for a family man."

"You want to marry her?"

"Marry her. Live with her. Have children with her. Grow old with her. You name it. But I'll settle for a combination of the above."

Happiness for him blossomed inside her. "As much as I'd like to accept responsibility for getting you two together, Tyler was the one who spilled the beans to Lauren about us not dating." She made a face. "Maybe I shouldn't have said that. Tyler wouldn't react as favorably to a kiss from you as I did."

"Very funny," Chris said, the trace of sarcasm in his voice mitigated by his laugh. "Speaking of Tyler, what's going on with you two? Still trying to avoid him?"

If not for the concern in his eyes, Diana might have believed Chris was ignorant of the answer. "Lauren told you she saw us kissing, didn't she?"

"Yeah," he confirmed. "And now for a piece of unsolicited advice. Be careful, kiddo. He's not the kind of man who'll always find time for you. He'll be too busy running his kingdom from behind the bench."

"Then you think he'll get the judgeship?"

"Why wouldn't he? Even I couldn't think of anything bad to say about him when the nominating commission guy called to grill me. And at the time I still thought Benton was interested in Lauren."

"You don't have to worry about Tyler and Lauren," Diana said. "Or Tyler and me, for that matter."

"Can't help it. I know he's been paying a lot of attention to you, but a guy as ambitious as that will ultimately put his career first."

"He has to, especially now," Diana said. "But he'll be able to relax some after he finds out if he gets the appointment. Then his life won't be under such a microscope."

"Where'd you get that idea?" Chris asked. "Whoever the governor appoints has to run in the next general election, if he or she wants to continue in the job."

The fluorescent lights overhead seemed to dim, as though a black cloud had passed over them. "I thought the appointment was for the life of the term."

"Not for a circuit judgeship, it isn't. The guy on the phone explained it to me. The governor appoints a temporary replacement until the election can take place."

Maybe this wasn't so bad, Diana thought. The next general election was fast approaching. "Then if Tyler gets the appointment, he'll run to keep the position in November?"

"Not this November. Next November. The law states that the interim judge must serve for at least one year before running to retain the spot."

Diana fought dismay as the implications of this new piece of information crystallized. During that year, Tyler shouldn't date a former drug addict. Neither should he suddenly produce a preteen daughter.

Diana could well imagine how politically damaging either of those things could be. If the facts got skewed, voters could even believe that Tyler had shirked his responsibilities toward the drug addict's daughter rather than accepting that he hadn't known Jaye existed.

If Tyler failed to get the appointment, he'd have to safeguard his reputation just as carefully. Because he'd surely be considered for future judicial openings, his actions could be scrutinized for years to come.

"Diana, are you okay?" Chris asked.

Diana felt so numb, she couldn't be sure whether she nodded. "Stop worrying about me, Chris. But do me a favor, okay? Don't tell anyone about Tyler and me. We're keeping it quiet."

Chris's mouth thinned, clearly indicating his feelings about the matter. "I'll do it for you, Diana, but I hope you realize what you're getting into with Tyler Benton."

"If I didn't before," Diana said softly. "I do now."

CHAPTER TWELVE

ELAINE SMITH SHOWED her granddaughter to the frilly pink bedroom on the second floor of her home, two doors down from another bedroom that looked exactly as it had ten years ago.

Elaine hadn't changed a thing in either room, behavior a psychologist would probably label unhealthy. But Elaine found comfort in reminders of the happy, uncomplicated time when her younger son was still alive and her daughter hadn't yet run away from home.

"Was this my mother's room?" Jaye spun slowly in a circle to take it all in. The Judy Blume books cramming the shelves. The stuffed animals above the bed. The hot-pink accent wall. The perfume bottles on the dresser.

"Yes, it was. Do you like it?"

Jaye set her suitcase and her violin case down on the carpet, then plopped onto the bed. "It's okay, I guess. If you like pink."

Elaine refrained from commenting that Jaye not only wore a pink long-sleeved shirt, but matching pink tennis shoes. She was fair where Diana and the rest of the Smiths were dark, her coloring reminding Elaine of someone or something she couldn't quite put her finger on. But the girl's eyes were a copy of J.D.'s, and something around her mouth reminded Elaine vividly of Diana. Elaine's throat constricted. With Jaye sitting there on the bed, it almost seemed as though Elaine had her daughter back.

"Your mother was a huge fan of the color." Elaine picked up a pink-and-white polka dot accent pillow and fluffed it before returning it to the bed. "She even bought some pink hair color once and dyed her hair."

"Really?" Jaye's eyes widened. "Did you get mad?"

"If she'd succeeded in turning her hair pink, I might have. But the dye didn't take because her natural color is so dark. That didn't stop her, though. She was determined to dye somebody's hair pink."

"Whose?"

Elaine pointed to a dresser where a row of Barbie dolls sat with their shapely plastic legs outstretched, all sporting identical pink tresses. "She used to call them the Pink Ladies."

Giggling, Jaye leaped from the bed and picked up the prettiest of the dolls, whose salmon-colored dress matched her pink hair. "Do you think maybe I could have her, Grandma?"

Elaine's heart broke at the longing in Jaye's voice, the question reconfirming Elaine's belief that she'd done the right thing in bringing Jaye to Bentonsville for the weekend.

"I'm sure that would be okay," Elaine said. "But when you see your mom, you might want to check with her."

The girl's body language changed, her shoulders

growing tense and her entire body stiffening. She stared down at her pink tennis shoes. "I don't see my mom much."

"I know that, but we'll probably run into her today at the community center."

Jaye's expression turned guarded. "Why would we go there?"

"You know that I tutor students in math. I need to drop by for an hour or so today in case anyone needs homework help."

"But what will I do when you're tutoring?" Jaye's voice held a touch of panic.

"You'll have fun. The center has pool tables and video games. And I'm pretty sure they're showing a movie this afternoon."

Jaye sank back onto the bed, the doll clutched in her hand. "Maybe I could stay here and practice my violin."

Elaine considered waiting to see if Jaye would confide in her, then thought better of it. She'd made that mistake with Diana, who'd never entrusted her at all. She lowered herself next to her granddaughter. "I'm a good listener if you'd like to tell me why you don't want to see your mother."

"You've got it wrong," Jaye cried. "My mom doesn't want to see me."

Elaine placed a hand on the little girl's back, which shook with her effort not to cry. "Why would you think that, Jaye? Your mother loves you."

"She doesn't love me. If she did, she wouldn't have left me with Uncle Connor. She'd want me with her."

Elaine couldn't speak about what had led to the estrangement between her daughter and granddaughter, but she might be able to help breach it. "I happen to know she does want you with her."

The tears that had gathered in Jaye's green eyes stayed put. "How do you know?" she asked, the question laced with suspicion.

Elaine repeated what Valerie, the talkative daytime receptionist at the community center, had told her about visiting Diana's apartment. "Your mother decorated her second bedroom just for you."

"Is that the truth?"

"Of course it's the truth. Now let's get over to the center." Elaine stood up and held her hand out to the granddaughter who had her son's eyes. After a long hesitation, the little girl let herself be helped off the bed.

"Grandma," Jaye said in a quiet voice when they were in the car heading for the center. "That bedroom my mother's saving for me. Do you know what color it is?"

"Why, yes I do," Elaine said, glad she'd thought to ask Valerie the same question. "It's pink."

HEAD DOWN, Diana dashed up the sidewalk, futilely trying to outrun the raindrops. A jagged bolt of lightning flashed in the sky, followed seconds later by the booming crack of thunder. She picked up her pace, fairly bursting into the center, wetter than she wanted to be.

Ruth Grimes, one of the group of senior citizens who regularly met for bridge, stood at the window of the center peering through her tiny glasses at the slashing rain outside.

"Hey, Mrs. Grimes," Diana said in greeting.

"What were you doing out in that weather, Diana?"

Diana held up two raindrop-dotted plastic bags. "Getting tonight's entertainment for our teenagers. The lengths I'll go to for microwave popcorn and a bunch of DVDs."

"You should have gone to those lengths with an umbrella, dear."

"I will next time, Mrs. Grimes. Excellent advice." Diana shook her head slightly to dislodge the raindrops, a warm feeling spreading through her at the strong sense that she'd become part of the center's community.

She headed in the direction of the teen room, waving to Valerie, who was on the phone. Valerie held up a finger, covered the receiver and mouthed. "Your mother wants to see you in the study lounge."

Diana formed an okay signal with her thumb and forefinger, but Valerie wasn't through speaking.

"She's adorable," she said, then went back to talking on the phone.

Diana wouldn't have used that adjective to describe her mother, but she supposed Elaine Smith did have her moments. Her mother had taken more care with her appearance lately, wearing makeup and dressing in brighter colors.

It surprised Diana that her mother had shown up to tutor on a Saturday, but she supposed there wasn't much else to do on a rainy day. Except, of course, watch movies.

She could have delivered the DVDs first, but optimism propelled her toward the study lounge. Did she dare hope her mother planned to issue an invitation? Coffee, dinner, a movie. Diana would agree to any of them.

Before she could enter the lounge, her mother spotted her through the window and slipped out the door to meet her in the hallway. "If you're going out in the rain," her mother said with a frown, "you really should use an umbrella."

The admonition sent another wave of warmth through Diana. "So I've heard. What's up?"

Before her mother could answer, the hinges on the restroom door creaked. Diana automatically gazed toward the sound. Jaye stepped into the hallway, then froze in place.

Diana stared at her daughter, hardly able to believe that the piece of the puzzle that would make her life complete—the most vital piece—stood only yards away.

"I need to get back to my students." Her mother's voice seemed to come from a great distance. "I thought you could give Jaye a tour of the center and see that she has something to do while she waits for me."

Diana vaguely registered the sound of the study lounge door opening and closing. She didn't move for a pregnant moment, afraid to do the wrong thing. Then she walked slowly forward, not stopping until she was a few paces from her daughter. "Hi, honey. I am so happy to see you."

Looking small and vulnerable, Jaye crossed her arms over her chest, gripping the backs of her biceps with her fingers. Diana's own hands longed to reach for her daughter and draw her close, but fear of rejection held her back.

Swallowing the lump of emotion in her throat, Diana asked, "I gather you're spending the weekend with your grandmother?"

Jaye nodded mutely.

"I bet that'll be a lot of fun," Diana said, then grew silent. How could she be at a loss for words with the child she'd carried for nine months, raised for nine years and would love forever? "I'm heading for the teen room now. Why don't you come with me?"

Jaye said nothing but uncrossed her arms and followed her mother down the hall. Diana acted the tour guide, brightly pointing out Chris's office and the multipurpose room where the senior citizens were playing bridge. She herself had no clue how to bridge the gulf that had formed between herself and her daughter.

"Grandma showed me your pink ladies," Jaye suddenly declared, the first words she'd spoken. "She said to ask you if I could have one of them."

The pink ladies? The term yanked Diana into the past, when she'd played amateur hairdresser on a bunch of unsuspecting Barbie dolls.

"Of course it's okay." Diana tried not to read too much into Jaye wanting something that had been hers, but her hope still soared. "I forgot about those dolls, but I remembered you like pink. In fact, I was thinking of you when I painted the second bedroom in my apartment. Would you like to see it?"

"Yes," Jaye said in a small voice.

Diana could no more hold back her next question than her next breath. "Then what do you think about staying with me tonight?"

Apprehension built in Diana like the water behind a dam, pulsating inside her with such force she could barely stand it. Jaye's answer, when it finally came, was barely audible. "Do you think Grandma would let me?"

The anxiety receded, and Diana had to force herself not to shout for joy.

"Why don't I ask her and see what she says?" Diana thought about how her mother had arranged for her to be alone with Jaye. "Somehow I'm betting her answer will be yes."

Jaye didn't respond, but neither did she pull away when Diana reached for her hand. With her daughter's small, soft hand enfolded in hers, a peace settled over Diana that she hadn't felt in a very long time.

She and Jaye still had a long way to go, but this was a very good start.

DIANA WATCHED her daughter bite into a slice of New York–style thin-crust pizza with extra cheese and thought about the unpredictability of life.

Never would she have dreamed when she awoke that morning that she'd be eating with her mother and daughter at a teenage hangout that evening. Although at the moment mostly families filled the restaurant, the hour too early for the teens to turn out in force.

When Jaye was through chewing, she said, "This is the best pizza ever."

"Your mother always thought so," Elaine Smith said. "We had dinner here a couple times a month when she was growing up. She always wanted to order the same thing you're eating now but her brothers usually talked her into adding pepperoni."

"Talked me into it?" Diana asked incredulously. "They outnumbered me. They didn't ask me what we were having. They told me. Then J.D. would eat really fast so he'd get the most pieces."

Her mother smiled wistfully, a hint of sadness in her eyes. "Boys have bigger appetites."

"Tell that to your granddaughter. She's on her third piece."

Jaye grinned and took another bite, adding to the nearly surreal feel. The entire afternoon had been like that. From the way the teenagers invited Jaye to watch the DVD of *Napoleon Dynamite* to Chris telling Diana to take off early so she could enjoy an evening with her mother and daughter.

"Isn't that Tyler Benton?" Her mother gazed past Diana. "Now there's a man I wouldn't expect to be alone on a Saturday night."

Diana's eyes swung to the entrance, where she spotted Tyler scanning the restaurant, as though searching for somebody. She'd meant to call and tell him she'd be unavailable tonight, but things had happened so quickly with Jaye she hadn't had the chance. He smiled, his eyes crinkling charmingly at the corners, and headed straight for their table.

"Who's Tyler Benton?" Jaye asked.

Your father.

"Tyler's a friend." Diana automatically reached into the pocket of her slacks for her lucky stone, telling herself not to panic. She'd known it was inevitable that Tyler and Jaye would eventually meet. She reassured herself it was highly unlikely that Tyler would guess Jaye was his daughter—even if he discovered her birth date.

Diana had fled Bentonsville soon after getting pregnant, and Jaye had arrived two weeks after her due date. Thanks to the story her mother had concocted, it was entirely feasible that Diana had gotten pregnant in Virginia.

Despite all that, now that the moment father and daughter would meet was upon them, Diana wasn't prepared.

"Hey, Diana." Tyler's gaze touched on Diana, his smile soft and intimate. A lover's smile. He switched his attention to her mother. "Hello, Mrs. Smith."

His smile grew, his dimple appearing as he focused on Diana's daughter. On *their* daughter.

"And you must be Jaye." He bent at the waist and stuck out a hand. "I'm Tyler."

Smiling tentatively, Jaye put her much smaller hand in his. "Hi, Tyler."

Diana's gaze ping-ponged between the two of them. She'd always known they shared certain features, but now that they were together the similarities stuck out like a crow in a flock of gulls. They had the same high foreheads and fair coloring, although Jaye's hair was lighter. The same eyebrow arch and nose shape. Even the same long fingers.

"Your mom's told me a lot about you," Tyler said, still smiling at Jaye.

"She talks about me?"

"All the time," Tyler said. "I don't know what I'm

looking forward to more. Hearing you play the violin or seeing you play soccer."

"I'm better at the violin."

"The violin, it is."

"Would you like to join us?" Her mother gestured at the empty chair at their table for four.

"I'd love to," Tyler said before Diana could catch his eye. She got his attention when he sat down, giving a barely perceptible shake of her head. He frowned, but answered her silent plea. "But only for a few minutes."

Even that might be too long. Now that he sat adjacent to Jaye, the resemblance was glaring. But Diana was being ridiculous. Nobody could know for certain that Tyler was Jaye's father because she'd never told anyone.

Diana had almost convinced herself to relax when she noticed her mother's narrowed eyes as she, too, gazed back and forth between father and daughter.

After a long moment, her eyes focused on Diana.

She knew. If her mother had shouted out the words, the message couldn't have been more clear. Diana's heart beat uncomfortably hard.

"You're welcome to have dinner with us, Tyler." Her mother kept her gaze on Diana. "I feel as though I should get to know you better."

Tyler glanced at Diana, and she tried to convey with her eyes that he should refuse the invitation.

"Thanks, but I can't. I only stopped because I, uh, saw Diana's car in the parking lot. I thought now might be a good time to talk about the teen program. But it's not, so it can wait." He lapsed into silence, perhaps realizing he was the world's worst liar.

"If you're hungry," Jaye piped up, "you can have one of our pieces."

"Thanks for the offer, Jaye, but I'll take a rain check," he said. "Diana, I'll catch you later. Nice to see you again, Mrs. Smith. And it was great to meet you, Jaye."

Diana avoiding looking at him when he pushed his chair back and stood up, feeling lower than the floor beneath her feet. He'd shared her bed and fathered her child, yet she'd clearly conveyed he wasn't welcome at the table.

"What's a rain check?" Jaye asked as soon as he was gone.

While Diana tried to process her daughter's question, her mother supplied the answer. "It's an agreement to get together in the future."

Not a good idea, Diana's brain screamed.

"Cool," Jaye said. "I'd like that."

"I'm sure Tyler would like that, too." Her mother pinned Diana with a look that erased any lingering doubt that she'd ferreted out Diana's secret.

Diana tried to tell herself that no one else would guess, that her mother had only figured it out because she knew Diana had been pregnant before leaving Bentonsville.

But the family resemblance between Tyler and Jaye was so strong it was only a matter of time before tongues wagged and the story her mother had invented was exposed for the lie it was.

Jaye might even notice the similarities between her

and Tyler herself. Thus far Diana had managed to deflect Jaye's questions about her father, but she'd been fooling herself to think she could avoid them forever.

It was only a matter of time before Diana's house of cards came tumbling down—unless she left Bentonsville.

But, no, that was unthinkable. She couldn't leave now. Despite her initial misgivings about returning to her home town, everything was falling into place. She had a job she loved, an apartment with room for Jaye and improving relationships with both her daughter and her mother.

Best of all, Tyler lived in Bentonsville.

Tyler, whose judicial future could be ruined if word got out that an ex-drug addict was the mother of his mystery daughter.

Could she live with herself if she was responsible for sabotaging Tyler's longtime dream of becoming a judge? Especially because the steps she'd taken to rebuild her life in Bentonsville had demonstrated that she possessed a reservoir of strength she hadn't known existed.

If she could succeed in Bentonsville, where the ghosts of the past still dwelled, she could make it anywhere.

Pain lanced through her at the prospect of leaving Bentonsville, but she realized she'd hit on the only solution. Once again, she must move away from the town—and the man—she'd come to love again.

JAYE OPENED HER EYES the next morning to a world that had turned pink. Slowly realizing she'd pulled the bedspread over her head sometime during the night, she dug out from under the covers.

She sat up in the double bed and surveyed the room, spotting her old Raggedy Anne doll and a Kelly Clarkson poster like the one that had hung in her bedroom when they lived in Tennessee.

Grandma was right about her mom wanting Jaye with her. This room was proof. So was the stone she'd seen her mother fiddling with last night, the one Jaye had painted her for good luck.

A familiar smell drifted through the door, making her mouth water and her heart soar. French toast. Her favorite. Not bothering to change out of her pajamas, she made a quick pit stop in the bathroom before hurrying to the kitchen.

Her mom stood at the stove, her dark hair shining, her eyes smiling. Nobody, Jaye thought, had a prettier mom.

"Good morning, sleepyhead." Her mom transferred two slices from the frying pan to a plate she set on the table. "Ready for some French toast?"

"I love French toast," Jaye said.

"That's why I made it."

Feeling happier than she had in a long time, Jaye sat at the table and polished off two pieces in record time while her mother sat across from her drinking a cup of coffee.

"Can I have some more, please?" Jaye held out the plate like Oliver begging for food.

Her mom laughed, got up and turned on a burner before dredging another piece of bread in the egg-and-milk mixture.

"We should have French toast every morning when

I move in with you," Jaye said. "Are we going to get my stuff from Uncle Connor's today?"

Her mom shut off the burner and turned around very slowly to face Jaye. "Don't you like it at your uncle's?"

"Sure, I do, but you're my mom." Jaye confidently played her trump card. "And you have a bedroom for me."

Leaving the French toast soaking in the milk and egg, her mom crossed the kitchen to the table and sat down. She was no longer smiling, Jaye's first clue that something was wrong.

"There's something I need to tell you, Jaye. I'm leaving Bentonsville."

The words hit Jaye like boulders thrown by a giant, because she knew what they meant. The conclusion was so terrible that her voice shook when she voiced it. "You don't want me to come with you," she whispered.

"Oh, no, honey. That's not it at all. It's just that I can't justify uprooting you from your school and your music and your friends until I'm settled somewhere else. You understand, don't you?"

Jaye understood that her mom was leaving her. Again. She struggled not to cry. "Yeah."

Her mom seemed not to know what to say, but then she clapped her hands once. She didn't exactly smile but looked like she was trying to. "Okay, then. How about that third piece of French toast?"

"I'm not hungry anymore," Jaye said.

Her eyes welling with tears, she pushed her chair back from the table and headed for the pink room that would never be truly hers.

MOLLY SAT alongside two other students in the study lounge on Monday afternoon, her head spinning as Mrs. Smith talked about x's and y's and distributive principles and multiplication.

She couldn't concentrate on the tutor's words no matter how hard she tried, not when her mind was still processing the terrifying fact that her period was three days late. She put a hand over her heaving stomach, praying a baby didn't grow there.

It was killing her not knowing one way or another.

Unable to sit still another second, she got abruptly to her feet, inadvertently knocking her algebra book off the table. It thudded to the floor.

Mrs. Smith's gaze zeroed in on her, concern etched on her features. "Molly, is something wrong?"

Molly reached down to pick up her book, then mumbled, "I don't feel good. I think I should go home."

"You don't look well." Mrs. Smith rose from her chair and laid a hand across Molly's forehead. "No fever, though. Still, somebody should drive you home."

Molly was about to insist she could walk home when she spied Diana passing in the hall. Mrs. Smith saw her daughter, too, and wasted no time in flagging her down and arranging a ride. Before Molly knew it, she was inside Diana's car.

"You really don't need to drive me home. I'll be okay." A lie if Molly had ever told one. If she was pregnant with Bobby's baby, she definitely would not be okay.

"It's no trouble," Diana said, sounding sincere. "What's wrong, exactly?"

Molly didn't think about her answer. She just blurted it out. "I think I might be pregnant."

CHAPTER THIRTEEN

DIANA DIDN'T NEED to read the directions on the back of the box to figure out how the pregnancy test worked. She remembered only too well, even though it had been ten years since she'd shoplifted a test from the very store where she'd purchased this one.

The teenage clerk had protested when Diana insisted on paying double for the test, taking the money only when Diana had set it on the counter and left.

Thankfully Diana had the foresight to instruct Molly to wait in the car. Not that the girl was any more eager to be seen buying a pregnancy test than Diana had been a decade ago. Or in watching to see if a second blue line would slowly materialize.

Molly couldn't even look at the indicator. She waited on the edge of the closed toilet seat in Diana's bathroom, her eyes shut tight. With her long, straight hair and lack of makeup, she hardly looked older than Jaye.

Diana had a fleeting thought of Valerie, who so desperately wanted to get pregnant and how differently she'd react to taking the test. But Valerie wasn't sixteen.

Diana glanced down at the test strip, then back up at the bathroom clock. Thank God.

"You can open your eyes, Molly," Diana said. "It's been more than five minutes, and I still only see one line."

Molly's eyes blinked open. "So I'm not pregnant?"

"Most likely, not. These tests are supposed to be effective as early as six days after conception and one day after a missed period."

Molly's entire body slumped in relief. Diana vividly remembered having a similar reaction, except she'd collapsed in fear. The dread had gradually transformed into hope that her relationship with Tyler could survive the unexpected pregnancy. She'd dreamed of marrying him, of raising their baby together, of a fairy-tale ending.

She'd been so young then. So stupid.

"I was so stupid, Diana." Molly shook her head. "I didn't even think about asking him to use birth control."

"You'll be smarter next time."

"I'm never having sex again. Never. I'm never letting Bobby near me again, either." Molly swiped at her face, as though angry at the tears that streamed down her cheeks. "We only had sex the one time. I thought it would make him like me more, but it didn't."

She sniffed loudly. Diana tore off some toilet paper from the roll and handed it to Molly. The girl noisily blew her nose, then tossed the tissue in the trash can.

Diana blew out a breath, aware the girl waited for her to spout words of wisdom. Surprisingly, Diana realized she had some. She'd seldom done the right thing in the past, but she had learned from the wrong ones.

"Any boy worth spending time with will like you regardless of whether you have sex with him," Diana said. "It's far more important to like yourself than for a boy to like you."

"I like myself," Molly mumbled, not entirely convincingly.

"Not as much as you should. You're going through a tough time with your parents getting divorced and you moving to a new town, but you can get through it." Diana put a hand on Molly's shoulder, trying to cushion the blow she was about to deliver. "You just need a little help."

Molly's wide, trusting eyes met hers. "You're helping me."

"Not from me, from your mother," Diana said. "Hear me out, Molly. You need to tell her. I can't be the one who takes you to the doctor."

Panic rolled off Molly, so palpable Diana could almost see it. "If I'm not pregnant, why would I go to a doctor?"

"You've been sexually active. You need to have the test result confirmed. And even if you don't want to be put on the birth control pill—"

"I don't," Molly interrupted hotly.

"You should be checked for STDs. And, no, I don't think you have an STD. But visiting a doctor is the responsible thing to do."

"I can't tell my mom about this," Molly cried.

"You have to, Molly."

Molly stood up abruptly, sweeping the box that had contained the pregnancy test into the trash can. She stormed out of the bathroom, then whirled to glare at Diana. "You don't know what any of this has been like for me."

Despite the fiction her mother had invented for her, Diana couldn't let Molly believe that. "You're wrong, Molly. When I was sixteen, my pregnancy test came out positive."

The anger visibly seeped from Molly, and her mouth dropped open. "You have a baby?"

"She's not a baby anymore. Jaye's nine years old."

"But where is she?"

"Living with my brother." Diana could no longer add that Jaye would be living with her soon, because she didn't know when they'd be together. "She visited last Saturday. You would have met her if you'd been at the community center."

Molly's smooth brows wrinkled, as though she was having trouble processing the information. "Was her father somebody like Bobby?"

The question called for more truth, highlighting the reasons Diana had to leave Bentonsville. Diana's answer wouldn't entirely blow the cover off the story her mother had invented, but it would loosen it.

"He wasn't like Bobby, but things still didn't work out for us. The bottom line is I shouldn't have had sex at sixteen. I probably wouldn't have if I'd talked to my mother about what was bothering me."

"Do you mean your brother dying?" Molly asked.

"Yeah," Diana said, "I do."

"You should have talked to her. Your mom's nice. She probably would have understood."

"Maybe she would have." Diana's mind spiraled backward, remembering her mother tucking her into bed when she was a child and saying she'd always love her. "Tell you what. Let's make a deal. You talk to your mother, I'll talk to mine."

Molly's brows scrunched up, but Diana found it encouraging that she didn't outright refuse the suggestion. Then again, Molly was a smart girl. She must know that Diana would have to tell her mother if Molly didn't.

"I don't understand what you have to talk to your mother about," Molly said.

Because she couldn't give Molly the entire, complicated answer, Diana boiled it down to one word: "Regrets."

DIANA PRESSED HER BACK against the cool plaster of the wall outside the teen lounge the afternoon after her talk with Molly, fighting nausea and nerves while she tried to gather her courage.

Rejection loomed as a distinct possibility, causing the chef salad she'd eaten for lunch to toss in her stomach. She inhaled slowly and deeply, concentrating on breathing through her diaphragm in an effort to calm herself.

If Diana couldn't manage to ask, there was no chance her mother would agree to meet with her. She also had Molly to consider. They'd made a deal, and Molly had already honored her part of it. Molly reported that her mother had cried after hearing about the pregnancy scare, but she'd also confided that they'd talked more last night than they had since the divorce.

"Are you avoiding me?"

Tyler Benton appeared as if from nowhere, looking like a dream in a navy blue suit that fit his lean, hard body so well it could have been tailored just for him. And maybe it had been. Her heart turned over, like one of the pieces of French toast she'd flipped for Jaye. She preferred the casual, unshaven Tyler to this elegant version of the man, but couldn't resist either of them.

"Avoiding you?" She parroted to buy herself time. "Why would you think I was avoiding you?"

"The way you just avoided answering that question, for starters." He tucked a piece of hair behind her ear, brushing her cheek in the process and creating a cascade of tiny shivers that danced over her skin. "If I didn't see that look in your eyes, I'd be getting worried."

"What look?" she asked.

"The one that says you want to get naked with me." His eyes roamed over her face, and her own bones seemed to melt, her entire body going weak. How was she ever going to find the strength to leave this man for a second time?

"You can have your way with me later." He feathered his fingers across her chin and down her neck, further wrecking her equilibrium. "After you tell me what's going on."

"You know what. We're keeping things quiet."

"That explains the way you acted at Angelo's on Saturday, but not why you ignored my phone calls today and Sunday."

She hadn't called because she needed to learn how to get along without him, but she wasn't quite ready to tell him that. She had something else to share, however, if only to get his reaction.

"I've had a lot on my mind. For one thing, I withdrew from my business classes today. The more I thought about it, the more I realized business wasn't for me."

"Good for you," he said. "Do you know what you'd like to do instead?"

"Not yet. I've been trying to figure out how to solve some of my other problems."

"Are you talking about Jaye?" he asked, but didn't wait for a response. "She's one of the reasons I called. I wanted to see how you two got along over the weekend, although you seemed to be doing fine when I saw you at Angelo's."

"We were," Diana said, reluctant to tell him that things between her and Jaye had headed swiftly downhill the following morning.

"She's beautiful, your Jaye. I'd love to hear more about her."

A vice seemed to clamp down on Diana's vocal cords, preventing her from speaking.

"How about you tell me more tonight? I have to work late, but I can stop by your place afterward," he said. "My week's so busy that if we don't see each other tonight, I won't be free until Thursday."

The prospect of spending another night in his arms was so tempting that Diana nearly agreed, but she couldn't lead him on that way. Not when she planned to leave Bentonsville. She found her voice. "Tonight's not good."

"Why not?"

"Because I'm going to my mother's house tonight."

He touched her cheek, understanding without words how important it would be for her to mend the rift with her mother. "I'll be home after ten tonight if you want to talk."

Without bothering to check if anyone was around, he kissed her softly and sweetly on the mouth and then left. Diana touched her fingers to her lips, where she could still feel the imprint of his mouth.

Straightening from the wall, she walked purposefully toward the teen lounge. She *would* get an invitation to her mother's house tonight and not only because of the deal she'd made with Molly. She simply couldn't bear to have told Tyler another lie.

AN ENORMOUS MOON lit the night sky, but the dim wattage of the bulbs in the mission-style table lamps cast the inside of the house where Diana had grown up in shadows.

She stood alone in the middle of the living room, waiting for her mother to return with the drinks she'd offered to get. Like the rest of the house, the room looked remarkably as it had ten years ago with polished tables, framed prints and overly formal upholstered furniture.

The Queen Anne sofa was directly under what used to be Diana's second-floor bedroom. Outside the tall, paneled window, she spied the sturdy oak tree that had served as her nightly escape route. She'd climb out her window after everyone had gone to bed, grab onto a branch and scramble down the tree.

After she'd told her mother she was pregnant, Diana hadn't needed to sneak out. Elaine Smith had all but shown her the door. "I just lost a son. And now you're pregnant," her mother had wailed. "How could you do this to me?"

There'd been more histrionics and flinging of blame, especially when Diana refused to name her unborn baby's father. And in a fit of defiance, she'd repeated the same lie she'd told Tyler, that the rumours about her loose reputation were true.

The lies, she knew, had to stop.

Sadness seemed to permeate the very air, unsurprising in a place where memories of that dark time abounded. Diana supposed it was only fitting that she reveal the secret she'd kept about her late brother in this house.

Her mother entered the room carrying two mugs of coffee she insisted had to be decaffeinated because of the late hour, then stopped suddenly when she noticed Diana wasn't sitting. "Is something wrong?"

Yes, something was wrong. This had been her house. Elaine was her mother. She should not be treated like a guest.

"Can we talk in the kitchen?" Diana asked.

"If you'd like," her mother said, then led the way to the kitchen where the family used to gather around the large, oak table. Diana claimed the chair that had once been hers, next to the one where J.D. used to sit.

Nerves seized Diana's throat, but her mother appeared composed. She drank from her coffee mug, then said, "Is this about Tyler Benton being Jaye's father?"

Diana hadn't anticipated the question, not even after it had become abundantly clear that her mother knew her secret. So much had been left unsaid between mother and daughter over the years that she figured they'd ignore this, too.

She didn't expect to feel the way she did, either. Because instead of anxiety, she felt relief. "How did you figure it out?"

"A better question would be why didn't I figure it out sooner. Those stories about you sleeping around when you were a teenager, they weren't true, were they?"

"No more true than the story you made up about my dead fiancé."

"I should have known they weren't true." Her mother didn't say she was sorry for what she'd believed or the fiction she'd spun, but Diana heard the apology in her voice nevertheless. "If you came over here tonight to make sure I won't tell him, rest assured that I won't. That's not my place. But I'm here if you want to discuss what you're going to do about it."

A part of Diana longed to accept the offer, but she feared her mother would try to talk her out of leaving Bentonsville. Besides, with Connor's wedding only two days away, she and her mother had something even more pressing to discuss.

"No. I don't want to talk about Tyler." Diana shook her head to add emphasis to her denial. "I want to talk about J.D."

James Dennis Smith, the brother Diana had loved with all her heart. The brother she'd failed.

Her mother stiffened. "Why?"

"I met Connor's fiancée."

The softness that had temporarily touched her mother's face disappeared. "Then I assume you've heard I'm not going to the wedding."

"I had heard that." Connor had confirmed it a few nights ago when he'd called, apologized for the eleventh-hour request and asked Diana to be in the wedding party. Diana chose her next words carefully. "But I wish you'd reconsider. I won't pretend I wasn't shocked when I met Abby or that having her in the family won't be an adjustment, but we can hardly blame her for what happened to J.D."

"I can blame her for keeping in contact with the man who killed my son," her mother snapped.

"That's not fair," Diana said. "Drew Galloway is Abby's brother, just like J.D. and Connor are my brothers."

"I know that." Her mother ran a hand over her face, looking far older than her years. "And I'm trying to get past it, for Connor's sake. But it's hard. The years go by, but I don't miss J.D. any less."

"I miss him, too, Mom." Diana's voice broke, because here in this kitchen, she felt closer to J.D. than she had in years. But overriding the mental picture of his young, handsome face crinkling in laughter as he told one of his corny jokes was his voice, urgent and convincing, as he extracted a promise from Diana. A promise she was finally going to break. "But I still think it's unfair of you to blame Abby for anything."

Diana grasped one of her hands with the other, praying for strength to say what she should have said so long ago. "If you need to blame someone besides Drew Galloway for J.D.'s death, blame me."

"You?" Her mother's voice spiked. "Why should I blame you?"

Memories swamped Diana. Of bursting into J.D.'s room to ask for help with homework. Of J.D.'s guilty expression when he looked up from his desk, where he was applying a crystalline powder to what resembled tobacco leaves. Of his admission that he was lacing marijuana with PCP. Of her promise to keep quiet after he insisted it was no big deal.

"Because..." The secret rose up in Diana, like lava from a volcano she could no longer keep from erupting. "Because I knew he was using drugs."

There it was. The ugly, damning truth. Spoken aloud for the very first time. The guilt that always lurked inside Diana surfaced, threatening to drown her. She didn't dare look at her mother but stared down at the table and doggedly finished her admission.

"He swore me to secrecy, but I shouldn't have listened to him. After I overheard you and Dad talking about drugs being found at the crime scene, I could barely function. Because if I'd told you J.D. was on drugs, he wouldn't have been at the field that night. He never would have died."

Silence reigned, so absolute Diana could hear the roar of blood in her ears. She lifted her head, expecting to see condemnation in her mother's eyes. But the older woman's face crumbled, grief carved into the lines around her nose and mouth. Tears poured from her eyes.

"It's not your fault J.D.'s dead. It's mine," she said in a strangled voice. "If you'd told me, it wouldn't have changed anything. Because *I already knew.*"

Diana must not have heard right. Her mother had known about the drugs *after* J.D.'s death, when she'd told Diana's father they had to preserve their son's reputation at all costs by making sure word of his drug use didn't get out.

Nobody else had been aware her brother was using drugs before he died. Not Chris, from whom J.D. had distanced himself months before. And surely not her mother, the one person J.D. had most feared finding out.

"I came across tobacco paper and powder residue in his room a few weeks before he died," her mother said, contradicting Diana's silent denial. "I tried to tell myself he wasn't experimenting with drugs, but then I noticed little changes in him and I knew. I *knew.* I couldn't decide what to do about it, so I did nothing. And now he's dead. Because of me."

Her mother's behavior after J.D.'s death suddenly made sense. The inconsolable grief. The failure to let go of the past. The inability to find happiness in the present.

The grief and the guilt rolled off her mother in a wave that caught Diana in its undertow. Her heart aching for her mother, she reached across the table and grabbed both of the other woman's hands in hers. "Did you know J.D. planned to go to the field that night to buy drugs?"

"No," her mother said, "but—"

"There are no buts. J.D. was so strong, so larger than

life somehow. You probably thought the same thing I did, that the drugs were a temporary phase."

"I was his mother," she cried. "I should have stopped him. I should have known what could happen."

"But you didn't know. Not that J.D. was planning to buy drugs or that Galloway would stab him. All you knew for sure was that you loved him." Diana waited until her mother's eyes met hers. "Listen to me, Mother. It wasn't your fault J.D. died."

Her mother's lips trembled, then the tears fell again. But this time Diana hoped she was crying because she'd finally forgiven herself. She released her mother's hands and slid her chair to within a few inches of where her mother sat. Then, somehow, they were in each other's arms, both clinging to each other as though never intending to let go.

As Diana hugged her mother, a truth slammed into her.

If J.D.'s death wasn't her mother's fault, it wasn't Diana's, either.

The guilt that had festered inside her lifted, like a cloud that dissipates and lets the blue sky shine through. How ironic that unburdening herself of her terrible secret had proved to be her impetus to forgive herself.

But Diana's conscience was far from clean, because she'd kept so many other secrets and told so many lies to cover them. And now, she knew, she had to stop.

THE DOOR to the meeting room emitted a creak loud enough to drown out speech, drawing every eye to Diana's entrance.

The eyes belonged to about two dozen people sitting in a circle who defied common description. There were the old and the young, men as well as women, Caucasians and minorities.

About the only trait they seemed to hold universal was promptness, something that set Diana apart. She'd found out about the meeting, the only one in a fifty-mile radius that met on Thursday afternoons, in the brochure she'd picked up at the community center. But she'd miscalculated how long it took to get to Fredericksburg from Bentonsville.

"Sorry," she said.

"That's okay." A stout, bearded man at the apex of the circle spoke. "Take a seat and join us."

Diana quickly identified the only empty seat as the one next to the bearded man. The one farthest from where she stood.

You can do this, Diana, she told herself.

Her head high and her heels clicking on the tile floor, she walked to the seat.

"Go on, Trudy," the bearded man urged. "You were telling us about how you used to search the bathrooms in your friends' houses."

"That's where a lot of people keep their prescriptions." The speaker was an attractive young woman with a long face and glasses, dressed in a brown sweater that matched her brown hair and eyes. "I always claimed I had to go. Then I'd carefully go through the bathroom looking for drugs."

At the other Narcotics Anonymous meetings Diana had attended, she'd heard a version of Trudy's story.

People probably swore by the meetings, she theorized, because so many of them had common experiences.

"Did you ever get caught?" a man with graying hair and a deep baritone asked Trudy.

"I got questioned a couple times. But I swore I didn't touch anything, and they bought it. I got really good at covering up around the people I loved. My boyfriend thought the money disappearing from our joint account went to charity. My parents believed I got fired because my boss was a jerk. Nobody knew it was all because of drugs."

A good number of heads in the room nodded, including Diana's. Disregarding teenage shoplifting and skipping out on the check at Angelo's, Diana had never stolen. But she related to Trudy's desperation to keep her addiction a secret.

"The thing is, I was deeply ashamed," Trudy said. "It was only after I started coming here that I could stop lying and admit to what I am."

The shame that burned inside Diana had been more searing because she'd fallen prey to the vice that played a part in dooming her brother. Her inability to expose her addiction to those closest to her, in fact, was why she'd convinced herself she'd never need any more help to kick her habit.

Yet now she realized she'd been a fool for believing she'd triumphed over her addiction simply because she no longer abused pain pills. Now she understood she'd continued to practice the behaviors that marked an addict.

She'd lied so much, in fact, that she'd tricked herself into believing lying was acceptable behavior.

"Thank you for sharing, Trudy." The bearded man gazed around the circle. "Who'd like to go next?"

Diana raised her hand, drawing the man's attention. He nodded to her. "Why don't you start by introducing yourself?"

Diana drew in a deep breath, filling herself with the resolve to finally do the right thing.

"My name's Diana," she said in a loud, clear voice that extended to every corner of the room, "and I'm a drug addict."

THE INTERIOR of Tyler's house on Farragut Street had a decidedly unlived-in feel. Upscale leather furniture, bland white walls and pristine beige carpeting all strongly suggested that the man who lived here wasn't often home.

Diana mentally added splashes of color—throw pillows in orange and yellow, leafy green plants and eye-catching accent walls.

If she'd been the type of woman Tyler needed by his side, she would have suggested redecorating his home in a style better suiting his warm personality.

But as the woman who'd deceived him, she had no right to suggest anything. After she made her revelation, she fully expected to no longer be welcome in his home. Or his life.

She waged war with her threatening tears, determined not to let her vision blur now that she could finally view the past clearly. Narcotics Anonymous advised its members to take a personal inventory and admit when they'd been wrong. Diana had wronged Tyler.

"That's the ten-cent tour." Tyler held her hand, which he'd captured when she arrived at his house. "I hope you're hungry. After you called and said you were coming by, I picked up some steaks."

She wrinkled her nose and inhaled, finally identifying the scent that had been teasing her nostrils. Except the touch of acridness didn't seem right.

"Is something burning?" she asked.

The scent must have reached him, too, because he dropped her hand and ran for the kitchen. She trailed behind him, watching smoke drift from the oven as he used a padded mitt to pull out a tray containing two charred steaks.

The smoke detector finally kicked in, emitting shrill eardrum-piercing chirps. Tyler set the steaks down on top of the stove, then dashed for the overhead detector, wrestling with it until he managed to remove the batteries.

"I am so sorry," he said into the sudden silence, the smoke swirling around him. "I meant to warm up the steaks, not turn them to charcoal."

He didn't seem to realize that the mistake endeared him to her even more. Appearing less than perfect somehow made him more ideal. Her heart contracted, squeezed by the knowledge that she was about to lose him.

"We still have salads." He spoke as he turned on the fan above the stove and opened a window. "They have a crumbly blue-cheese topping, and they're supposed to be delicious. And I could always order out for pizza."

He turned on her a smile so charming it nearly killed her resolve to confess.

"I appreciate all the trouble you've gone to, but could we just talk?" she asked. "I don't think I could eat just now."

He frowned. "Well, sure. Would you like a glass of wine first? I've got merlot and cabernet."

"No, thank you." Since weaning herself off prescription drugs, coffee was the only vice she allowed herself. She craved a cup now, but stifled the urge to ask for one. "All I need is to talk."

He indicated for her to precede him into his den, which featured an oversized, flat-screen television she'd wager he seldom watched. Lowering himself onto a cream-colored leather love seat, he patted the place beside him. She shook her head, preferring to remain standing. If she got too near him, she might lose her nerve.

"I went to a Narcotics Anonymous meeting this afternoon, stood up in front of the group and admitted I'd had a problem with drugs," Diana said.

"Good for you," Tyler said. "That took a lot of guts."

"Guts are something I've been lacking most of my life, but I figure it's not too late to get some." This part of Diana's preplanned speech would be the easiest to get through. "You asked me the other day if I knew what I wanted to do now that I'm no longer taking business classes. I do now. I'd like to get a degree in counseling and specialize in helping teens."

"That'd be the perfect career for you."

"I think so. But it's a long-term goal. In the short term, I want to give talks to teenagers about what I've been through."

A worry line appeared on his forehead. “I thought you didn’t want anyone to know you’d been addicted to drugs.”

“I changed my mind.” She paced to one side of the room and back, realized what she was doing and stopped. “If I want to be any help at all, I need to be open about my past. That includes my teenage pregnancy and my brother’s murder, too. I can’t keep quiet any longer about who I am or what I’ve done.”

He edged forward on the love seat, his brow still furrowed. “These talks you’re planning to give, will they be at the community center?”

“Not at the Bentonsville Community Center.” She forced herself to meet his quizzical gaze. “I’m leaving town, Tyler. In fact, I already gave Chris notice. I can’t stay here and risk ruining your chances of becoming a judge. I couldn’t live with myself if I did.”

He ran a hand through his golden hair, his expression disbelieving. “So you’re leaving because of me?”

“I already told you. I can’t keep my past a secret any longer.”

“I never asked you to,” he retorted. “I admire you for fighting your addiction and winning. You know that.”

“Not everyone thinks that way. I know how politics work, Tyler. There have to be people who don’t want to see you on the bench. They’ll use our relationship against you.”

“You’re presuming some hypothetical muckraker has nothing better to do than dig up dirt on the woman I’m dating.”

“I admit that’s unlikely,” Diana said. “But I do think

somebody might look into the background of your child's mother."

He grew very still. "What are you talking about?"

She closed her eyes, praying for strength that didn't come. Still she had to make sure he understood. *No more lies,* she reminded herself.

"Jaye's your daughter, Tyler."

HER WORDS DIDN'T COMPUTE. Jaye's father was a stranger who'd gotten the young Diana pregnant, promised to marry her, then wrecked their future to hell with a car.

Even as the scenario ran through Tyler's mind, it rang false. It sounded like a story a mother might invent to cover the shame of her teenage daughter's promiscuity and subsequent pregnancy. Hadn't Elaine Smith, after all, been the one who'd spread the tale around town?

But Diana hadn't been promiscuous. She still wasn't. That was how Tyler had instantly seen through the fiction when she'd claimed to be dating Chris Coleman. Diana would never be involved with two men at once, let alone multiple men.

"You never slept with anybody but me when we were teenagers," he said, as much to himself as to her, amazed he hadn't figured it out before now.

Until she'd confirmed the ugly rumors that she was an easy lay, he'd believed with every pore of his teenage being that she loved him. Her false admission had blinded him to everything, including reason. Another conclusion he should have reached years ago spilled forth. "You were never engaged, either."

"No." Her voice was as soft as his.

He'd never asked about her alleged fiancé because he couldn't bear to hear about him, but he did now. "This other man, did he even exist?"

She shook her head, cementing the fact that Jaye was his daughter. He pictured the blond, green-eyed little girl, belatedly realizing his daughter had inherited his fair coloring and the general shape of his features.

My God. His daughter.

He'd shaken her hand the other day, and he hadn't even known who she was. Worse, Jaye thought of him as a stranger.

"Did you lie to Jaye, too?" he asked harshly. "Does she believe her father died in a car accident?"

"That was my mother's story, not mine. I didn't even know what she'd told people until I came back to town."

"Then what did you tell Jaye about her father?"

She couldn't meet his eyes. "I told her not everybody has both parents, that I loved her enough for two people."

Except Tyler would have loved her, too. He already did, with a fierce intensity that made the blood rush through his veins. Anguish and betrayal combined to make his voice harsh. "How could you have kept this from me?"

"You'd been accepted into Harvard. You were one of Bentonsville's golden boys. I couldn't let you throw your future away because I'd gotten pregnant."

Since Tyler had believed at the time that Diana was his future, her logic was skewed. "So you decided it was better to break my heart by lying to me about sleeping with half the boys at school?"

"I never meant to hurt you." Her eyes pleaded with him for understanding, but they seemed like the eyes of a stranger. "I couldn't have stayed in Bentonsville even if I hadn't gotten pregnant, not after what happened to J.D. I thought it would be best for both of us if I left without any ties."

"You left with my baby!"

"I left you with no reason not to fulfill your potential. And you've done that, Tyler. Look how successful you've become. You're on the verge of fulfilling your dream."

Except Diana had been his dream. How could she not have known that?

"I wanted to tell you. That's why I came to your house, but then I found out how political the process of becoming a judge was."

"So you kept on lying to me. Not only about Jaye, but about the reason you couldn't date me, about dating Chris and about God knows what else."

"I was wrong to lie to you. I know that now. But I lied to protect you. So the commission wouldn't find out you have an illegitimate child by a former drug addict."

He could barely process what he was hearing. "Are you proposing I don't tell anyone about Jaye?"

"Nobody else knows for certain that she's yours except my mother, and she won't tell. If neither of us says anything, either, nobody needs to know."

"Like hell they don't." The anger that had been simmering inside him boiled to the surface. He got to his feet and crossed to within a foot of her. "How could you possibly believe I'd deny my daughter?"

"The judgeship—"

"Is not nearly as important to me as she is. As you used to be. What kind of a man do you think I am, Diana?"

"An ambitious man. Becoming a judge is all you ever talked about."

"That's because I thought my sixteen-year-old girlfriend would panic if I told her my main ambition was to love her for the rest of my life."

HIS MEANING DAWNED on Diana, drying the tears that had formed in the backs of her eyes.

After discovering her mother had spread the fake story about the identity of Jaye's father, Diana had suspected that Tyler had genuinely cared for her when they were teens. This was the first time she knew for certain that he'd loved her.

Exactly the way she'd prayed he did when their child grew inside her. She'd daydreamed that he'd discover her pregnancy and come charging into her aunt's house, declaring that nothing was more important than the two of them.

But then it registered upon Diana that Tyler had spoken in the past tense. Mere hours ago, he might have loved her still. But she'd killed whatever feelings he once had for her.

"What happens now?" she asked in a small voice.

He raked his fingers through his hair, looking like anything but the calm, collected judge she'd always believed he would become.

"I need to think about it, to process what you've told

me, then I'll be in touch. But I can tell you right now that I am going to have a relationship with my daughter. She will know that she has a father who loves her."

She swallowed, hardly daring to ask the question. But it slipped from her lips. "What about us?"

The look he turned on her was cold. "There is no us anymore, Diana. Because of you, I've missed almost ten years of my daughter's life. I won't ever be able to forgive you for that."

Although she'd expected them, his words sliced into her, the pain emanating to every part of her. She'd thought nothing could hurt more than losing him that first time.

Now she knew she'd been wrong.

CHAPTER FOURTEEN

"WHAT'S WITH YOU today, Tyler?" his father asked between bites of roast beef sandwich during their weekly Friday afternoon lunch at Custer's. "You passed Frank Collins without even saying hello."

Collins was a longtime city councilman with spidery ties in the Bentonsville community and an abrasive personality that grated on Tyler. Still, Tyler hadn't deliberately ignored him.

"I didn't notice him," Tyler said.

"You can't afford not to notice the movers and the shakers, son. But I understand you're preoccupied with your interview this afternoon. What do you say we go over some of your answers?"

Tyler finished off the last of the reuben sandwich he'd ordered and washed it down with lemonade before answering. "Thanks for the offer, but I'm not in the mood."

His father's dark eyebrows, a startling contrast to his gray hair, drew together. "How can you not be in the mood? This is one of the most important days of your life. To be prepared is half the victory."

"I have some other things on my mind."

"Things beside your interview? Like what?" His father put his elbows on the table and leaned forward. "Is it Lauren Fairchild? I heard she was dating that community center director. Surprised the hell out of me. I thought she had her heart set on you."

"It's not Lauren, Dad. I'm happy for her and Chris." Tyler hadn't intended to confide in his father until he had things figured out but recognized his father wouldn't stop until he had all the answers. "It's Diana Smith."

"Diana? I warned you about her at the spaghetti buffet. She seems nice enough, but her family's had problems since J.D. was killed. She's not the woman for you."

"I used to think she was the one for me. When I was a high school senior, right around the time her brother died, I was crazy about her."

His father frowned, the revelation obviously news to him. He stroked his chin. "Didn't she move to Virginia and get pregnant by some guy who died in a car accident?"

"That's the story her mother spread around town, but I've learned Diana was pregnant before she left town." Tyler met his father's worried gaze. "I'm the father of her daughter, Dad."

"What?" His father glanced around to check if anyone else had heard Tyler, then continued in a hushed voice. "You can't believe that. If she's trying to pin this girl on you, it's because she knows you'll help her support the kid. We'll demand a DNA test, is what we'll do."

"I don't need a DNA test," Tyler said quietly.

"Like hell, you don't." His father kept his voice down, but didn't disguise his exasperation. "Do you know how damaging an allegation like this could be to your career?"

"That's not my uppermost concern."

"It should be. We can't let this get out, son. If it's money she wants, we'll pay her to keep quiet until we can prove she's lying."

Tyler felt his muscles bunch. "Diana's not lying."

"Be reasonable, son. If she's not lying, why wouldn't she have told you about the baby before now?"

"Because she loves me," Tyler snapped, "and she has this screwed-up notion that she and Jaye could stop me from living out my dream."

Why had it taken his father criticizing Diana for Tyler to realize that? Tyler had been so angry over Diana's lies that he hadn't recognized her motivation until this instant. She loved him. Loved him deeply enough to sacrifice her own happiness for his. Except, without each other, neither one of them would ever truly be happy.

"Keep your voice down, son." His father reached across the table and covered Tyler's hand, peering at him intently. "If this gets out, that's exactly what could happen. You might never become a judge."

Tyler couldn't rouse any anger, because his father clearly wanted what he thought was best for Tyler. But it was past time for Tyler to act on his own desires. Tyler deliberately drew his hand out from under his father's.

"You're right. I have always aspired to become a judge, partly because that's what you wanted for me.

But here's the rub. A judgeship pales in comparison to what's truly valuable to me." Tyler pushed his chair back from the table and stood up.

"Son, where are you going?" his father asked, panic lacing his syllables.

"I have an interview this afternoon, remember?"

"Don't do anything stupid," his father's voice trailed after Tyler as he headed to the exit of the restaurant without meeting the eyes of a single mover or shaker.

His father had finally issued some advice Tyler intended to follow. Although Tyler suspected his interpretation of what constituted stupidity differed a great deal from his dad's.

DIANA REARRANGED the baby's breath in her daughter's silky blond hair, ridiculously thankful that Jaye had allowed her this close. They were in the guest room at Connor's house, with Jaye sitting in front of a mahogany dresser equipped with a large mirror. Diana stood behind the little girl, surveying her handiwork.

"You look beautiful, honey." The tiny white flowers graced the crown of Jaye's blond head, and the lilac of her bridesmaid dress beautifully complemented her fair skin. "Abby picked out the perfect dresses."

Diana's own dress flowed silkily around her ankles and matched her daughter's. There'd been some doubt Diana would be able to find the right dress days before the wedding, but the bridal shop had one left that happened to be her size. Abby said it was karma.

"That's because Abby loves me," Jaye said. "She tells me so all the time."

Diana would not let herself get jealous of a woman to whom she owed a world of gratitude she could never repay. She'd spent the better part of two days with Abby, helping her future sister-in-law get ready for today's wedding while pretending the breakup with Tyler hadn't devastated her.

"Then we're lucky your Uncle Connor fell in love with Abby." Diana meant every word. Over the past two days, she'd begun to think of Abby as a friend. No matter who her brother was.

"Grandma loves me, too," Jaye said. "She's staying with me this week while Uncle Connor and Abby are on their honeymoon."

Diana very carefully didn't react. She herself couldn't stay with Jaye in Silver Spring because she needed to fulfill her obligation to the community center in Bentonsville. "Your grandmother told me that. I'll visit you. And maybe you can come to Bentonsville for the weekend to visit me, too."

Jaye's lower lip thrust forward, the way it did whenever she was upset. She stared into her lap.

"Whatever it is, Jaye," Diana prompted, "you can tell me."

Jaye's eyes lifted, wet and vulnerable, and met Diana's in the mirror. "I love Grandma, but I'd rather stay with you," she mumbled. "Unless you don't want me."

"Of course I want you. Why would you even think I didn't?"

"Because you left me." Jaye didn't cry, but her voice sounded teary. "You left me and didn't come back for a long, long time."

"Oh, Jaye." Diana moved to the side of the dresser so she gazed at her daughter instead of her reflection. "I couldn't come back."

"Why not?"

"For the same reason I left. I should have told you this before, but I was ashamed. So very ashamed." Diana summoned the strength she'd tapped into at the Narcotics Anonymous meeting. She was through lying to the people she loved, no matter how much the truth cost her. "I had a drug problem, and I needed to take care of it before I could be around you again."

"You mean those little white pills you swallowed?"

Shock pulsed through Diana. "You knew about those?"

Jaye nodded solemnly. "You acted funny after you took them. But you didn't have to leave, Mommy. I could have taken care of you."

Diana bent down so she was eye level with her daughter, the backs of her eyes stinging. "I'm the adult. It was my job to take care of you. But I couldn't trust myself around you after the car accident. That's why I left you with Connor."

"But why did you take so long to come back?"

"Because I wanted to make things up to you by getting a better job and a nicer apartment. By going back to school so I can make more money."

Anger flashed on Jaye's face, as bright as lightning. "I don't care about any of that stuff. I only care about being with you."

And then Jaye did cry, great, gushing tears that streamed down her face in thick rivulets. Her thin body became rigid when Diana embraced her, but then she collapsed into her mother's arms.

Diana held her tight, regretting the time they'd lost and the pain she'd caused Jaye. By trying to do the right thing, she'd done the wrong one. She, of all people, should have known better. She had the same fierce desire for her mother's love.

"I've been so stupid. About everything," Diana said into her daughter's sweet-smelling hair. "But I'll make it up to you if you'll let me. If you want to live with me, of course you can."

"I want that." Jaye's words were hardly recognizable through her sobs. "I love Uncle Connor and Abby. But I love you more."

Humbled, Diana hung on tight to her daughter, aware that she'd never hold anything more precious. For perhaps the first time, she realized exactly what she'd deprived Tyler of. Because a possible judgeship paled in comparison to the love of a child.

She hadn't only been unfair to Tyler. She'd shortchanged the daughter she loved with her whole heart out of knowing her father. Because she finally realized how wrong she'd been in keeping them apart, she'd call Tyler and suggest a meeting with Jaye at the earliest possible date.

"We'll break the news to Connor and Abby after their honeymoon that you're moving in with me." Diana kissed the top of her daughter's head. "As soon as I find another job and an apartment, we'll be together."

"We can't stay in Bentonsville?" Jaye asked.

"I'm afraid not."

"Then will you tell my dad about me before we leave?"

At the softly voiced question, Diana drew back from her daughter so she could search her face. Her heart thudded painfully in her chest. "Why do you think your father is in Bentonsville?"

"He is, isn't he?"

Diana's throat tightened. "Yes, honey, he is."

"Does he know about me?" Jaye seemed almost afraid to pose the question, causing Diana to realize how obtuse she'd been. Her evasive answers to Jaye's questions hadn't stopped the girl from wondering about her father—or from fearing he hadn't wanted her. She wiped a tear from under her daughter's eye with the pad of her forefinger.

"He didn't know about you until a few days ago," Diana answered. "Now he wants more than anything to get to know you."

Jaye had stopped crying, and her green eyes appeared huge. "It's Tyler, isn't it?"

Diana stared into the face that looked so much like that of the man she loved. "How did you know Tyler was your father?"

"I didn't. I just wanted him to be," Jaye said, breaking into a smile that was a duplicate of Tyler's. "When can I see him?"

"Soon," Diana promised. "But right now we have a wedding to go to."

A wedding where she'd pretend that her happiness for Connor and Abby, not to mention her joy for Jaye, blotted out the painful realization that her own love story wouldn't have a happy ending.

TYLER SLAMMED on the brakes of his car, parked at the curb and followed Elaine Smith into the county library.

Only a desperate man, he acknowledged, would trail the mother of the woman he loved through town.

But he'd been nearly out of options when he spotted Elaine Smith. He hadn't been able to get in touch with Diana last night to tell her what had happened at his interview. She hadn't answered her telephone or door this morning either. The woman who'd picked up the phone at the community center was a stranger, possibly even Diana's eventual replacement. She'd known Diana had taken the day off but didn't know why.

Locating Diana would be a whole lot simpler if Diana owned a cell phone. If she ever forgave him for being so dense, he'd buy her one first chance he got.

The small library seemed too crowded for its size, with young mothers helping their children choose books and adults perusing the bestsellers.

He wound through the library, greeting by name three or four people he recognized, and found Elaine Smith in the nonfiction section flipping through a book entitled *Cooking for Children.*

"Morning, Mrs. Smith."

She looked up from the book. "Tyler? What a surprise. I wouldn't have expected to run into you in the cookbook section."

"I didn't expect to be here myself until I spotted you going into the library." He saw no need to disguise his motive, not when he'd gladly shout his love for Diana through a loudspeaker in the middle of town if that's what it would take to get her to forgive him. "Do you know where I can find Diana?"

"Why, yes I do." A strange look passed over her face. "She's at her brother's wedding."

"I knew Connor was getting married, but I didn't realize it was today." Tyler noticed that Elaine Smith was dressed in her usual skirt and blouse, perhaps a little formal for a morning at the library but not dressy enough for such an important event. "Excuse me for asking this, but why aren't you at the wedding?"

She raised one eyebrow as though the answer was obvious. "You do know who my son is marrying, don't you?"

"Abby Reed," he answered, deliberately not referring to her as Drew Galloway's sister. "I vaguely remember her from high school. A nice, quiet girl who I've heard has grown into a remarkable woman."

Elaine set her jaw. "A woman with unfortunate family connections."

Tyler could have let the matter drop. Everybody in Bentonsville knew Elaine Smith had been devastated by her younger son's death and unforgiving of his killer. Except Abby Reed hadn't killed anybody, and Mrs. Smith had more than one son. A son who happened to be the brother of the woman Tyler loved.

"This may be none of my business, but I'm going to say it anyway. Are you sure you won't have regrets for skipping your son's wedding? Because if you do, you'll have them for the rest of your life."

She didn't say anything for long moments, her chin high as she regarded him with frost in her gaze. "You're right."

His shoulders slumped in defeat. "About it being none of my business?"

"About the regrets." She checked her watch. "How fast can you drive? Connor's wedding starts in less than an hour, and I don't go above fifty-five miles per hour."

He smiled at her. "I'll gladly drive you there."

"I don't want you to simply drive me to the wedding. I want you to *escort* me. As the mother of the groom, I'm entitled to bring a guest. You can be it."

"Are you sure?" he asked, his heart beating faster at the prospect of seeing Diana. "Even though, I think you're aware, I am family."

"I did know that." She hooked an arm through his. "Why do you think I asked you along in the first place?"

IT HAD BEEN SO LONG since Diana had attended a wedding that she'd forgotten how wonderfully hectic the minutes before the ceremony could be.

After assuring that the organist did indeed plan to play "The Wedding March" from *A Midsummer Night's Dream,* Diana headed back to the room where Abby was sequestered. The sight of Connor in a corner of the vestibule derailed her.

He looked darkly handsome in a gray tux that fit his tall form to perfection. But not only was he alone, he was fidgeting. Frowning, she took a sharp right turn.

"Didn't you know that nobody's supposed to see you before the ceremony?" Diana asked as she approached.

A corner of his mouth lifted, but only slightly. “Nobody’s supposed to see the bride. The guests don’t care what I look like.”

She straightened his lapel and smiled up at him. “Well, I think you look very handsome and that Abby is one lucky lady.”

“I’m the lucky one,” he said, his sincerity evident.

Okay, Diana thought. Prewedding doubts were out. This was a man sure about his decision to get married.

“Have I told you yet how glad I am that you’re here?” A muscle twitched in his jaw. “As much as I’m going to miss her, I’m also glad Jaye’s moving back in with you.”

“Jaye told you about that?” Diana asked in dismay. “She was supposed to wait until after the honeymoon.”

“My guess is that she couldn’t help it. She was practically bursting with the news.” He placed a hand on Diana’s shoulder. “She told me about Tyler Benton, too. Are you sure he’s the one?”

“He’s the only boy I slept with, Connor. I lied about the others because I didn’t want anyone to know Tyler was the father.” Diana closed her eyes. “I lied about a lot of things, including the reason I left Jaye with you. I had a problem with prescription drugs, Connor.”

“I suspected that,” he said. “I also know you’re clean now and that Jaye belongs with you. I don’t have any doubts about that.”

“Then what’s bothering you?” Even as Diana asked the question, the answer occurred to her. Of course. Why hadn’t she figured it out before? “It’s because neither of our parents are here, isn’t it?”

"Actually, Dad showed up. He's in the church, but he left his pregnant wife at home. He didn't bring Ben, either," Connor said, referring to their seven-year-old stepbrother. "He's also leaving partway through the reception. Something about needing to get back to Richmond because Ben has a basketball game tomorrow morning."

"Those games are important to him," Diana said. "When I spoke to him on the phone, he talked my ear off about how good Ben is at sports."

"He does that."

Diana bit her lip. "If it's not Dad, it must be Mom. You're upset that she isn't here."

"Yeah." He drew out the word. "I know she said she wasn't coming, but I thought she might...changed her mind."

Diana assumed Connor had mixed up his tenses, but then it dawned on her that he was staring over her shoulder with a smile brighter than the white of his bride's dress.

She turned. Their mother stood a few steps inside the church. Dressed no differently than usual except for the smile she wore, she headed directly for them.

"You look beautiful, Diana." She briefly touched Diana's upper arm before turning her full focus on her son. "And you look very handsome, Connor. Do you think you can forgive an old lady for even thinking about missing her son's wedding?"

Connor blinked a few times, then grabbed for their mother's hand, which he pressed in both of his. "I already have."

Diana backed away, giving her mother and brother their moment, her heart swelling as Connor bent down to embrace their mother. Everything would be perfect, Diana thought, if only Tyler was here.

And then Tyler walked into the church.

She did a double take, sure she'd conjured him up. But, no, the man in the casual slacks and long-sleeved shirt was definitely Tyler. Even if he hadn't been one of the only men in the church not wearing a suit, he would have stood out because of his height and fair good looks.

As though sensing her staring at him, he turned and their eyes met. Without breaking the gaze, he walked toward her, the entire scene seeming to take place in slow motion.

"Hello, Diana."

She had a hundred things to say to him, but only managed one. "What are you doing here?"

"It's complicated." He nodded toward Connor and her mother, who still held each other, both seeming to be talking at once. "Suffice it to say I'm your mother's escort, and I need to talk to you. How long before the ceremony starts?"

Her mind spinning with possibilities of what he wanted to discuss, Diana answered, "Maybe ten minutes."

"Then I'll talk fast." He grabbed her hand and led her through a door and down a hall into a small room with a blackboard and rows of miniature desks. A religious education class, no doubt. But what were they doing here?

"Do you know how many times I've called you yesterday and today?" he asked, his eyes roaming over her.

"I was at Connor's helping Abby get ready for the wedding, but I don't understand why you were calling. Or why you're here." A terrible thought occurred to her, causing an ache in her chest. "If it's because you think I'll be difficult about Jaye, you're wrong. I should tell you, though, that she's already guessed you're her father."

His Adam's apple bobbed as he swallowed. "And how does she feel about that?"

"She's excited. Don't worry. I told her you didn't know about her until a few days ago. I'll make things as easy as possible for both of you. I won't move far from Bentonsville and I'll be generous with visitation." She bit her lip, forcing out the next words. "I only hope you and I can be friends."

"All you want from me is friendship?"

She lowered her eyes, which must be filled with regrets for all the mistakes she'd made and the lies she'd told. "I'd be lying if I said that was true, and I've made a vow to stop. But I've accepted that you'll never be able to forgive me."

"Even if it's finally gotten through my thick skull that you lied because you loved me?"

Her mouth lifted, and her chin jerked up. She stared into his eyes and could hardly believe what she saw there: love.

"I didn't come here about Jaye," he said. "Well, not entirely about Jaye. I came to tell you I took my name out of consideration for the judgeship."

Shock rippled over her. "Why would you do that?"

He touched her cheek and gazed at her with a tender smile. "Because I'm not about to subject you or Jaye to unfair scrutiny because some political type might not want me to sit on the bench. I've decided instead to go into law practice for myself and concentrate on juvenile law."

Even though the profession would be a natural for him, his sudden change of heart didn't make sense. "But you've always wanted to become a judge."

"I want you and Jaye more," he said certainly. His bottom lip wavered slightly, and he'd never looked more vulnerable. "The question is, do you still want me?"

"Still?" Emotion rose in her throat, and she touched his face, trailing her fingers along his jawline. "I've always wanted you, Tyler. And I always will."

"That's a very good thing," he whispered, "because I'm partial to the idea of raising my daughter with the woman I love."

Sweeping her into his arms, he lowered his head and kissed her, filling Diana with hope for the future. She'd made mistakes in the past and suspected she'd make her share of them in the years to come, but the difference was that she'd face them head on. With Tyler by her side.

A loud bang pierced the silence, the interruption so unexpected that Diana didn't recognize it had been the sound of a door bursting open until Tyler broke off the kiss. Still in Tyler's arms, she saw Jaye staring at them openmouthed.

Tyler recovered first, gently putting Diana from him and stooping so he was at eye level with Jaye. “Hi, Jaye. I hope you don’t mind that I was kissing your mom.”

Jaye’s eyes grew round. “Why were you kissing her?”

Tyler glanced up at Diana. “I was about to persuade her the three of us should become a family, but I don’t want to move too fast. I want to give you time to get used to me being your father first.”

Without warning, Jaye launched herself into his arms, hugging him tightly around the neck. Tyler hugged her back, his jaw clenching hard and eyes closing tight. Her own eyes filling with joyful tears, Diana placed her hand on Tyler’s back, completing their family circle.

The tap-tapping of high heels striking tile flooring announced the arrival of another interruption. This one, a harried-looking bridesmaid who was one of Abby’s coworkers, had no difficulty finding her voice.

“Diana. There you are,” the bridesmaid said in a somewhat frantic tone. “Jaye was supposed to find you and tell you the wedding’s about to start.”

“We’ll be right out,” Diana said, speaking not only for herself but for her daughter and the man she loved.

It seemed fitting that they were about to witness a new beginning, especially because theirs was already underway.

* * * * *

Happily ever after is just the beginning...

Turn the page for a sneak preview of DANCING ON SUNDAY AFTERNOONS by Linda Cardillo

PROLOGUE

Giulia D'Orazio
1983

I had two husbands—Paolo and Salvatore.

Salvatore and I were married for thirty-two years. I still live in the house he bought for us; I still sleep in our bed. All around me are the signs of our life together. My bedroom window looks out over the garden he planted. In the middle of the city, he coaxed tomatoes, peppers, zucchini—even grapes for his wine—out of the ground. On weekends, he used to drive up to his cousin's farm in Waterbury and bring back manure. In the winter, he wrapped the peach tree and the fig tree with rags and black rubber hoses against the cold, his massive, coarse hands gentling those trees as if they were his fragile-skinned babies. My neighbor, Dominic Grazza, does that for me now. My boys have no time for the garden.

In the front of the house, Salvatore planted roses. The roses I take care of myself. They are giant, cream-colored, fragrant. In the afternoons, I like to sit out on the porch with my coffee, protected from the eyes of the neighborhood by that curtain of flowers.

Salvatore died in this house thirty-five years ago. In the last months, he lay on the sofa in the parlor so he could be in the middle of everything. Except for the two oldest boys, all the children were still at home and we ate together every evening. Salvatore could see the dining room table from the sofa, and he could hear everything that was said. "I'm not dead, yet," he told me. "I want to know what's going on."

When my first grandchild, Cara, was born, we brought her to him, and he held her on his chest, stroking her tiny head. Sometimes they fell asleep together.

Over on the radiator cover in the corner of the parlor is the portrait Salvatore and I had taken on our twenty-fifth anniversary. This brooch I'm wearing today, with the diamonds—I'm wearing it in the photograph also—Salvatore gave it to me that day. Upstairs on my dresser is a jewelry box filled with necklaces and bracelets and earrings. All from Salvatore.

I am surrounded by the things Salvatore gave me, or did for me. But, God forgive me, as I lie alone now in my bed, it is Paolo I remember.

Paolo left me nothing. Nothing, that is, that my

family, especially my sisters, thought had any value. No house. No diamonds. Not even a photograph.

But after he was gone, and I could catch my breath from the pain, I knew that I still had something. In the middle of the night, I sat alone and held them in my hands, reading the words over and over until I heard his voice in my head. I had Paolo's letters.

* * * * *

Be sure to look for
DANCING ON SUNDAY AFTERNOONS
available January 30, 2007.
And look, too, for our other
Everlasting title available,
FALL FROM GRACE by Kristi Gold.

FALL FROM GRACE is a deeply emotional story
of what a long-term love really means.
As Jack and Anne Morgan discover,
marriage vows can be broken—but they
can be mended, too.
And the memories of their marriage have
an unexpected power to bring back a love
that never really left....

COMING NEXT MONTH

#1398 LOVE AND THE SINGLE MOM • C.J. Carmichael
Singles...with Kids
When Margo almost loses her bistro...and custody of her children...she realizes a real family is about more than owning a pretty house and being a perfect mother. And then there's Robert... But like the other single parents in her support group, she has to make sure he wants the whole package. Is it really possible to find true love the second time around when you're single...with kids?
The first in a wonderful new series!

#1399 THE PERFECT DAUGHTER • Anna DeStefano
Count on a Cop
Detective Matt Lebrettie can't be the man for Maggie Rivers. She just can't watch him face danger every day. But will keeping her heart safe rob her of her chance for happiness?

#1400 THE RANCHER NEEDS A WIFE • Terry McLaughlin
Bright Lights, Big Sky
After his divorce, Wayne Hammond resisted making anyone the second Mrs. Hammond. Topping the list of the women he wouldn't pick is Maggie Harrison Sinclair, who's taken refuge at her family's ranch until she can figure out which big city is for her. He's not about to make the mistake of picking a city woman again. Or is he?

#1401 BECAUSE OF OUR CHILD • Margot Early
A Little Secret
More than a decade ago, Jen Delazzeri and Max Rickman had a brief, intense love affair—and then disappeared from each other's lives. Now Jen's work as a TV reporter brings her into Max's world again, the world of smoke jumpers and Hotshots, of men and women who risk their lives to fight wildfires. Should she use this opportunity to tell him the secret she's kept for twelve years—a secret named Elena?

#1402 THE BOY NEXT DOOR • Amy Knupp
Going Back
In Lone Oak, Kansas, Rundles and Salingers don't mix. Not since the tragic accident involving Zach Rundle's brother and Lindsey Salinger's mother. But when the well-being of a young boy is at stake, Zach and Lindsey are unwillingly dragged together again. Fighting the same attraction they'd felt twelve years ago.

#1403 TREASURE • Helen Brenna
Jake Rawlings is a treasure hunter and Annie Miller is going to lead him to the mother lode. But what he finds with beautiful Annie is much more than he bargained for.

HSRCNM0107